**"I DIDN'T**
**ENGAGE**

He held her gaze for a moment before his eyes dropped to the hand captive in his.

She attempted to maintain a casual tone while she became more and more troubled by the warmth of his hand over hers. "Floyd gave me this ring."

"Don't you ever get lonely for a man's company, Rachel?"

She snatched her hand away from him. "I have male friends, Cole Braxton. Is that why you took me out today? You think I'm so starved for male companionship that I need your pity?" She jumped up from the table and began to clear away the dishes.

"Pity is one emotion I don't feel for you, Rachel."

There was something in his voice that Rachel wasn't ready to acknowledge....

## ABOUT THE AUTHOR

A devoted wife and mother of two, Pamela Bauer recently returned to college to complete a degree in nutrition science. After taking a professional writing course, however, Pam found herself spending less time on nutrition and more on writing . . . luckily for Harlequin readers! A supertalented new author, Pamela writes unusual and emotional stories that are sure to please.

Pamela Bauer

# HALFWAY TO HEAVEN

Harlequin Books

TORONTO • NEW YORK • LONDON
AMSTERDAM • PARIS • SYDNEY • HAMBURG
STOCKHOLM • ATHENS • TOKYO • MILAN

Published November 1986

First printing September 1986

ISBN 0-373-70236-1



Printed in Canada

More than three hundred thousand American soldiers were wounded during the United States's involvement in the Vietnam war. This book is dedicated to one of them, my husband, Gerr.

# *CHAPTER ONE*

"READY FOR ANOTHER?"

Cole glanced at the bartender holding the bottle of Scotch near his empty glass, nodded briefly, then turned his attention back to the scene reflected in the mirrored wall behind the bar. He puffed a cloud of gray cigar smoke into the already hazy atmosphere, ignoring the friendly smiles around him. They were strange faces in a strange town and he wasn't in the mood for company, male or female. But then, neither did he feel like spending the evening in a hotel room. If it wasn't for Robert, he thought, a surge of irritation rising within him, he would be back in Minneapolis sipping his Scotch in the familiarity of Fletcher's Place, rather than killing time in a Chicago singles' bar.

He swallowed the liquor with a grimace. Who was he trying to fool? It wasn't Robert he was angry with but himself. Instead of telling his grandfather that he trusted Robert's judgment, he had given in to the old man's demand that he investigate his cousin's professional integrity. Thirty-eight years old and he was still dancing to the tune of an eighty-year-old man. A very shrewd, analytical eighty-year-old man, Cole reminded himself, whose still-sharp mind was the reason why he was here in Chicago second-guessing Robert's motives.

He surveyed the patrons of the bar through the mirrored wall and his eyes fell upon a tall, slender blond. He watched her move through the crowd, coyly smiling as she nudged her way between closely packed bodies on the tiny dance floor. She reminded him of a wild filly, her tawny mane of hair trailing down her shoulders like shimmering gold while her head bobbed to the beat of the music. From a distance she appeared to be a sophisticated woman, but as she came closer, he could see the youthfulness she was trying to conceal. She looked like a child playing at being grown-up, her eyes heavily lined in black, her cheeks dusted with dramatic color and her lips painted bright red. The nearer she came, the more obvious it was that she had been drinking more than she was accustomed to.

He watched as she perched herself precariously on a leather stool, setting her empty glass down with a thud. Immediately there was a male arm draped around her shoulder possessively. Cole turned his head away, disinclined to watch the invading fingers that had wrapped themselves around her slender figure and were stroking the creamy skin exposed by the skimpy dress. It meant nothing to him if some childlike woman allowed a potbellied man to paw her in public.

He swallowed the remainder of his Scotch, a scowl marring his handsome features. He didn't want to look at the female next to him, but his eyes were drawn to her sylphlike figure. Through the mirror he could monitor her every move: the way she continually brushed back her gold-streaked hair with a flick of her hand; the way she attempted to shrug away from the man's touch. He couldn't help but overhear the blatant advances her companion was making, nor could he ignore her obvious lack of experience in dealing with propositions. When her companion excused himself, Cole felt his whole body relax. But a quick glance around the bar told him that she would not be alone for long. She turned her blue eyes in Cole's direction, holding his glance for a moment before looking down, and some alien emotion stirred inside of him.

"Are you having a good time, Angel?" he drawled, sliding over to the empty stool beside hers. He had been accurate in his assessment of her age. She was a real beauty, but definitely not old enough to be hustling men in a bar.

"Even better since you've arrived," she returned, batting eyelashes heavy with mascara. She fumbled with the clasp of her purse, finally extracting a cigarette, which she proceeded to dangle under his nose.

Cole held her unsteady hand in his while he lit the cigarette. "Didn't anyone ever tell you, Angel, that cigarettes are bad for you?"

"Maybe I'm just a bad girl," she returned with a deep, throaty laugh. "And what about you?" She pointed toward his cigar smoldering in the ashtray.

He picked up the small stub and blew several smoke rings. "Bad, too, it would seem."

"Do you think a big bad guy like you could buy a bad little girl like me a drink?" She held up her empty glass, and twirled it in the air. In the mirror Cole caught a glimpse of the pot-bellied man.

Taking the glass from her hand, he expertly slid his arm around her waist. "An angel should be drinking champagne among the stars instead of beer in a crowded bar. I know just the spot. It's right across the street." Sensing her uncertainty, he added, "It's way up at the top of the hotel... almost high enough to touch the clouds. Wouldn't you rather dance on a cloud than on some tiny, crowded dance floor?" He didn't like the way her blue eyes gleamed in response to his insincere flattery. If it hadn't been for the lecherous leering of the pot-bellied man, Cole would have felt guilty at his own deceptive interest.

As he led her out of the bar, a female voice called after them.

"Stacey! Where are you going?"

The blonde paused, casting an irritated glance at the scantily clad redhead following them.

"It's okay, Chelsea. I'm going dancing in the clouds." She pointed to the high-rise hotel with its mirrored glass facade rising majestically into the night, then giggled as she did a wobbly pirouette on the cement sidewalk.

"Stacey, I think you'd better come home with me," the other girl pleaded.

Stacey put unsteady hands on Chelsea's shoulders and turned her toward Cole. "Are you crazy, Chelsea? Just look at this guy. He's perfect."

"Don't you think he's a little old for you?"

"He's just like the man of my dreams... tall, dark and handsome. Don't worry, I just want to have a little fun."

"Stacey, he looks like he wants more than a little fun."

"I can take care of myself," she returned, giggling. "I'll be home later." She turned back to Cole, who was leaning against a lamppost puffing on his cigar.

"But Stacey..."

"See ya." And with a flounce of her tawny hair she thrust her arm through Cole's.

RACHEL KINCAID was unsure whether it was the loud crack of thunder or her mother's intuition that suddenly woke her. She had been restless all night long, not knowing if it was the unseasonably warm air, heavy with the threat of thunderstorms, or her suspicions about her daughter's whereabouts that was causing her nervousness.

Maybe it was the look in Stacey's eyes as she had asked her mother if she could spend the night with her friend Chelsea. Rachel didn't like the uncertainty that had come into her relationship with her daughter. And she didn't trust Chelsea. The time—eleven forty-five—was illuminated on the clock radio. If she were to call Chelsea's home, would Stacey be there? She started to dial, only to reluctantly replace the receiver. No, the slender thread of trust between mother and daughter would only be strained if Stacey thought she was checking up on her.

Still, she couldn't help but stare at the telephone on the nightstand. She remembered the cautious glances exchanged between Chelsea and Stacey when they had spoken of their plans to study for their upcoming exams. Were they actually studying or had that merely been an excuse to enable Stacey to go out on a school night? How many times in the past few months had she lied about her whereabouts, or missed classes at school? Rachel picked up the phone once more and began to dial, only to drop it on the cradle at the sound of the doorbell.

A brief sensation of fear charged through her as she pushed aside the percale sheet and reached for her blue satin dressing gown. Wrapping herself in the smooth fabric, she tied the belt and quickly moved through the apartment, flicking on a light switch on the way.

Through the peephole in the door, she saw Chelsea's distraught features. "Chelsea!" she cried in confusion. The young girl rushed into the apartment, agitation showing in her every movement.

"Chelsea, what's happened? Where's Stacey?" Rachel demanded.

"Oh, Mrs. Kincaid, I'm so scared. You've got to do something."

"Chelsea, please. You have to tell me what's wrong. Where is Stacey? Has she been hurt?" Rachel's voice rose slightly as she grabbed the girl's shoulders.

"I don't know," Chelsea whined. "We went to this singles' bar and Stacey met this guy, and the next thing I knew he was practically dragging her up to his hotel room, and now I'm so afraid that he'll rape her or something and I didn't know what to do so I came here." Her words ran together as her voice rose in hysteria.

"A singles' bar! You mean you've been drinking?" Rachel said accusingly. "You're not old enough to be allowed into a bar."

"We have fake IDs," Chelsea explained.

"Oh, my lord!" Rachel said and let out a long sigh, running her fingers across her furrowed brow.

"We just wanted to have a little fun," Chelsea returned defensively.

"Fun!" Rachel bit back the reprimand that sprang to mind, clasping her hands together tightly. "We've got to find Stacey."

"I know where she is because I followed them." Chelsea's eyes widened as she spoke.

"Do you know which room he took her to?"

Chelsea nodded.

"You wait here while I get dressed," Rachel called over her shoulder, rushing into her bedroom.

Her limbs trembled as she quickly pulled on an old pair of slacks and a shirt. She was so preoccupied with thoughts of Stacey that she didn't even notice she had misbuttoned her raincoat. She grabbed her purse, ran out of the apartment with Chelsea following close behind, slammed the door and hustled Chelsea out into the pouring rain.

Had any of her neighbors seen her rushing from the apartment building they might easily have mistaken her for Stacey. Not once in the three years Rachel had been a tenant at Lakeshore Manor had they seen her silky golden tresses free of the constriction of a tightly braided chignon. Her normally pale complexion was flushed with anger and the blue eyes that were usually hidden behind wire-rimmed glasses now sparkled with emotion as she contemplated her daughter's predicament.

"We're going to have to take the El," she told Chelsea. "My car's in the garage being repaired." Although Rachel had an umbrella, the gusty wind quickly turned it inside out, rendering it useless against the pelting rain. By the time they reached the rapid transit station, both were drenched from head to toe.

The ride on the elevated train seemed never-ending to Rachel. Apart from a handful of second-shift workers, their car was nearly empty. She stared silently at Chelsea's painted face. The rain had caused tiny streaks of color to run down in rivulets across her cheeks. Her once stylish hairdo now lay plastered to her head. Rachel wanted to blame Chelsea for Stacey's erratic behavior; ever since they had moved to Chicago she had thought Chelsea a bad influence on her daughter. But the fact was that Stacey was the one in a hotel with a strange man. She shuddered at the images the thought provoked.

Oh God, where had she gone wrong? It had not been easy raising a child without a father, but she had done the best she could. Stacey's welfare had always come first in her life. She had worked hard to provide a good home and to be a responsible parent. She had been a model of virtue, determined that Stacey would not make the same mistake she had. Yet here she was rushing off to some strange hotel expecting to find...no, she wouldn't dwell on the worst possible consequence. She could only pray that she wouldn't be too late.

By the time Rachel and Chelsea stepped off the train, the rain had diminished to a steady drizzle. They hurried toward the hotel. Once inside Chelsea indicated they should take the elevator. Oblivious to the curious stares she and Chelsea were drawing as they marched across the plush carpeting of the lobby, Rachel clutched her purse defensively. When the elevator doors slid open, Chelsea hesitated until Rachel's firm grip on her elbow forced her to move inside.

Within seconds they were at the top floor. "It's that last door on the right," Chelsea whispered, pointing her finger down the hallway. "Can I wait here?"

Rachel took her by the arm. "I think you'd better confirm that this is the correct room first."

Chelsea gave a small moan in protest, then reluctantly followed Rachel.

"You're sure that this is the right one?" Rachel repeated, her teeth tugging at her lower lip. At Chelsea's nod, she knocked loudly on the door. Her heart was beginning to pound in her ears and she could feel the familiar swell of nausea she experienced whenever she became extremely frightened. She was about to raise her fist once more when the door was suddenly thrust open.

Rachel stared in dismay at the masculine occupant of the hotel room, who appeared to have been aroused from his sleep, his chest and feet bare, a pair of silk pajama trousers slung low on his narrow hips. She had automatically assumed the man would be nearer Stacey's age than her own, and was unprepared for his disturbingly attractive good looks, or for the naked torso staring her in the face. She had to tip her head back to look at him.

"Well?" the man drawled, running his fingers through coal-black hair, his mouth twisting in irritation.

Rachel glanced sideways at Chelsea, who, after a brief nod of her head, withdrew like a scared kitten. At Chelsea's confirmation, all Rachel's protective instincts surfaced and the momentary terror she had felt at the size of him fled. With a feeling of desperation, she pushed through the doorway past his imposing figure.

"Stacey! Stacey, where are you!" she called out, her eyes frantically searching the luxuriously furnished room. But before she had taken more than a couple of steps a firm arm grabbed her by the shoulder and swung her around.

"Just what do you think you're doing?" he demanded, kicking the door shut with his foot.

"Get your hands off me before I call the police and have you arrested for assault," she threatened with more conviction than she was feeling, tugging her arm out of his grasp. "You picked up a young girl from the bar across the street and brought her up here. Where is she?" Rachel stood with both hands on her hips, unaware of the defiantly childlike image she projected. Her hair hung in wet clumps around her pale face, her wide eyes anxious.

"In my bed—which is just where she wanted to be, judging by her actions in the bar," he retorted, his eyes narrowing as she glared at him. "She was acting like a two-bit hussy, and if it weren't for the fact that she was stinking drunk she might just have gotten what she was begging for."

Rachel's reaction was instinctive. Raising her arm she slapped his cheek with a stinging blow, then stepped back in shock, her palm burning from the contact. In all of her thirty-four years, she had never struck another human being. Her heart beat heavily in her throat and her body trembled with emotion.

"You little..." he swore under his breath, moving toward her with a fierceness that caused Rachel to recoil in horror. But just as quickly as his anger had erupted, restraint intervened and he stopped abruptly. He leaned back against the closed door, his thin, tanned fingers gingerly trailing across his reddened cheek. If he had been drowsy when he had answered the door, he was wide awake now. He turned on the overhead light, illuminating the hallway, and surveyed the woman facing him.

Cole could see that she was a smaller version of the female in his bed, but definitely more mature. She had the same blue eyes the younger girl had, except hers lacked the glittering eye shadow and heavy mascara. There was no mistaking the resemblance of the high cheekbones and the small, straight nose. They had to be sisters. But it was obvious that in this case the older sister was not the more experienced. There was a fresh innocence about her, a simplicity evident in the hauntingly beautiful eyes that now wore a pained expression.

Rachel shifted unsteadily under his gaze, swallowing with great difficulty as she realized the vulnerable position she had placed herself in. She thought about the self-defense class she had taken when she had first moved to Chicago, and wondered how effective her efforts would be against a man his size.

Cole simply let his dark eyes rove over her bedraggled appearance until suddenly he said, "She's in there," indicating a doorway to Rachel's left. He watched her as she quickly moved toward the bedroom.

Rachel could feel a knot of repulsion inside of her as she surveyed the room. Lying in the center of a king-size bed, Stacey looked small and forlorn. Her tawny hair covered the part of her face that wasn't buried in the fluffy pillow. At the sight of her red dress draped across the back of a chair, Rachel inhaled deeply. When the stranger stepped into the bedroom, she turned to him, her fists balled at her sides.

"My God, she's only seventeen! Young enough to be your daughter!" she raged. "What kind of a man are you to abuse a child?" Tears filled Rachel's eyes at the thought of such a man violating her only child's virtue. It had to be a bad dream, she told herself. This innocent sleeping girl was her baby, not some strange man's plaything.

"A child?" he repeated. "You call this the dress of a child?" He crossed the room and picked up the wisp of red material Stacey had been wearing, dangling it from the tip of his index finger. "Maybe you had better take a closer look. You might discover she's seventeen going on thirty," he retorted, gazing at her with a speculative scowl.

Rachel only glared at him. Reaching across the large bed, she tugged on Stacey's shoulder.

"Stacey, wake up." Her voice trembled with urgency. She had to get her daughter out of this man's bed and back home where she could take care of her. When it became evident that Stacey was not going to wake up, Rachel straightened and faced the man across from her.

"What have you done to her?" she cried out. "Did you give her drugs?" Her face was tormented, her dark eyes anxious. Without waiting for an answer, she reached for the telephone. "I'm going to call the police. You can't get away with this, no matter how much money you have," she said, flinging her arm in the air.

Like a bolt of lightning, Cole was across the room, pulling the phone from her hands. His eyes narrowed as he focused them on Rachel. "The only drug in her body is the alcohol she consumed in the bar across the street. She passed out, but not before she was violently sick, which is why she took off the damn dress," he said curtly. "You should be thanking me. There were dozens of men in that bar who wouldn't have blinked twice at taking advantage of a girl in her condition. Now, if you want to take her into the bathroom and get her under the shower, you can probably sober her up enough to get her home. I've already cleaned up after her once this evening; I'll leave you to finish the job," he finished irritably, then moved past her with the same swiftness of a few moments ago, leaving her alone with Stacey.

Rachel breathed a shaky sigh of relief, hoping that if nothing else, Stacey's intoxicated condition had at least prevented her from being sexually abused. The problem now was how to get her up and out of the hotel room. Unfortunately, her own petite figure was no match for her daughter's five foot nine-inch limp body, and there was no way she was going to ask the man for any assistance.

Rachel found a facecloth in the bathroom and ran cold water on it. She rubbed the cloth across Stacey's fair skin, shaking her gently as she urgently repeated her name. When Stacey finally stirred, it was with a moan.

"Oh, my head," she groaned, pulling the sheet up closer to her face. When she realized it was her mother bending over her, a startled gasp escaped from her parched lips. "Mom! What are you doing here?"

"That should be obvious," Rachel admonished her quietly. "The question is, what are you doing here?"

"I can explain—" she began, sitting up, only to have her mother interrupt her.

"Stacey, you have to get dressed so that I can take you home. We'll talk about all this after we're out of here." She retrieved the red dress from the nearby chair.

"Oh God, I hope I'm not going to be sick again." Stacey pulled a hand across her mouth, her pale face contorting in discomfort.

"For goodness' sake, Stacey! You've got to try to get yourself together. Please get dressed while I phone for a taxi," Rachel implored. "Do you realize what that man might have done to you? Or still could, for that matter. We've got to get out of here."

"Oh, Mom, I feel so awful, I don't think I can go anywhere." Stacey lay back down on the bed, her dress partially covering her legs, while her mother made the phone call.

"Come on, the taxi will be waiting." Rachel lifted Stacey back up to a sitting position, pulled the garment down over her daughter's waist and hips, then slipped her black sandals onto her bare feet. "You can make it down the elevator and out the lobby, can't you?" Rachel persuaded, helping the woozy girl up, her smaller frame supporting Stacey's larger one. She removed her raincoat and draped it around Stacey's wobbly figure.

Dreading any further contact with the suite's occupant, Rachel moved as quietly as she could, silently praying that Stacey wouldn't be sick again until after they were out of the hotel. As she struggled toward the door with Stacey's heavy form hanging on to her every step, she saw him staring out at the Chicago skyline through the large plate-glass windows of the suite, the glow from his cigar the only light in the room. Any hope Rachel had of sneaking out unseen vanished as he crossed the room at the sound of their footsteps.

Rachel wasn't sure whether he was squinting because of the light in the hallway or because he was angry at the sight of the two of them leaving. Obviously, his evening hadn't turned out as he had expected, but she wished he would simply let them go without any further confrontation. Her heart leaped into her throat when he stepped in front of them, blocking the exit. Was he going to prevent them from leaving?

He had pulled on a white terry-cloth robe, which accentuated the darkness of his skin. There was a curious glint in his eyes as he surveyed the pair of them. When his glance strayed to Rachel's cream silk shirt, which had come partially unbuttoned, she shivered unconsciously.

"Please—leave us alone." Her voice faltered and she could feel the goose bumps creeping along her flesh.

Hearing the fear in her voice, he sighed heavily. "Believe me, the thought of making love to a female who has just emptied her stomach in my suite is not very appealing." He was irritated with himself for feeling the need to defend his actions. "As hard as this may be for you to believe, I actually thought I was being chivalrous this evening. You shouldn't jump to conclusions. Circumstances are not always what they seem," he told her as he opened the door for them.

Rachel eyed him doubtfully, remembering the feral look that had struck her when she had first confronted him. Stacey's weight was becoming increasingly difficult to support; with each passing moment she was seemingly closer to passing out again. Dragging her daughter with her, Rachel staggered through the doorway out into the hall where they were met by an anxious Chelsea.

"Wait." The deep command halted their steps. "I have something for you." He held out a paper bag, which Rachel recognized as the type provided by hotels for soiled laundry. "You might need this. She still looks a little green." He cast a disparaging glance at the three of them before returning to his suite.

"Oh my God, Stacey! What happened? You look awful!" Chelsea's voice was a near-whisper.

"I'm sick. What do you think happened?" Stacey grumbled thickly.

"Chelsea, please help me get her downstairs." Rachel tried to keep the anger from her voice, but her shoulder was beginning to feel numb and her emotions could no longer be denied. As the three of them struggled down in the elevator and out of the hotel, Rachel could feel sympathetic glances being cast her way, which only fueled her indignation.

Once inside the cab she told the two girls precisely what she thought of their actions. Not that it did any good, for Stacey was drifting in and out of consciousness, and she finally passed out cold not far from home. When the two of them couldn't rouse her, Rachel was forced to ask the cabdriver for his help in carrying her up the two flights of stairs into the apartment building.

"Chelsea, you're welcome to sleep in the guest room," Rachel offered after they had managed to get Stacey to bed. "But I'm going to have to call your mother." She started toward the phone.

"No, wait, Mrs. Kincaid, please!" Chelsea pleaded, stepping hesitantly toward Rachel. "I already told her I was sleeping over here," she confessed.

"And Stacey told me she was sleeping at your house." The words were spoken more to herself than to the teenager. "Just where were the two of you planning on spending the night?" Rachel inquired.

"At my sister Ginger's apartment. I've got a key because I take care of her cat when she's out of town. She's an airline stewardess."

There were several minutes of silence before Rachel finally said, "I won't call her now, but I'm going to have to speak to her in the morning." She acknowledged Chelsea's forlorn good night with a nod of her head.

It was a bone-weary Rachel who padded into her own room, her head drooping on her slender shoulders as she massaged her aching spine. Lightning sent staccato flashes of opalescent light around the bedroom, silhouetting her figure, and she glanced at her ghostlike reflection in the dressing-table mirror. She didn't bother switching on a lamp. Instead, she undressed in the shadows created by the electrical storm, allowing the khaki pants to fall in a heap at the foot of her bed, followed by the oversize cream-colored shirt and her lacy undergarments. Wrapping herself in her periwinkle-blue satin robe, she moved across the dusty-rose carpet to the closet and pulled the oak door wide open so that the life-size photo poster of the uniformed soldier was smiling directly at her.

It was yellowed at the edges, the once distinguishable details now dulled by time, the paper worn thin around the facial features from the constant stroking by gentle fingers. Rachel pressed her forehead against the paper soldier's wide brow, her fingers once again tracing the outline of the full, sensuous mouth and then the uneven white teeth that gave a boyish charm to the man's face. She didn't need a light to see the individual features of his face; she knew them by heart.

"Oh, Floyd," she whispered almost reverently. "Everything would have been so much easier if only you had come home." There were no tears in her eyes, only a dull ache in her heart. The pain hadn't disappeared even after eighteen years. "Time has taught me to be strong, but I still need you . . . and your daughter needs you. Oh, Floyd, please come home." The words were so softly spoken Rachel wasn't even sure she had uttered them aloud. With a disconsolate quiver of her drooping head, she turned away from the poster and stumbled toward the bed.

Stacey was only seventeen—the same age Rachel had been when she gave birth to her. No, she would not take the blame for Stacey's behavior. It was not like mother like daughter. She and Floyd had been in love, and they would have been married had it not been for the Vietnam war.

She lifted the diamond solitaire off the crystal ring holder on the nightstand and placed it on her finger, remembering how her heart had nearly burst with joy when it had arrived by registered mail from Vietnam. Before Floyd had left for the war, he had told her they would be married as soon as he returned from overseas. She would be finished with school by then and he would be eligible for his discharge from the service. Rachel hadn't wanted to wait, but Floyd had had definite ideas about their wedding day. He didn't want to sneak off to some justice of the peace; he wanted a big church wedding with all their friends and relatives present. But after being in Vietnam only a couple of months, he had sent her the ring with instructions that she meet him in Hawaii to get married as soon as he was scheduled for the personal leave every combat soldier was granted from the war. He had spoken to other GIs who had gotten married while on their brief respites from combat, and he would make all the arrangements for the two of them. Knowing that he wanted to marry her as soon as possible had given her the courage to tell him about her pregnancy and had dispelled any regrets about having anticipated their wedding vows. But the honeymoon in Hawaii never transpired, for during his tour in Vietnam, Floyd was separated from the United States Armed Forces and became an MIA—Missing In Action.

Floyd had been only twenty years old, so unlike the man Stacey had chosen to give herself to tonight. Rachel shuddered once again at the thought. But there was no use in torturing herself until she actually had an open discussion with Stacey. Nevertheless, the thought of such a conversation, of what she might learn about her own daughter, frightened her.

A loud clap of thunder echoed Rachel's fears and in her mind she could hear her father's harsh voice saying, "You will pay for your sins, Rachel. The devil will own the soul of that child." They were the last words he had uttered, the night Stacey had been born, the night he had urged her to give the baby up for adoption or be punished . . . the last night she had ever seen him.

# *CHAPTER TWO*

"STACEY!" Rachel called out as she pushed open the door to her daughter's bedroom. "You're going to be late for school if you don't get up now." She had always respected Stacey's pleas for privacy and rarely entered the overcrowded room where rock stars' posters hid the lemon-yellow walls and stuffed animals competed with record albums for space. But after last night's events, she knew that Stacey would need more than a knock on the door to awaken her. Trying to disregard the half-empty package of cigarettes lying on the bureau, she jabbed at a silver button on the stereo system, which sent a cacophony of rock music blaring into the silent room.

Stacey mumbled a few incoherent words, then rolled over, pulling the feather pillow over her head.

With deliberate steps, Rachel crossed the room and opened the yellow venetian blinds, allowing the early-morning sun to penetrate the darkness of the room. Then she swooped the pillow off Stacey's head. "Up right now," she repeated firmly.

"I can't go to school." Stacey pulled her arm across her eyes, her face twisting in vexation. "I'm sick."

"You're not sick. You're hung over," Rachel retorted. "You miss one more day of school and you won't be graduating in June."

"The way I feel right now I don't really care."

"Well, I do!" Rachel raised her voice, causing Stacey to sandwich her head between her forearms with a shudder.

"All right! I'm coming," she returned irritably. "Just don't shout anymore." Slowly edging herself out of bed, she tiptoed toward the bathroom, one hand on her forehead, the other outstretched as though she were a blind person groping for something to hold on to.

After two aspirin and a shower, Stacey reappeared, looking like a young, innocent girl, very different from the siren of the previous evening. Her appearance was her only defense, she knew. Her hair was brushed straight back and tied with a yellow-and-orange-striped scarf, and her face was devoid of all makeup except for a golden peach blush to hide the pallor of her skin. She wore a tangerine cotton-knit dress her mother had sewn especially for her, a style Stacey thought was much too juvenile for her, but necessary under the circumstances. As she caught sight of her mother on her hands and knees scrubbing the ceramic tile in the kitchen, she knew she had made the right choice. There was only one reason why her mother would be washing the floor for the second time that week. Some people paced away their anger or others banged drawers and closet doors, but Rachel simply attacked her housecleaning. Wisely, Stacey waited until Rachel had scrubbed the last corner clean and had tossed the gray rag into the plastic bucket with a resounding sigh of accomplishment before she opened her mouth.

"Aren't you going to be late for work?" She eyed her mother cautiously.

"I made arrangements to start later since I have to pick up the car from the garage. I didn't think you'd feel up to any breakfast," she explained, indicating the wet kitchen floor.

"No. I'm not hungry." Stacey smiled weakly. "Besides, I don't want to miss the school bus."

"I think we'd better have a talk before you go."

"But I'll be late," she protested, quickly forgetting her earlier reluctance to even attend school.

"I phoned Mr. Hammond and he assured me you could make up your study period after school." She lifted the plastic bucket and carried it to the bathroom with Stacey following close behind.

"You phoned the principal?" With a greater effort, Stacey bit back the expletive that threatened to escape. "That's just terrific," she replied with heavy sarcasm, watching her mother rinse out her scrub rag. "Everyone else is going down to BJ's after school, and I have to sit in detention with the rest of the losers because my mother decides to have a heart-to-heart talk with me."

"I should think that a detention would be the least of your worries after what you pulled last night." Rachel walked out past her to the utility closet where she tucked away the pail.

Stacey looked a little sheepish. "I can explain about last night."

"What possible explanation can justify your presence in a bar or the fact that you allowed a strange man old enough to be your father to take you to his hotel room?'' Rachel stood with one hand on her hip, the other clutching the doorknob.

''It wasn't like that,'' Stacey protested.

''Suppose you tell me what it was like.''

Stacey placed her hand on her mother's elbow. ''Please try to understand, Mother,'' she pleaded, leading her into the living room. ''Chelsea and I simply wanted to go dancing—someplace where they have a live rock band instead of taped music. I am almost eighteen, you know.''

''Still not old enough to drink,'' Rachel reminded her, inviting Stacey to sit beside her on the blue floral print sofa, an invitation Stacey ignored.

''All right. I shouldn't have had the beer, but I guess I didn't realize how quickly it would affect me. I wasn't looking to be picked up. I simply wanted to meet some guys who could carry on a normal conversation. Honestly, Mother, the boys in school are all so immature and boring. But like I said, I didn't realize what a couple of beers could do to me and the next thing I knew I was pretty dizzy. Cole actually rescued me from some creepy old guy.''

''Cole is the man whose room I found you in?''

Stacey nodded. ''I told him I wasn't feeling well and he offered to take me someplace where he could get me some coffee. I didn't know he meant his hotel room.''

''That's not what Chelsea said.''

Stacey rolled her eyes heavenward. ''Chelsea always did fantasize a lot, Mom. Where is she, anyway?''

''Her mother came and picked her up earlier this morning.''

"You didn't tell her mother about last night, did you?"

"Of course I did. You told me you were sleeping at Chelsea's and Chelsea told her mother she was staying over here. Neither one of us was told the truth."

"If I had told you we were staying at Ginger's you wouldn't have let me go, would you?"

"So instead you sneaked around behind my back."

"I'm sorry, Mother. I just wanted to have some fun. I never meant for things to turn out the way they did."

"You don't know how frightened I was last night. When I think of what could have happened." Rachel rubbed her temples with two forefingers.

"Nothing happened, Mother." Stacey emphasized each word. "I'm seventeen, not twelve, and you've already given me the lecture on the birds and the bees. Besides, Cole had no intention of seducing me."

"Men pick up women in bars for one reason, Stacey, which is why girls who hang out in them earn a reputation for being easy."

Stacey laughed sarcastically. "Easy? Mother, this is not the Victorian age. Your ideas of what nice girls should and should not do are so dated. Times have changed since you were my age."

"I wouldn't say it's old-fashioned but merely common sense that a woman shouldn't march off to a hotel with a stranger, a man who could easily be a rapist or even worse."

"Cole certainly is no rapist. Give me credit for having some judgment, Mother. Didn't you know the very first time you met Daddy that he was trustworthy and honest? And you were even younger than I am."

"Yes, but that's a whole different set of circumstances. And we didn't run off to a hotel the first night we met. You don't seem to understand the consequences of such actions."

"Oh, Mother," Stacey drawled in exasperation. "I've already told you I didn't go to Cole's room to sleep with him."

"He seems to think you did."

"Why? What did he say?" She shifted her weight from one foot to the other, a curious glint in her eyes.

"He was rather crass about the whole situation."

Stacey shrugged. "He was a perfect gentleman to me. You wouldn't believe how gentle he was when I was sick." While Rachel was wondering if they were actually talking about the same person, Stacey was silently berating herself for having drunk too much.

"Oh, Stacey, you're so naive. I saw this...this Cole fellow and believe me, he wasn't simply looking for a nice young woman to have a pleasant conversation with. Older, more experienced men spell trouble for a girl your age. What if he was married?"

"He told me he wasn't."

"I doubt any businessman away from home is going to walk into a singles' bar with a wedding band on his finger and announce he's happily married."

"Well, what difference does it make now?" Stacey grumbled. "I mean, I'm hardly likely to see him again after my mother came storming in like some brood hen after her lost chick. It's over with and as I told you, nothing happened."

"A lot happened," Rachel countered. "You lied to me and you were drinking, and now I'm wondering if I can trust you anymore."

"Oh, Mom, don't say that," Stacey pleaded, placing her hand on Rachel's shoulder as she sank down beside her on the sofa.

"I'm going to take away your driving privileges for two weeks and you're going to have a ten o'clock curfew."

"Ten o'clock? You've got to be kidding! There's a concert next weekend and I promised my friends I'd drive. Oh, Mom, please! You can't do this to me." Her lower lip quivered, and one large diamond-shaped tear trickled down her cheek, followed closely by several others.

Rachel felt the familiar stirrings of maternal sympathy, but the image of her daughter in the stranger's king-size bed had been seared into her memory. "The tears aren't going to change anything, Stacey."

Wiping her cheeks with the backs of her fingers, she sniffed loudly, the tears continuing to come in a steady downpour. "I bet if Daddy were here he wouldn't be so strict with me." She walked over to the rolltop desk, picked up the picture of Floyd Andrews and clutched it close to her bosom. "You're so worried I'm going to make some god-awful mistake you won't let me have any freedom. Mom, you can't stop me from growing up. I know I was wrong last night and I'm sorry, but can't you accept the fact that I'm not a child anymore?" She returned her father's picture to its place on the desk, then went to sit beside her mother, placing her arm around her shoulder. "You can trust me, Mom. I promise I won't do it again."

If the memory of the night before hadn't left such an ugly stain Rachel might have yielded to the temptation to lessen her daughter's punishment. She thought of a few of the many times when she had succumbed to Stacey's contrite appeals and been disappointed. She had been lenient too often; the time had come to be firm. Avoiding Stacey's pleading gaze, she rose and picked up her tan smock from the back of a chair. "I have to get ready for work," she said quietly. "If you'd like to walk with me over to the garage, I can give you a ride to school."

"I'd rather take a bus," Stacey said with a stubborn set to her jaw.

"It's your choice," Rachel replied.

"You mean you're actually allowing me to make such a big decision?"

Rachel ignored the sarcasm and went to change her clothes. When she was ready to leave, she said to Stacey, "And one more thing. You'd better stop asking Chita to make up design samples for you. Not only will you lose your opportunity to model for Annalise, but you may cost Chita her job as well."

"I don't see what the big deal is. She just zips them off for me from the leftover fabric," she said sullenly.

"The big deal is that it's against company policy. And anyway, that red dress was from Julian's Eclipse collection; it wasn't designed for a teenager."

"Chita didn't make it exactly the same."

Rachel exhaled in exasperation. "There's a casserole in the refrigerator. Put it in the oven when you get home from school." And without waiting for a reply, she let herself out of the apartment.

The image of Stacey's tearful face stayed with her as she drove to Annalise Fashions. In the past she had always made sure that she and Stacey didn't part on a sour note. She was determined that their relationship wouldn't deteriorate to the point that her own relationship with her mother had. Unresolved differences left her feeling anxious and discontent and it was with a stiff discipline that she continued on to the fashion house.

Rachel loved her work. Next to Stacey, it was the most important thing in her life. Creating fashions was a high for her, as were the satisfied comments she received from those who wore her dresses. She tried to cling to those feelings rather than think about the mockery that had been in Stacey's voice as they had argued. It hadn't gone unnoticed by Rachel that Stacey had put on the tangerine cotton knit. Stacey had always been precocious, wanting to wear grown-up dresses even as a child. And even though she would scoff at the clothes Rachel would sew for her, she couldn't hide the proud gleam in her eyes when admiring glances and compliments came her way. But to a child, homemade dresses, no matter how stylish, were not the same as store-bought dresses with a designer label.

It was on mornings such as this that Rachel would weigh the trade-offs involved in her decision to move from the obscurity of dressmaking into the competitive field of fashion design at Annalise Fashions. Life had seemed so simple back in Milwaukee; Stacey hadn't had any behavioral problems then, and the dressmaking profession hadn't been nearly as demanding of her time.

Ever since Stacey was a baby Rachel had worked as a seamstress, which enabled her to stay at home and see that Stacey received the attention only a mother could give. She had always earned enough to support the two of them sufficiently, but she'd always hoped that one day Floyd would reappear and take over as head of the family. But Floyd hadn't reappeared, and the older Stacey became, the more expenses had seemed to escalate, until finally Rachel admitted to herself that she would have to find a more lucrative job.

Annalise's offer had seemed like a godsend at a time when Stacey was feeling the need to keep up with her peers both socially and fashion-wise. Any misgivings Rachel had as to the suitability of such a big city for a teenager were dispelled once she saw the opportunity for intellectual and artistic expression in Chicago. Stacey loved the city. But it wasn't easy for Rachel to relinquish her parental responsibilities, and leaving Stacey on her own was a source of never-ending worry.

Once Rachel arrived at Annalise she was quickly ensnared by someone in the construction department who needed her assistance in altering several of her dress samples for one of the new collections. By the time the lunch break arrived, she had successfully put aside her conversation with Stacey, but the headache she had awoken with sat like a dull weight over her temples. She didn't realize what a glum picture she was presenting until a soft voice caused her to look up.

"Is my brother responsible for you looking as though your best friend died?"

Rachel couldn't prevent the smile that tugged at her cheeks as the perky blond office manager, Katie Conroy, sat down across from her in the cafeteria. "No, he fixed the car for practically nothing, as usual. You're going to drive him out of business if you keep sending all your friends in for service. He's too sweet to even charge what he should."

"Sweet, eh?" Katie grinned slyly. "To you, maybe." Ever since Rachel had moved to Chicago three years earlier, Katie had figured she was the perfect match for her brother Bud. They were both quiet, sensitive individuals who had lost their mates, except Rachel wouldn't admit that she had lost Floyd. Katie squirted the packaged salad dressing onto her chef's salad. "Seriously, Rachel, is everything all right? You look a bit pale."

"I'm just tired. The storm kept me awake last night."

"And that's why you haven't eaten but two bites of that chicken salad?" she probed gently. "Are you certain those dark circles under your eyes weren't caused by worry over one teenage daughter?"

Instinctively Rachel replaced the wire-rimmed glasses that were hanging on a chain around her neck. "It's a mother's prerogative to worry," she defended herself, meeting the inquisitive glance of the closest friend she had made since moving to Chicago. She wanted to confide in Katie, but for seventeen years she had managed her emotions privately, and she found it extremely difficult to open up. She knew that the younger woman suspected she was having problems with Stacey, but Katie prudently respected her friend's reluctance to discuss her private life. Katie didn't have any children, but she understood Rachel's devotion to Stacey.

Their friendship had taken Rachel by surprise. They were such opposites: Katie was vivacious and outgoing; Rachel, quiet and introspective. Twenty-eight and divorced, Katie Conroy loved the Chicago nightlife, whereas Rachel preferred to avoid the singles scene. To Katie, vogue was everything, and it was evident in her appearance. Lots of makeup, the latest hairstyle and the most chic fashions made her stand out in any crowd, in contrast to Rachel, whose simple appearance allowed her anonymity in a group. Yet their friendship had grown, despite the fact that they came from different backgrounds.

"How's your morning been?" Rachel asked, eager to change the subject.

"Hectic. Julian had a couple of announcements that created quite a stir."

"You mean about Marshall Field devoting an entire bank of its State Street windows to the Eclipse collection?"

"You've heard about it?"

"Yes. I think it's wonderful. Eclipse has been his baby and he's put so much of himself into it. He must be terribly excited."

"Rachel, I know that a good part of that collection was your idea." Katie eyed her carefully.

She shrugged. "I simply made a few suggestions."

"Which he called his own."

"Katie! If it weren't for Julian, I wouldn't be here right now. I'd still be trying to fit a size-ten dress on Mrs. Donley's size-sixteen figure in Milwaukee. He's a genius when it comes to design."

"And so are you, yet you're not temperamental and difficult to work with."

"Nor do I have the responsibilities or reputation to uphold that Julian has. Let's face it. He *is* Annalise."

"He couldn't do it without his assistants," Katie insisted, finishing her salad and pushing the bowl aside. "I'm not saying he's not worthy of the applause, I just wish it was spread around a little more."

"You don't hear me complaining."

"You're too modest for your own good."

"I don't think Julian shares your opinion. I asked for a raise when I heard about the Braxton account."

"Good for you!" Katie enthused. "If Julian lands that contract he'll be able to afford it. Rumor has it that Owen Braxton's grandson and Julian were once very close friends." The words were softly spoken.

"And just what's that supposed to mean?" Rachel asked innocently.

When Katie didn't say anything but shrugged her shoulders carelessly, Rachel said, "Katie, you can't possibly think that a corporation as prestigious as Braxton's would base a decision of that importance on the basis of a personal relationship between the grandson of the board of directors and a friend?"

Katie raised her eyebrows. "You don't think decisions have been made in boardrooms all across the country as results of bedroom performances?"

It was no secret around Annalise that Julian preferred the company of men to women, and although no one had ever run into Julian with any of his lovers, rumors of his numerous affairs circulated among the employees.

"You mean that this Owen Braxton III is..." Rachel never ceased to be embarrassed by talk concerning Julian's private life.

"The word is gay, Rachel. And yes, I have heard that the grandson of Owen Braxton is a brilliant, successful businessman who is charming, witty, sexy and..." She paused, then added seriously, "Gay." She glanced at the wall clock, then heaved her shoulder-strap purse over her arm. "In any case, you'll be able to see for yourself. Julian's bringing him through the studio later this afternoon. I've got to scoot. See ya later."

It wasn't long after lunch that Rachel, sitting with her feet tucked around the legs of her high-backed stool, noticed a small commotion out of the corner of her eye. Peering through the glass partition that separated the designers from the production area of the studio, she watched as a small group of employees offered their hands in introduction while Julian escorted a tall stranger through the studio, a stranger Rachel assumed could only be Owen Braxton III.

Julian was laughing at something the other man was saying, his right hand resting comfortably on Braxton's shoulder. Their backs were turned to her, but there was something disturbing about their physical contact. Rachel mentally shook herself. Darn Katie for having told her of the rumor, anyway. She wouldn't have even noticed if she hadn't been looking for it. She removed her glasses to get a better look. Owen Braxton definitely had an athletic physique and he was just as tall as the lanky Julian. It was obvious he was a charmer; even elderly Pauletta was bashfully smiling up at him. When he turned around, Rachel pressed the palms of her hands to her face in horror. He was the man who had taken Stacey to his hotel room. She groped eagerly for her purse, then scrambled off her stool and headed toward the ladies' room.

Under the unflattering fluorescent lights of the lavatory, she grimaced at her pale features. Maybe he wouldn't even recognize her. After all, last night she hadn't been wearing her glasses and her hair had been hanging straight. She glanced at her watch. If she stayed in there long enough she might be able to avoid him completely. She was still resting on the chaise lounge after fifteen minutes had passed when Katie came in.

"Rachel! What are you doing in here? You're missing all the excitement. Julian's introducing Owen Braxton III to all the employees."

"I'm not feeling well, Katie." She looked down at her white knuckles clutching her purse. "I thought it might help if I just relaxed in here for a few minutes."

"Can I get you anything? A soda or some aspirin?" The other woman's features were anxious and Rachel felt a fraud.

"No, thanks. I've already taken some tablets."

"If you're sure..." Katie hesitated before turning to leave. "Rachel, just wait until you see this Owen Braxton. What a waste of masculinity. It never ceases to amaze me how these gay men can look so macho. And you should see how Serina is ogling him. I can't wait until she hears he's a fruit."

"Katie, I think you've got to be wrong about that."

"Oh, God, don't I wish!" she said dreamily. "Listen, I have to go. Julian will be expecting me to get coffee for his friend. Don't worry about a thing. You just stay here and rest and I'll tell Julian you're not feeling well, okay?"

Rachel nodded and smiled weakly. The way Katie had said "his friend" sent a chill down her spine. Even though she had limited experience with men, she was certain that this Owen Braxton couldn't be gay. But then if by some remote possibility he was, it made what had happened the night before seem even more horrible. Just what type of character was this Owen Braxton III, wealthy grandson of a department store magnate, seducer of innocent young women and who knew what else? She glanced at her watch. Nearly twenty-five minutes had passed. Surely by now they had to be back in Julian's office. Hopefully, Mr. Braxton had liked what he'd seen and was signing the contract. If Julian was going to take charge of the exclusive collection, she would never have to see Braxton again.

There was no sign of Julian or his "friend" when Rachel made her way back through the studio. Taking a deep breath, she got down to work and tried to concentrate on her sketches, but so much had happened in the past twenty-four hours. She recalled Stacey's behavior the previous evening and their argument that morning. Then, to top it all off, she had discovered that Stacey's Cole was Owen Braxton III. Her normally serene features were troubled and pale, and then she saw the memo stuck to the corner of her desk. It was from Julian, instructing her to bring her sketches to his office as soon as she returned.

Rachel's pulse quickened as she strolled toward the chief designer's office, her sketchbook tucked under her arm. It was hard not to panic when she thought about her confrontation with the man who was so important to Julian yet so repulsive to her. But maybe she was worrying over nothing and he wasn't in Julian's office anymore, she tried to reassure herself.

Such hopes were quickly dashed as she came near to the open doorway and heard several voices. Forcing herself to look into the room, she saw Katie, Julian and the man from last night. She entered as unobtrusively as possible, clinging to her sketchbook as though it were a life preserver.

"Ah . . . here she is now. The last of our designers. This is the gal I've been telling you about, Cole." Julian greeted her by taking hold of her hand. "Katie said you weren't feeling well."

Rachel felt all eyes move to her face, which rapidly changed from ashen white to crimson red. She shook her head in denial. "It was only a headache, but I took some tablets and I'm fine," she said, struggling not to sound as uncomfortable as she felt.

"Cole, meet Rachel Kincaid, my right arm," Julian said encouragingly, extending Rachel's hand to Cole's. "Rachel, Owen Braxton III, better known as Cole."

Rachel lifted her chin and faced him, forcing a businesslike smile that revealed perfectly even teeth. Her fingers burned from the slight contact of his gentle grasp as he took her small hand in his large one, acknowledging the introduction. In the light of day she saw that the lean angular features had obviously been tanned by a climate warmer than that of the Midwest and that the dark eyes framed by thick dark lashes had a faintly bored expression. She couldn't prevent the blush that suffused her flawless skin as his dark eyes gave her an appraising glance. She quickly averted her eyes, grateful for Julian's intercession.

"Coffee, Rachel?"

"Please," she accepted rather nervously, seating herself beside Katie on the modern velveteen sectional in a manner she hoped conveyed self-confidence.

While Julian carried on in his usual theatrical style, using dramatic gestures and an elaborate vocabulary, Rachel sat self-consciously, aware of Cole's eyes upon her as he listened to her boss expound on how he discovered his protégée.

"It was simply providential that my sister Yvonne went to Milwaukee. If she hadn't gone visiting an old school chum she would never have discovered Rachel's talent. And you can imagine my skepticism when Yvonne told me I must fly to Milwaukee to see a dressmaker! Well, when I saw what a flair Rachel had, I knew I had to sign her to work for Annalise. She's an absolutely marvelous designer."

Rachel was certain she was blushing from head to toe. She and Katie exchanged glances that conveyed Rachel's discomfort and Katie's sympathy. She was determined to avoid Cole's gaze, preferring not to know if his eyes still held the same bored expression. She had seen the way he had hastily given her the once-over when they were introduced, and she was certain that no amount of praise from Julian would alter his opinion of her.

It took Cole several minutes to figure out why Rachel seemed oddly familiar. Then he realized that she was the same woman who had accosted him last night over her sister's virtue. He felt a ripple of aggravation start at his forehead and slither right on down to the tips of his toes. He studied her nondescript appearance, noting the plain brown pumps, the beige skirt and smock that allowed her to sit unnoticed against the muted tones of the sofa, and the outdated hairdo. A bun! Not even his grandmother wore her hair screwed up into a knot anymore! If she was such a *marvelous* designer, then why did she look as if she belonged in the factory running a sewing machine instead of creating fashion trends?

Cole glanced once more from Rachel to Julian, carefully guarding his expression. It appeared as though his grandfather had been justified in sending him in Robert's place. He walked across the thick carpeting to the plate-glass windows overlooking Lake Michigan. Forrest had insisted that Rachel assist him on the project, even though there were other Annalise designers equally as qualified. Robert might have been accurate in his assessment of the talents of the fashion house, but in the advertising campaign planned for the Braxton golden anniversary celebration, the designer would be appearing in promotional spots and the person chosen would have to fit the image of the Mr. B's salon. Cole sincerely doubted that this woman would fit that image.

He turned his attention back to the chief designer, who had been interrupted by an office messenger.

"Cole, unfortunately something urgent has come up that requires Katie's and my immediate attention. I'm going to have Rachel accompany you to the showroom, but first she can show you the sketches she's brought along." Then he turned to Rachel. "Start with the Eclipse Collection, please Rachel. Take the van to the Apparel Center and when you return we'll sit down and discuss some business, yes?"

Cole refrained from releasing an impatient sigh, opting for a reluctant nod. Julian had assured him that after seeing the collections in the showroom, he would have a better idea of the talent of the staff. Now it seemed that this dressmaker was going to be the one to convince him of Annalise's suitability. He could imagine what his grandfather would have had to say if he were present. He didn't realize that he had chuckled aloud.

"Mr. Braxton?" Rachel rose to her feet, as the second stretched into a minute of silence and Cole made no effort to even look at her.

"Mr. Braxton," she repeated, when he didn't answer but continued to stare out at Lake Michigan.

"Yes?" He looked at her as though she were a bothersome child.

"If you'd like to step over to the table I'll show you the sketches," she suggested.

"About last night." He spun around, finally giving her his undivided attention.

"What about last night?" she echoed softly.

"Are we going to pretend that last night didn't happen?" he asked in a wry tone.

"You're making this rather awkward for me," she murmured uncomfortably, avoiding his eyes.

"I wouldn't want to make you uncomfortable." Again the sardonic tone that had Rachel's spine stiffening.

"What I'm trying to say, Mr. Braxton, is that it was unfortunate we had to meet under such unusual circumstances. But I'm certain we are both professional enough to put aside personal feelings that could be detrimental to business."

"I think that after last night we can cut out any pretense at being pleased about the prospect of working together, don't you agree, Ms Kincaid?"

"Considering your personal life-style, Mr. Braxton, I have absolutely no desire to have any kind of a relationship with you, be it personal or professional. But it seems I have no choice in the second instance."

As soon as the words were out, she regretted them. Insulting a client like Braxton could seriously jeopardize her future at Annalise Fashions. Before she spoke again, she swallowed to steady her voice. "Forgive me, Mr. Braxton. That was uncalled for. If you'll come over here I'll show you what we've accomplished so far on the fall collection." She walked over to the large display table and began arranging the sketches she and Julian had worked on so diligently over the past few months.

"That won't be necessary, Ms Kincaid." He spoke from across the room, making no attempt to follow her.

That brought Rachel's bent form up with a jerk. Cole thought that amid the surprise he caught a trace of hurt in her expression, but was certain he must have been mistaken, for he could see she was having a difficult time even being civil to him.

Rachel's stomach did a tiny flip-flop. "Is it that you don't want to see them, Mr. Braxton, or that you've already made up your mind they aren't any good without even having looked at them?" As hard as she tried, Rachel couldn't keep the slight edge from her voice.

"I have no doubt that if you are employed by Annalise, your fashions are quite good, Ms Kincaid. But

I think Julian neglected to tell you that we are looking not only for a creative designer, but for someone who is experienced with the promotional end of fashion. Those involved with Mr. B's collection will be featured in a great portion of our advertising."

Rachel was seething inside. She wished she could summon a fairy godmother who would wave a magic wand and replace her serviceable work clothes with one of her most feminine designs, and turn Owen Braxton into a frog at the same time. She couldn't prevent the blush of humiliation that she knew blazed across her cheeks, but she refused to show this insufferable man that he had hit a vulnerable spot.

Cole could see that she was trying to hold her anger firmly in check, but her eyes sparkled with emotion. It had been her bright blue eyes that had caught his attention last night, and if she hadn't been wearing glasses now, he would have attributed their coloring to prescription contacts. He altered his initial opinion of her slightly. Anyone with eyes that bright a blue couldn't be described as nondescript.

"Mr. Braxton, I think you're making a professional judgment based on personal feelings." Her voice was husky and sexy in contrast to her appearance. "Which just goes to show how wrong I was about you. Earlier today, when someone insinuated that Annalise was in consideration for the coveted Braxton account simply because of Julian's personal relationship with you, I defended you. I presumed that a man of your professional integrity would keep his private life separate from his business affairs and wouldn't allow personal feelings to influence professional decisions. But it seems I was mistaken."

With only a couple of strides Cole had crossed the room until he stood with his face only inches from hers. Rachel mentally prepared herself for the scathing comments she knew he was capable of. But he did the last thing she expected of him. He smiled, a devastatingly attractive smile.

With his face close to hers so that she was aware of the aroma of his after-shave, he said, "You really shouldn't listen to office gossip, Ms Kincaid. It's my cousin, Robert, who has had the personal relationship with Julian. I only met Julian for the first time today. As I told you last night, you shouldn't jump to conclusions. Circumstances are not always as they seem."

While Rachel searched for her tongue, he bent over the design table.

"On second thought, I do want to see your sketches, Ms Kincaid."

## *CHAPTER THREE*

"I'LL DRIVE," Cole announced, automatically reaching into his pocket for his keys as they stepped out of the elevator into the underground parking lot. "I have a rental car." His softly but firmly spoken words bounced off the concrete walls like bullets. He crossed the gray pavement without checking to see if Rachel was following.

If anyone else had made the suggestion, Rachel would have been more than happy to acquiesce. Maneuvering the Annalise van with its standard transmission up the exit ramps and out of the underground garage was a challenge she avoided whenever possible. But somehow the prospect of riding as a passenger in Cole Braxton's car was equally unappealing.

"Mr. Braxton, even Chicagoans find traffic unbearable at this time of day." Her voice was slightly breathless from having to increase her pace to keep up with his long strides.

Cole paused as he realized that he had been rushing with no regard for her stature. "In that case, Ms Kincaid, you'll appreciate my offer. Look at it this way. I'm the prospective client, you're the merchant. Humor me."

Rachel shrugged her shoulders. "Very well." She wondered if he thought she would be an incompetent driver or if he simply disliked being chauffeured by a female.

Because of the close proximity of the parked cars, it was necessary for Cole to back the car out of the space before she was able to get in. Trying to act as though she had not expected him to hold the door for her, she quickly slipped into the plush velour interior and fastened her shoulder safety belt, unconsciously straining toward the window. After the pungent odor of exhaust fumes in the garage, she was once again aware of the fresh scent of his after-shave.

He drove much too fast for her peace of mind, paying no attention to her sudden intakes of air as he squealed the tires and ascended the narrow spiral exit ramps. When they reached street level, he turned to look at her.

"I'll need a few directions. It's been a while since I've been in Chicago. My cousin Robert usually handles business in this area," he reminded her with a mocking grin.

Rachel ignored the innuendo. It was more than likely, judging by his tan, that he spent most of his time in the sun, and cousin Robert probably didn't have a choice in the matter. "You can take a left at the corner," she directed as they exited the parking lot, refusing to glance over at him. "Then stay on State Street until you get to Randolph." Irritation put an edge onto her words as she tried to stifle her disapproval of him and concentrate on winning the contract for Annalise. After his silent survey of the sketches, she could only assume that he liked what he had seen, since he had been the one to suggest they leave for the Apparel Center. However, his next words dispelled any such notion.

"I want you to understand, Ms Kincaid, that I am going to look at these collections because I know there are six other designers at Annalise." He didn't know why he felt so annoyed by the fact that he had liked the sketches, any more than he knew why he kept noticing how smooth her skin was.

"If you're trying to tell me that you didn't like my sketches, I got the message," she managed to bite out between clenched teeth.

"It's not a question of liking them. Your designs are not what I'm looking for, and to be perfectly honest, I doubt that anything you are going to show me is going to change my mind about Annalise being wrong for Braxton's."

"Then why bother?"

"Because I owe it to Robert. He was quite insistent that we use Annalise for the Mr. B's collection, so much so that my grandfather became suspicious when he learned about his relationship with Julian and began to question his motives."

"He doesn't approve?"

"Do you think any eighty-year-old grandfather would?"

She merely shook her head.

"Robert is a sharp businessman. I have a lot of confidence in his abilities even though Grandfather is skeptical of his motives."

"Which is why you're here," she mocked him.

"I'm not trying to discredit Robert, but to ensure that Braxton's golden anniversary is appropriately honored. Grandfather worked his way up from pauper to department store magnate on sound business decisions, earning Braxton's a reputation that is synonymous with both quality and fashion. I'm almost certain that Mr. B's will be the last project he'll be able to take part in. It will be his final mark on our family name. *That's* why I agreed to investigate Annalise."

As traffic came to a standstill, he drew out a thin cigar and placed it between his teeth, then lit the tip with the car's cigarette lighter. As the sharp aroma filled the interior, Rachel's eyes began to water. Cole had opened his window a crack, but it wasn't enough to dispel the smoke that filtered through the air, tickling Rachel's nose until finally she sneezed. Digging through her purse she extracted several tissues, then removed her glasses to dab at her runny eyes. When she blew her nose loudly, Cole turned her way.

"What the . . . are you sick?" he asked impatiently.

Rachel shook her head and honked like a duck once again. "It's my allergies . . . the cigar smoke," she managed in between coughs. She turned her head away from his gaze, certain that her eyes were puffy.

Cole stuffed the almost whole cigar in the metal ashtray, then snapped it shut. Why the hell hadn't she said something before he lit the damned thing? He jabbed at the control panel on his door handle, creating a hum as all four tinted windows slid open.

Some gentleman, Rachel thought, as crosscurrents of air tugged at her neatly pinned hairdo. He hardly seemed to notice her, let alone worry about whether she would object to his smoking. Apparently it was only in the movies that men asked their female companions if they would mind if they smoked. He looked even more disgusted than he had when they first met in Julian's office.

"Better?" Cole asked, closing the windows from his controls.

"Thank you," Rachel replied stiffly. Several wisps of fair hair had come loose from the wind, giving her a much softer profile, and Cole wished she would look at him when she talked. He liked to look people in the eye when he spoke with them, but she seemed to take pleasure in staring straight out the window. When she lifted her hands to replace the wire rims, he wanted to reach across and stop her. He looked at her fingers, not surprised by the lack of a ring.

Rachel shifted uncomfortably in her seat, finding it extremely difficult to relax. Not only was Cole driving like a reckless cabbie, but his proximity was unnerving. Never had she been around a man who caused her to feel so self-conscious. Not one to worry about opinions of the male population, she was puzzled by the annoyance she felt at knowing he held her in so little esteem. It didn't matter what he thought about her personally, she told herself. It was her work she wanted him to respect.

If only she hadn't mistaken him for his cousin. Normally she disregarded company gossip, even Katie's. But when it came to Cole Braxton, she found herself acting completely out of character. Last night she had slapped his face and today she had hidden in the ladies' room like some schoolgirl avoiding an unwanted boyfriend. Then she had reacted so emotionally toward him, she had nearly lost the Braxton account for Annalise. Now she was sitting like a frightened rabbit, and it was with a great effort that she warned him of the detour ahead.

"You might want to take a left at the next corner. They're doing some road repairs up ahead."

Cole followed her directions, keeping his eyes on the road while she indicated what moves to make. When a tour bus pulled over in front of them, he let out a sigh of impatience. Camera-toting visitors climbed out one by one and crossed the street.

"It's the Picasso mystery sculpture at the Daley Plaza," Rachel responded to the unasked question. "It's even worse in the summer when there are free concerts there. No one has ever really figured out what the sculpture is supposed to be. Officials say it's a woman, but people have been known to think it's a cow with its tongue hanging out."

"I've never been one to attempt to understand modern art." He gave her an odd little smile, and Rachel mistook it for an olive branch.

"Chicago is virtually an outdoor museum of modern art. We can take an alternate route back that will give you an idea of the array of massive abstractions in downtown Chicago."

Cole acted as though he hadn't heard her friendly overture and once more Rachel felt anger color her cheeks. With a businesslike tone she gave him concise directions to the Apparel Center. Once there, she didn't wait for him to come around to open her door, but climbed out of the car.

"Annalise is on the third floor," she said, leading him across the art deco-styled mall to the escalators. She would have had to be blind not to notice the looks women cast his way, which only added to the irritation she felt at having to be with him. When she missed her step coming off the moving stairs, Cole's arm shot out and went around her waist, and she became aware once again of how sensuous his lower lip was, as she looked up into his face. It was no wonder Stacey had succumbed to his charms. She quickly averted her glance. No matter how hard she tried, she couldn't forget the fact that he had taken Stacey to his hotel room. For a man with an abundance of good looks and wealth, there was no excuse for weeding out a girl young enough to be his daughter. Her animosity toward him increased again, and it was with a supreme effort that she concentrated on the fact that this was a client who was very important to Annalise. "Thank you," she murmured unwillingly. "Have you been here before?"

"Several years ago. Recently we've dealt mainly with the New York houses."

Rachel made no comment. Chicago's Apparel Center boasted more than four thousand lines of clothing and was a source for many big-name designers, including Annalise.

For the next hour, the talk was strictly business. They looked at rack after rack of clothing, Cole questioning, Rachel responding and offering suggestions for similar styles or modifications of a particular design. When he saw a copy of the red dress Stacey had worn the previous night, he was quick to comment.

"This one looks familiar. Does Stacey also work for Annalise?"

"Stacey is a high school senior," she said defensively, intent upon reminding him he had seduced a schoolgirl. "She has done some modeling for Annalise, but certainly nothing from this collection."

"Oh, she can wear an Annalise original all right."

Rachel blushed angrily.

"Let me give you a piece of advice, Ms Kincaid. I know you believe that Stacey is a young, innocent seventeen-year-old who needs your protection against all the bad men in this world, but she is more worldly-wise than you'll ever be. Why get yourself all worked up over what she does? She's practically an adult, and the fact that she's attractive, sexy and alluring is one that you cannot change. The two of you are light-years apart in your attitudes. Your parents are the ones who should have disciplined her as a child, and if anything, I hope you've told them about what she did last night."

"For your information, Mr. Braxton, I am the parent. I'm not Stacey's sister, I'm her mother. And I feel that after seventeen years I know my daughter a little bit better than you do after your brief encounter with her last night." Rachel shoved the offending dress between two other garments.

"Daughter?" He stood staring at her incredulously, finally understanding why she'd been so repulsed by the previous evening's events. And now he had just repeated the fact that he had found her daughter sexy and alluring. No wonder she was looking at him with barely concealed disgust.

"That's what I said, Mr. Braxton, my daughter," Rachel repeated, feeling pleased that she had caught him at a loss for words. Without waiting for him to make any further comments, she waved for a sales representative to come over, then introduced her to Cole.

"Nancy, will you take care of Mr. Braxton for me?" Rachel asked the impeccably dressed woman, who looked more than willing to accede to Rachel's request. "I have a few business matters to attend to and Mr. Braxton has seen all but the at-home collection." She had had more than enough of Cole Braxton's company and there was no way she could handle showing him the delicate lace teddies and diaphanous caftans of the intimate apparel lines. Walking away at a brisk pace, she cast a quick glance over her shoulder, only to discover that Cole had already turned his attention to Nancy's tall willowy figure.

Actually the only business matter Rachel had to transact was a phone call to Stacey to let her know that she would be later than usual since she had to stop for groceries on the way home. But rather than use Nancy's office, she opted for a long walk, stopping to use a pay phone in the mall. After a brief conversation with Stacey, she returned to the Annalise showroom to find Cole and Nancy laughing together inside Nancy's office.

"Stop in and see me next time you're in Chicago," Nancy said in a tone that indicated much more than a professional interest in Cole, as she offered her hand to him. Rachel looked away, as though indifferent to the affinity that had sprung up between the two of them.

"Seen enough, Mr. Braxton?" she asked on their return to the parking lot.

"More than enough, Ms Kincaid."

Cole did not appear eager to make conversation. He only spoke when he required directions back to the studio. He made no comments about what he had seen, and once again she found herself wondering if he had found the collections unsatisfactory. She wanted to ask him if he had changed his mind about using Annalise, but her recent attempts at communication had proved ineffective and she figured it was wiser to say nothing than to risk losing the contract. Cole seemed to be lost in thought when she stole a glance at his solemn profile. Judging by his somber expression, he was not pleased, and Rachel only hoped it was not her fashions that had caused the creases in his forehead.

Actually Cole was not very happy with himself at the moment. Rachel's revelation had done today what she had wanted to accomplish last night. It had driven home the fact of how young the girl was. Rachel was his contemporary, which did make him old enough to be Stacey's father, and also served to remind him of Melinda Sue. Were she alive, she could have been a classmate of Stacey's, and the thought that his daughter could have been in the same predicament as Stacey was sobering. The trouble was that Rachel's mind was made up. She had cast him as the villain in the scenario and he doubted whether anything he could say would change her mind.

As soon as they arrived back at the studio, Julian was there to commandeer Cole's attention, and Rachel politely excused herself, grateful to be out of his presence.

Cole sat across from Julian mulling over the events of the past few hours. He had been surprised by the extent of creativity displayed in the collections he had viewed at the Apparel Center. It was obvious that the Annalise staff was talented. He had been as impressed with the dress collection as he had been with the subtly alluring designs of the at-home apparel.

"Well, Cole? What did you think?" Julian was eager to hear Cole's impressions.

"I have to admit I was pleasantly surprised," Cole acknowledged in a guarded tone. "I'm not certain that Ms Kincaid is the right woman for the promotional spots, however."

"I'm certain your staff would find her very easy to work with. She's not at all temperamental, but quiet and dedicated to her work." He raised his fingers to his lips thoughtfully, noticing Cole's skeptical look. "But of course I would be the one designing the collection; Rachel would merely be my assistant. And you can be assured that nothing leaves this house without my approval."

"I'm not questioning the talent of Annalise. It's the promotional image I'm concerned with. Now granted, we're not pushing lingerie specifically, but from what I saw of the leisure wear, there was a certain sensuality, a chic suggestiveness that I think would be closer to the image we're looking for. If you would allow me to speak with the designer responsible for that look, I could get a better idea as to whether we'll be able to do business."

Julian shrugged his narrow shoulders. "But you already have. That collection belongs exclusively to Rachel and myself."

"Ms Kincaid?" Cole straightened in his chair.

Julian nodded. "I've been trying to convince her to transfer some of those ideas into her dresses but she's reluctant to give up the classic style. Having been a dressmaker for so many years and being a bit conservative, she prefers to keep the two lines separate."

"She's something of a paradox, isn't she? Judging by her appearance, one would never expect her to have such a flair for style."

"Don't let Rachel's modesty fool you. As I already told you, she is one marvelous designer and an absolute gem."

"Modesty, however, does not fit with our promotional campaign."

"A little makeup and the right hairstyle can do wonders," Julian reminded him.

"I'm sure you can appreciate that a decision such as this takes careful consideration." Cole rose to leave.

Julian could see he was wavering, and the important contract that had been dangling under his nose was not as sure a thing as Robert had led him to believe. "Robert was very impressed with Annalise's fall collection." He couldn't help but bring his friend's name into the discussion.

"I've always respected Robert's opinions. He certainly has an eye for fashion, which is why he's such a successful buyer. I'll get back to you after we've spoken together." Cole paused at the doorway. "This Kincaid woman—is she married?"

"Widowed."

Cole simply nodded, then left. The hum of the sewing machines was absent as he walked across the studio, most of the workers having gone home for the day. He saw Rachel talking to one of the office employees near the exit, her petite figure dwarfed by the tall woman next to her. She was smiling, and Cole realized that it was the first time he had ever seen her look happy. The minute she noticed that he was looking at her, however, a polite mask of indifference chased away the spontaneous smile. He nodded as he passed, unaware that Rachel had unintentionally overheard part of his conversation with Julian. "Good night, Ms Kincaid."

"Good night, Mr. Braxton," she responded politely, watching his tall figure walk through the revolving door.

Katie turned toward Rachel. "What's with this Ms Kincaid and Mr. Braxton stuff? You spent the entire afternoon with the man."

"Yes, and it was the longest afternoon of my life. I'm certain he didn't want to call me by my first name any more than I wanted to call him by his." The two exited the building together, Katie accepting Rachel's offer of a lift home.

"So what's he like?" Katie asked.

Rachel shrugged her shoulders. "Like any other department store executive, I guess. Intelligent, perceptive."

"Come on, Rachel. You know what I mean."

"Yes. And I know that I am never going to listen to your office rumors again."

"You mean he's not gay?" she asked excitedly.

"I mean he's not Robert Braxton. Katie, Owen Braxton has *two* grandsons. Cole had never met Julian before today. It's his cousin who is Julian's 'friend.'"

"I knew it!" Katie snapped her fingers. "I knew by the way Serina sought him out like a bloodhound. She's never been wrong! Is he married?"

"I didn't ask him."

"Rachel!" Katie shrieked in dismay. "How can you be around a gorgeous-looking man like that for hours and not want to know if he's married? You must have noticed if he wore a wedding band."

"Since when do all married men wear rings?" Rachel thought Katie was as bad as Stacey.

"Well, at least if one was there I'd know for sure he was."

"Trust me, Katie. I don't think Cole Braxton would be the ideal boyfriend." Rachel could hardly believe she was giving the same advice for the second time in one day.

"So you did get to know him?"

"You don't have to know a person to realize that he doesn't share your values."

"What did he say that turned you off?"

"Nothing," she denied, wondering what Katie would say if she told her about last night. "Besides, it's hardly likely that we'll see him around here anymore. The way I understand it, Robert Braxton usually handles this end of the business, and my guess would be that he's the one Annalise will be dealing with, should we get the contract."

"Do you really think so?" Katie asked with a groan.

I'm praying for it, Rachel said silently. Aloud she said, "I got the impression that he was simply confirming Robert's recommendations to use Annalise in the first place."

"Thanks for the lift, Rachel," Katie said as the Honda Civic stopped in front of a tall apartment building. "I'm going out with Brian this evening and it was nice not to have to wait in line for the bus."

"Have a good time," Rachel called out as Katie climbed out of the car.

"He's no Cole Braxton, but at least he has good taste in entertainment. He managed to hunt down two tickets to *Cats*. See you tomorrow." And with a wave she disappeared.

Cole Braxton. Rachel didn't even want to think about the man. Of all the people there were to do business with, why did it have to be the one who had attempted to seduce her daughter? For the very first time since she had begun working for Annalise, she couldn't wait to get out of the studio. The place that had always been a haven for her, where the hum of the sewing machines was like music to her ears, now left her feeling agitated. And all because of Cole Braxton. What she needed was a shower and an uninterrupted night's sleep . . . and tranquillity with Stacey.

Stopping at the neighborhood grocery store, she contemplated what she would say to her daughter. She poked idly at the produce and checked dates on the dairy products. By the time she paid the cashier, she had decided against telling Stacey about her encounter with Cole Braxton. With a brown grocery bag in each arm, she scurried up the steps into the apartment building, then leaned against the door, her pinkie pressed into the tiny black button on the wall.

"I don't think anyone's going to answer. I've already tried pounding on the door and leaning on the buzzer."

Rachel nearly dropped the bags at the sound of Cole's voice.

"What are you doing here?" she demanded in a shaky voice.

"I'm leaving for Minneapolis this evening and I thought I should return this personally. Here, I'll make a trade," he suggested, holding out Stacey's black leather purse in exchange for the groceries.

Rachel reluctantly relinquished the bags and slipped Stacey's purse across her arm, then fished into her pocket for the large metal "R" with several keys dangling from it. The music of the Pointer Sisters, which could be heard through the thick door, became almost deafening as she entered the apartment. She quickly crossed the room and turned down the volume on the stereo.

Cole's eyes took in the femininely furnished apartment, the artistic flair evident in the interior design of the traditionally styled living room. Everything was just as he would have expected her home to be...neat and orderly, with doilies on the pecan coffee tables and all the books in perfect alignment on the shelves. No sheet music had been left sitting on the spinet piano. What he hadn't expected to find were the black wingtip shoes in the entryway. The possibility that she could be living with a man hadn't even crossed his mind. So whose shoes were they?

The piercing sound of an alarm had Rachel rushing into the kitchen to fetch a step stool from under the counter. Disregarding Cole's puzzled gaze, she hurried into the hallway where she steadied the legs of the stool before climbing the rungs and reaching up to disconnect the smoke detector. Cole had moved into the living room and was watching her tiny figure carry out its objective. He noticed for the first time how shapely her legs were under the calf-length skirt.

"It always goes off when the oven is on. It must be oversensitive," Rachel explained, stepping down again and coming back into the living room with the step-stool in hand. "At least it means Stacey remembered to put the casserole in."

"Where shall I put these?" he asked, armed with the groceries.

"I'll take them now, thank you." She reached for a bag with her spare hand.

Stepping around her he walked into the kitchen and plopped the bags down onto the Formica counter. "I hope you don't forget to put that thing back on," he reminded her, pointing toward the smoke alarm cover.

"Oh, no. I always put it right here so I see it as soon as we clean up after dinner." She placed it next to the sink.

Rachel had never realized how small her kitchen was until Cole's large frame stood in the middle of it. "Thank you again, for the help with the groceries and for returning Stacey's purse." She hoped he would take the hint that she was uncomfortable with his presence and leave. She had noticed how his sweeping glance had scrutinized her apartment, and she didn't want to know if he found her home lacking, just as he found everything else about her lacking.

"About Stacey..." he began, only to be interrupted by the girl's entrance.

"Hi, Mom. When did you get home?" Stacey was engrossed with rubbing her newly washed hair with a thick towel and didn't see Cole until she nearly walked into him. It didn't seem to bother her that the only thing covering her nude body was a towel, and Rachel felt the blood race through her veins as Stacey said nonchalantly, "Oh! Hi, Cole. You must have gotten my message. I wasn't sure when I called if you'd still be there," which only incensed Rachel even more.

"You called Mr. Braxton's hotel room?" Rachel gasped.

"I left my purse there last night," Stacey explained, sending her mother a look that dared her not to make a fuss.

"Stacey, I think you'd better get dressed."

"Oops! I almost forgot." She giggled as she ran out of the room. "Don't go away, Cole," she ordered, poking her head around the doorway.

"Mr. Braxton, I think it would be better if you left." Rachel said bluntly as soon as Stacey was gone.

Suddenly Cole was angry—angry that Stacey was a child, angry that she was making him look like the fall guy in this whole sordid mess, angry that he hadn't simply trusted Robert's judgment, and angry at Rachel for looking so damned offended when nothing had happened.

"For God's sake, will you quit looking at me as though I were something that crawled out from under the nearest rock? Any man who had seen your daughter in that bar last night would have assumed she was a consenting adult. If I had been looking for sex do you really think I would have chosen a female who was intoxicated and on the verge of passing out? I took her to my hotel room with the intention of seeing that she was able to return home, but she passed out in my bed and I ended up spending the rest of the evening sleeping on the couch."

Cole felt that with every word he spoke he was losing ground. All it had taken was for Stacey to prance into the kitchen half naked hinting at an intimacy that didn't exist, for Rachel to close her mind to logic. In her mind, her daughter wasn't provocative; he was a lecher. And he would bet a fortune that the young Stacey knew exactly what strings to pull with Mama.

"If you'll excuse me, Mr. Braxton, I have to get these groceries put away." Rachel no longer cared about the Braxton account. Here in her kitchen they were no longer department store executive and fashion designer. Without waiting for him to follow, she walked to the door. But before Cole had crossed the hallway, Stacey reappeared, dressed in skintight leather jeans and an oversized white top that dropped low on one shoulder.

"Cole, you're not leaving?" she exclaimed in dismay.

"My flight leaves at nine-forty."

"You can't just leave without having a drink . . . or better yet, stay for dinner. It's the least I can do to thank you for rescuing me last night." Stacey took his large hand in hers and tried to lead him over to the sofa.

"Stacey, Mr. Braxton is a very busy man and I'm sure he's already made plans for dinner," Rachel said, disliking the gleam that had entered Stacey's eyes.

"Mom, don't you have to check on something in the kitchen?" Stacey said pointedly.

Cole removed his hand from Stacey's grasp discreetly and thrust it into his pant pockets. "Your mother's right, Stacey. I have other plans.'' He tried to make the words sound gentle, for it was obvious today that Stacey really was a child, and he could see the admiration in her eyes when she smiled at him.

''But when will you be back in Chicago?''

Rachel stiffened.

''I have to go where business takes me, and I don't think it will bring me back here for quite some time.''

Was that a hint that Annalise had lost the contract? Or did it mean that he would allow Robert to handle this end?

''Business isn't the only reason to come to Chicago,'' Stacey said provocatively with a teasing smile. ''Thousands of people come for a weekend of fun.''

Rachel clenched her fists at her sides.

''Unfortunately, my work leaves me little time for pleasure.'' He glanced at his watch. ''Really, I must go. Take care.'' And as he walked out into the corridor, Stacey chased after him.

''Cole!'' He paused and she reached up to kiss his cheek. ''Thanks for being so wonderful about last night. I'm sorry I made a fool of myself.''

When Cole glanced back, Rachel was standing in the doorway, a look of disgust on her face. ''Take my advice, Stacey, stay out of bars.'' And as he walked out into the cool spring night he was annoyed with himself for even bothering to try to explain to Rachel. He should have left well enough alone.

## *CHAPTER FOUR*

"I COULD HAVE DIED of embarrassment! Mother, how could you?" Stacey stormed past her mother into the apartment.

"How could I what?" Rachel countered, following her.

"How could you be so rude? The first decent guy who pays me any attention and you treat him like he's got the plague. And why couldn't you have given me a little privacy with him?" She stomped into the living room and plopped onto a Queen Anne chair.

"Stacey, you can't possibly think he's interested in you?"

"Well, if he was he certainly isn't anymore." She slung one leg over the arm of the chair. "When are you going to let me grow up and choose my own friends? I'm seventeen. At my age you were having a baby! But you won't even let me talk to a man if you don't approve of him."

"Stacey, we went through all this earlier today." She sighed and sat down opposite her daughter, taking her hand in hers. "Did you ever think that maybe it's because I did have a baby at seventeen that I want you to be able to have all the fun that normal teenagers have?"

"Are you saying that I kept you from enjoying your youth?"

"You kept me from going half-crazy when your father disappeared in Vietnam. You were a part of him and I wanted you more than anything in the world. But that was seventeen years ago and that was me. Times have changed. There are so many opportunities for you that weren't there for me. I know how important it is to have a boyfriend in your life, but when I see you making bad choices, I have to tell you."

"I know why you're so against Cole. You seem to think I hop from bar to bar hustling older men, but Mom, last night was the first time anything like that happened. It wasn't what you're thinking it was. I knew the moment I laid eyes on him that he was special. He's really nice, Mom, and he wouldn't have gone to the trouble of finding out where I lived if he didn't like me, too."

Rachel chose not to tell Stacey about her encounter with Cole at Annalise, disinclined to encourage any further contact between the two of them. If Stacey knew of their association, heaven only knew how she would use Annalise to contact him.

"He simply wanted to return your purse."

"He didn't have to come over here. He could have left it at the hotel desk."

"Which is what he would have done had you not phoned him."

"But I wanted to see him again. And now I'll probably never see him . . . ever," she said, choking back a sob. "Well, at least that would make you happy, wouldn't it?" And with a jerk she brushed past Rachel, stamping off to her bedroom.

Rachel ate a solitary supper that evening, unwilling to plead with Stacey to quit sulking. She was simply too tired to argue. After soaking away some of her tensions in a warm bath, she tried to speak to Stacey once more before she went to bed, but was met with the petulant response, "Go away. You don't understand."

Was there a teenager alive who thought a parent would understand? She had said the same thing dozens of times to her own mother...because her mother never had understood, which was what frightened her. Would there always be this strain in her relationship with Stacey? She had read all the current self-help books on raising teenagers and had tried all the recommended strategies, but Stacey's growing pains didn't seem to go by the book. Rachel simply wished they could return to the closeness they had shared in earlier years. But the day Stacey would come to her for advice seemed as unlikely as Cole Braxton being gay. He had looked rather odd standing in the hallway with Stacey's purse hanging from his forearm.

And although she didn't want to, Rachel found herself wondering what Cole Braxton was really like. Was he married? Maybe he even had children of his own. How many other Staceys had passed through his life? She had detected a cynicism about him, but there was also a sensitivity in his eyes. Stacey had been right about that. She tried to push thoughts of him out of her mind, but he kept creeping in, even when she made her daily inspection of Floyd's picture, and she found herself noticing how gently Floyd's lips curved into a smile compared to Cole's sculptured mouth. She mentally shook herself. Why should she even be remembering those lips?

AFTER A COUPLE of days of sullenness, Stacey's usual bubbling personality returned. When a boy from school called to invite her to the spring dance, Rachel canceled her punishment, thinking that if Stacey became interested in another male she might quit mooning over Cole. Actually, Stacey hadn't mentioned Cole Braxton since the night he had returned her purse; it was Rachel who kept thinking about the man. She told herself it was because she was worried she might have jeopardized the contract, but it was a long time since she had felt such a strong reaction to a man, and as much as she wanted to deny it, she knew exactly why Stacey had been attracted to him.

Several weeks later, Julian announced his plans to have a dinner party to celebrate Annalise's being chosen for the Braxton label. "You are coming tomorrow night, aren't you, Rachel?"

"Yes, of course."

As much as she would have liked to say no, Rachel accepted his invitation. She had been trying to think of an appropriate excuse to miss the event, but this morning he had announced at a staff meeting that she was to assist him on the Braxton project, precluding any ideas of skipping the affair. The other significant factor had been her discovery that Robert Braxton would be the one she would be working with.

"Great. My sister Yvonne is visiting and she's looking forward to seeing you again. She's also brought Denise along, which is why I was hoping I could persuade you to bring Stacey. A dinner party is hardly exciting entertainment for two teenagers, is it? Maybe they could keep each other company, since Denise is only a year younger than Stacey. What do you think?"

"I'm sure Stacey would be happy to come. Thank you for inviting us both."

Stacey, however, did not find the prospect of spending Friday night with her mother at a dinner party very exciting. They were having supper at Stacey's favorite restaurant, a back-to-the-fifties-style hamburger stand, when Rachel brought up the subject.

"But, Mom, everyone's going to KiKi's party," Stacey protested, punching the buttons on the small jukebox in their booth. "Do you have any quarters?"

"Who's KiKi?" Rachel asked, digging into her purse for some change.

"Katherine Arneson. Everyone calls her KiKi. Her party is going to be so fantastic—I just can't miss it. Oh look, Mom. They've got that one you like by Lionel Richie." Stacey dropped the coins into the slot and within a few seconds a love song filtered around them softly. "Why don't you ask Bud? He usually takes you out to dinner on Friday evenings anyways."

"I don't think Bud would feel comfortable with that crowd. Besides, it's a business dinner to celebrate a big account Annalise has won." She toyed with the frilly toothpick sticking out of her hamburger, hesitant to reveal the Braxton name. "Actually, Julian has put me in charge, so to speak."

"Mom, that's great! Does it mean you'll get a raise?"

"Yes, but what's important is that Julian feels that my work is good enough to stand alone."

"Wait!" Stacey stopped Rachel's hand from raising the soda fountain glass to her lips. "This calls for a toast." Picking up her chocolate malt, Stacey gently clicked her glass with her mother's. "To my Mom... the fashion world's next superstar."

Rachel smiled. "I always said that behind every successful woman is a loyal daughter." She watched Stacey cover her cheeseburger with horseradish sauce. "Your father used to love horseradish on his hamburgers, too," she said wistfully.

"Mom, you say that every time we eat here."

"I know. I guess I just like remembering how like him you are. You have a lot of his mannerisms, which is strange, considering he hasn't been around."

"He's been with me in my heart," Stacey said simply. "So tell me, what's the name of this big account?"

"It's a large chain of department stores—" Rachel paused "—called Braxton's." She avoided Stacey's eyes, taking a bite of her hamburger and a sip of the chocolate milk shake. "They're mostly in the Midwest."

"I've seen their ads in magazines," Stacey acknowledged, making no reference to Cole.

"That's why I can't miss this dinner party. We wouldn't have to stay long at Julian's, but his niece is here from Boston and he specifically requested that you be invited. You could still go to Katherine's party a little later."

"Oh, all right. But promise me we can leave as soon as possible?"

"It can't be too soon for me, either," Rachel admitted.

"How formal is this thing? I suppose I have to wear a dress."

"That would be nice," Rachel said with a wry smile.

Nice was hardly the word Rachel would have used to describe Stacey's dress. Nor had the garment been created at Annalise.

"My God, Stacey, it looks like something Tina Turner would wear!" Rachel gasped when Stacey emerged from her room Friday evening.

"That's what it's supposed to look like. The girl at the boutique said they only got two of them in and I was lucky enough to be there when she was hanging them up. Isn't this fabric neat? It looks like leather, but it's soft. Do you think I should wear the black or the red shoes?" She carried a different one in each hand.

"I think that either of the shoes will work, but the dress won't."

"Mother, be serious."

"I am being serious, Stacey. That dress is not appropriate for a dinner party. In fact, I'd hate to see you wear it anywhere. It's so revealing!" She eyed the low-cut bodice disapprovingly.

"Just because you like your necklines up to your chin doesn't mean I have to. If it makes you feel better, I'll get the jacket that goes with it." She marched back to her bedroom, Rachel following close behind.

"There." She pushed her arms through a puffy-sleeved jacket of the same black slippery fabric that hid the décolletage, but still clung sensuously to her slender torso. "Better?" Stacey turned a full circle.

"Better, but still inappropriate."

"Mom, trust me. This is what girls my age wear. I don't want Julian's niece thinking I'm a nerd."

"Julian's niece is from Boston, not Hollywood." Rachel glanced at her watch. "Are you ready to go?"

"I haven't finished putting on my eye makeup."

"You don't need any color on your eyes. They're beautiful just the way they are and we're running late as it is."

"Just let me add a little sparkle," Stacey begged, bending over the ruffle-skirted dressing table.

"I'll meet you out front, but please hurry."

When Stacey appeared, she had added more than a little sparkle. Rachel had to admit that she did look older than seventeen. What had happened to the little girl with the ribbons and barrettes? Was it only a couple of years ago that she had worn braces on her teeth and wouldn't replace her blue jeans with a dress for anything? How many times had Rachel harped at Stacey to comb her hair—to dress up? Well, tonight she was dressed up, only Rachel wasn't sure if it was the same little girl.

"You look nice, Mom," Stacey remarked as they got into the Honda Civic. "Is that a new dress?"

"Yes. What do you think?" Rachel glanced sideways at her.

"It looks like you." Stacey knew her mother possessed a tremendous amount of creativity, but for some reason she always wore the same style dress, a classic for petite figures that deemphasized her large breasts, and always in a pastel color, this time pink.

Rachel never tired of the breathtaking view Lake Shore Drive afforded in the twilight as it traced Lake

Michigan's shoreline up what was known as the Gold Coast. A smudge of smoke curled into the pink sky as a passing freighter slowly moved across the shimmering water. The tranquility of twilight engulfed Rachel as she maneuvered her tiny car into a parking space, the setting sun casting golden beams on the bronze-tinted glass of Julian's lakefront apartment building. But not even the serenity of a spectacular sunset could chase away the uneasiness she felt as she looked at Stacey entering the exclusive apartment building.

"Rachel, you're the last ones to arrive." Julian greeted them. "Hello, Stacey. My, my." He clicked his tongue. "It is rather unique." He lifted both of her hands and held her at arm's length, appraising her outfit with a genuine smile. "I like it."

"At least you aren't like Mother. She gets upset if it isn't an Annalise."

"That's what I like to hear—loyalty. Come, and I'll introduce you to Denise. Don't go away, Rachel," he said, pointing his index finger. "I want to introduce you to Robert Braxton." He led Stacey across the posh room to a white velveteen sofa where a demure-looking girl sat alone, looking bored and out of place.

Rachel did a quick scan of the crowd and realized that, as usual, Julian's gathering had blossomed from a small dinner party for a few business associates to a large party.

"I had a feeling you two were going to be late." Katie's friendly voice sounded from behind her.

"Hi, Katie." Rachel smiled, grateful for the appearance of a friendly face. "It was Stacey."

"I figured as much when I got a look at her," Katie returned, glancing to where the two girls sat. "Somehow I don't think she and Denise are the same type. Julian told me Denise is studying violin at Juilliard. She won some sort of young people's award for the performing arts."

"Definitely not Stacey's type," Rachel confirmed. "I only hope my daughter remembers her manners."

"Don't worry about it. Kids are kids. They'll be just fine. What you need to do is mingle, take your mind off your daughter. There are people all over the place—on the patio, in the game room, in the living room. And wait until you see Sheila Garret's outfit. She looks like a gypsy going to the prom."

Rachel couldn't help but laugh at Katie's description of one of Julian's unconventional friends. "Stacey will probably love it."

Katie nodded in agreement. "I like your dress. It suits you."

"Thank you. That's the same compliment I received from my daughter earlier this evening. Am I supposed to be making an impression on someone tonight?"

"No, but you're so tiny I thought you might wear some of the petite fashions you created for the Sophisticate line."

"Katie, I'm the mother of a teenager, not a college coed."

"You would look great in them and you know it." Katie eyed Rachel's figure, wondering how anyone could be so unaware of her own assets. "If I had your shape..." She sighed enviously and thought to herself that with the right clothes and a different hairstyle Rachel could easily attract all sorts of attention from men. She had what Katie's mother called a plain prettiness, which could be elegant beauty with a little care. Katie turned her attention to the guests. "I think everyone's here. I wonder what time Julian's planning on serving dinner." She usually acted as hostess at Julian's catered business affairs.

"What's for dinner?" Rachel asked.

"Duck à l'orange with wild rice—in honor of our Minnesota guests. Have you met Robert Braxton yet?"

"No. I was hoping to see Yvonne first."

"Follow me and I'll take you to her. She could use a pleasant diversion. Ever since Cole Braxton arrived, she and Serina have been like two birds after the same worm."

"Cole Braxton?" Rachel stopped abruptly. "I thought you said Robert Braxton was here?"

"He is. But so is Cole."

"But why?" But before Katie could respond, Cole walked through the open patio door, looking even more attractive in his formal evening wear than Rachel had remembered him to be. Her first reaction was to turn and look across the room to see if Stacey had noticed his presence, an action that didn't go unnoticed by Cole. Rachel's eyes darted back and clashed head-on with Cole's for a brief instant before Yvonne's youthful figure emerged from directly behind him.

"Darling. How wonderful to see you." She rushed forward and embraced Rachel. "Julian just showed me the Eclipse collection and it is absolutely stunning. I haven't seen anything in New York that could even compare. Come, you must tell me what's been happening in your life." She took Rachel by the hand and led her out onto the balcony, under the watchful eyes of Cole Braxton. "You don't have any wine," she exclaimed.

"Oh, no thanks. None for me just now."

"No? What about a Perrier?" Yvonne waved to her brother. "Julian, get Rachel a Perrier."

Rachel made all the appropriate replies and smiled as Yvonne recounted her stories about New York and the designers there, but her eyes kept track of Cole Braxton through the open doorway as he mingled with the others. She let Yvonne introduce her to Robert Braxton, who Rachel discovered was pleasant and easy to talk to, unlike his cousin. She wanted to ask him why Cole had come back to Chicago, but she refrained, unwilling to show any interest in the man. Unlike Cole, Robert didn't make her feel incompetent or edgy.

When Cole slipped out of view, Rachel decided to go indoors. "Excuse me, but I think I'll check and see how Stacey and Denise are getting along."

"I'll come, too," Yvonne insisted. "It was sweet of you to bring Stacey to keep Denise from being bored," she commented as they stepped back into the elegantly furnished apartment. "You know how teenagers abhor being alone."

But Denise was alone. And looking very bored.

Rachel had a sinking feeling in the pit of her stomach that as soon as she located the tall, dark Cole Braxton, she would find Stacey.

"Denise, you remember Rachel, don't you, darling?" Yvonne asked, offering her hand to her daughter. "Where's Stacey? In the powder room?"

"She said she wanted to say hi to Mr. Braxton. They're over by the piano."

"Er... she met him last time he was here," Rachel offered apologetically. "I'd better say hello, too."

She arrived just in time to prevent Stacey from picking up a glass of champagne from the passing waiter's tray. "Here. Have mine. I didn't really want it." Rachel handed her daughter the champagne glass filled with Perrier, hoping to save her the embarrassment of forbidding her to drink. From the look in Stacey's eyes, she wasn't happy to see her mother.

"Hi, Mom. Look who's here." She hooked her arm through Cole's in a possessive manner, causing Rachel's stomach to contract.

"Mr. Braxton," she acknowledged coolly.

"Ms Kincaid." He didn't miss the way Rachel's eyes had darted from Stacey's arm wrapped inside his to his face.

"You'll have to excuse me a moment," Cole said, gently extracting his arm.

"Only if you promise me a ride in *Melinda Sue*," Stacey replied, clinging to his sleeve. "Please! I've never been in a hot air balloon before."

"You'd have to come to Minneapolis," Cole told her, his voice sounding slightly weary.

"I'd do anything, Cole," Stacey cooed provocatively.

Rachel wanted to gag her daughter. "Stacey, I want to talk to you privately," she demanded, steering her to the side of the room.

"Not now, Mother," she said, making a face as she sipped the Perrier and realized that it wasn't champagne. "I should have known you wouldn't be drinking." She set the glass down, then walked away.

Rachel watched as Denise attempted to get Stacey's attention. Stacey just ignored her and moved over to the group of people surrounding Cole. Rachel still couldn't help but notice how obvious Stacey's attempts to flirt with Cole were. As inconspicuously as possible, she followed her daughter and separated her from the others.

"Stacey, you're supposed to be keeping Denise company," she said, glancing toward the sofa where Denise sat thumbing through a magazine.

"Mother, do you think I want to spend my time talking to a girl about classical music when there's a great-looking guy like Cole in the room?"

"That great-looking guy is not interested in a teenage girl, Stacey. There's only one reason he's here and that's because of Braxton's contract with Annalise."

"You knew all along who he was yet you didn't tell me, did you?" Stacey accused.

"Since I didn't think we'd come into contact with him again I didn't see any point in it."

"You knew you'd be working with him."

"Julian told me I'd be working with Robert. Thank goodness, because personally I find Cole Braxton disgusting."

"Are you sure, Mother?"

"Of course I'm sure. He's been nothing but unpleasant ever since I met him."

"Maybe the reason you don't want me involved with him is because you're attracted to him. I've noticed the way you blush when he looks at you."

"That's because I'm embarrassed over the way my daughter is behaving."

"Oh, Mother, you're so old-fashioned."

Rachel watched her walk away.

"Teenage turmoil?" Katie gently inquired, coming to stand beside Rachel.

"No, just a typical mother-daughter conversation. She's a bit taken with Cole Braxton."

"Aren't we all!" Katie watched Rachel's eyes follow the young girl over to where Cole stood.

"No, we *all* aren't," Rachel returned a bit more sharply than she had intended. "Gosh, I'm hungry. I missed lunch today."

"Haven't you seen the hors d'oeuvres?"

"No, but I think a dose of sugar and caffeine would help. Does Julian have any cola?"

"I'll get you some. You wait here. It'll give Stacey something to do." Rachel watched her walk over to where Cole and Stacey stood, say something to Stacey, then lead the young girl by the arm into the kitchen. Cole immediately walked over to Rachel.

"You're not having a very good time, are you?" he asked.

Rachel detected no sarcasm in his voice.

"What makes you say that?"

"I've been watching you from the moment you arrived."

Warmth spread through her. She looked away from him, taking a few seconds to try to squelch the airy feeling in her stomach. "I'm not much for parties."

"The quiet-evenings-at-home-with-a-good-book type?"

"That doesn't make me sound very exciting."

"Do you want to be considered exciting?" His eyes met hers and Rachel could feel her heartbeat accelerate and her face grow warm under his gaze. Confusion clouded her eyes, the thick lashes fluttering as she realized that she had almost said yes.

"What made you change your mind about using Annalise? I didn't think I passed the test," she said stiffly.

"Obviously, you did. I'm here, aren't I?"

"I understood that Robert was in charge."

"He is."

"I'm surprised to see you here. You don't look like a man who would make unnecessary business trips."

Cole had been asking himself that same question all day. What was he doing in Chicago when he should have been in Phoenix?

"Robert asked me to come," he lied. What the hell did it matter what this woman thought, he asked himself. He owed her no explanation of his actions.

"Here's your cola, Mom." Stacey handed her mother a tall glass, glancing suspiciously from her mother to Cole.

"Thank you, Stacey."

Cole noticed how uncomfortable Rachel became the minute Stacey appeared. "Stacey, if you don't mind, I'd like to discuss some business with your mother."

"Sure." Stacey made a sulky gesture of acceptance, then left.

Trying to maintain her composure Rachel asked, "Why did you do that?"

"If we're going to work together successfully, I think we should get one thing settled."

"And what's that, Mr. Braxton?"

"I'm not interested in your daughter. This is a professional relationship and I'm not such a snake that I'm going to seduce the daughter of a business associate. So please stop looking at me as though I were going to ravish her the minute you turned your head the wrong way."

"She's got a crush on you," Rachel reluctantly admitted, annoyed that she found the scent of his aftershave disturbing.

"I know. She appears to be at that rather vulnerable period in life—somewhere between teenager and adult, which is why I haven't been more discouraging."

"Well maybe you ought to be, considering the circumstances."

"Would it make you feel better if I publicly humiliated her?"

"No...it's just..." Rachel was beginning to feel warm and tingly inside and a little bit silly. She finished her cola and looked around the room, hoping desperately that someone would come to her rescue.

"What is it you want me to do, Ms Kincaid?"

Suddenly Rachel felt as though her tongue was doing gymnastic maneuvers. "Pweez." She cleared her throat. "Please, don't hurt her." She couldn't understand why the words sounded so strange to her ears. She needed to get away from this man before she made a complete fool of herself. "Everything would be so much easier if you'd just leave us alone." She turned and sought Stacey.

"What were you two talking about?" Stacey demanded.

"I told him to leave you alone."

"Oh, my God, I could die of embarrassment." She rolled her eyes heavenward.

"Stacey, is it warm in here or is it just me? Maybe I shouldn't have worn this long-sleeved dress. I feel a little light-headed."

"Want me to get you another cola, Mom?"

"Okay." She smiled, then removed her glasses. It was much easier to see across the room without them. Unconsciously her hips started swaying to the calypso rhythm of the background music as she walked toward the sofa.

"Here, Mom. Maybe this will cool you." Stacey handed her another glass of cola, which Rachel quickly swallowed.

When Katie walked by, Rachel called out. "Dinner ready yet? I think the Gypsy's hungry." She nodded toward Sheila Garret who was sampling the caviar, then sank down onto the sofa, giggling.

"Rachel?" Katie dropped down beside her.

"Katie?" Rachel met her inquisitive gaze with a big smile.

"Have you been drinking?" She practically whispered the words.

"Drinking what?" she returned in a low voice.

"If I didn't know better, I'd say you have a buzz on."

"It's just so hot in here." Rachel undid the top three buttons of her dress, allowing a hint of cleavage to show, and causing Katie's eyes to bulge in astonishment. When Rachel had swallowed the remainder of the cola, Katie took the glass from her hand and sniffed.

"Katie, you didn't put something in my cola, did you? I'm really feeling strange."

Katie glanced over to where Stacey sat. "Rachel, I'm sorry, but you must have gotten someone else's glass by mistake. This one has booze in it."

"Booze? But Katie, you know I can't drink on an empty stomach." Rachel's voice was steadily increasing in volume and her words were becoming slurred, attracting several curious glances.

"Why don't you come out to the kitchen and we'll see how dinner's coming," Katie suggested.

Katie could hear the other guests murmuring quietly, but fortunately Rachel was oblivious to it. Katie set her down at the small wooden table out of the path of the caterers and placed a cup of coffee in front of her. "Here. Drink this. I'll be right back."

Within seconds, Katie returned with Julian. "Rachel, love." He dropped down onto his haunches before her. "What seems to be the problem? Katie says you're not feeling well. Shall I get Stacey to drive you home?"

"But Julian, I don't want to miss your dinner. I'm hungry. Everyone is! You really ought to be serving dinner."

The caterers looked away discreetly.

Upon seeing Cole walk through the swinging door, she added, "Mr. Braxton must be hungry, too. He's in the kitchen." At which Julian rose to walk over and confer with Cole.

"What do you suppose the big secret is?" Rachel asked Katie, attempting to stand. But the room was starting to spin, and she quickly dropped back down onto the cane-backed chair. "Katie, I don't think I do feel good."

"Rachel, I'm going to have Cole drive you home," Julian said soothingly, crossing the room.

"But what about my car?" she protested.

"Stacey can drive your car home," he said, placing his arm around her shoulder.

"But I took away her car keys. She's been misbehaving." She cast an accusing look at Cole. "I'll drive Stacey home myself." She wanted to give her tongue a good twist. No matter how hard she tried, she couldn't seem to articulate the letter "S."

Katie looked bewildered by Rachel's behavior. "Rachel, why don't you let Stacey borrow your keys just for tonight? You shouldn't be driving in your condition."

"I'm not drunk." She looked from Katie to Julian to Cole. "Am I?"

"Just a victim of circumstance, as they would say." Cole helped her to stand and placed his arm around her waist. Rachel wanted to protest, but when she felt the weakness in her whole body she was grateful for the strong frame to lean on. "Katie, would you see that Stacey meets us downstairs?" And for the second time in less than a few weeks, Cole found himself escorting a Kincaid female out into the fresh air.

## *CHAPTER FIVE*

"STUCK TOGETHER AGAIN," Rachel said, suppressing a giggle.

Cole smiled to himself as he walked arm in arm with her across the flagstoned courtyard of the apartment complex. Her eyes were slightly glassy, her cheeks flushed, and she was clinging to his arm as though she would fall off the edge of the earth without his assistance. Much to his surprise, he found her completely charming. There was an attractive vulnerability about her, which he had unwillingly responded to in Julian's kitchen.

When she drew to a sudden halt, he asked, "Are you going to be all right?"

"Are you?" she countered.

"That's what I asked you."

Rachel met his inquisitive stare with a capricious smile. "I feel silly," she said with a lilting voice. "Like I'm walking on a moonbeam."

Cole led her over to the car and gently helped her inside, securing her seat belt for her when her fingers fumbled with the clasp. As he climbed in alongside her, Rachel couldn't help but notice how his hair shone like the black satin on the lapels of his dinner jacket. He really was quite handsome, she thought to herself and felt an unfamiliar desire to rest her head on his broad shoulder.

"Is Stacey behind us?" She jerked around, suddenly remembering her daughter.

Cole nodded and swung the big car out into traffic. He didn't need to say much on the way back to Rachel's apartment. Her steady flow of conversation was enough for the two of them. She told him about Stacey's experience at summer camp and how she had won the baton-twirling competition in the fifth grade and a blue ribbon in her junior high school's science fair. By the time they reached the brick apartment building, he knew the names of every school Stacey had ever attended, the grades she had earned and all the organizations she had participated in. Cole knew Rachel felt the need to defend Stacey's character to him. And so he listened to her ramble, responding politely now and then. It was obviously important to her that he think Stacey was a good girl.

Even with the slight slur in her voice, there was a lilting quality about it as she giggled or sighed at the memories of Stacey's childhood. She was a completely different woman when she talked about her daughter, Cole mused, her voice filled with a warmth and gentleness he had not witnessed previously. What he couldn't figure out was how such a quiet and refined woman could have raised such a rebellious daughter. He found himself wondering how long Stacey's father had been dead and if there was another male figure in the picture. The black wing-tip shoes had to belong to someone, yet Julian had assured him that the two women lived alone. He glanced at the neckline of Rachel's dress, which only hinted at the shapely figure hidden within, and felt an inquisitive urge to know about the men in Rachel's life.

After parking the car, Cole reached over and released Rachel's seat belt. She didn't wait for him to come around, but opened the car door and stepped out onto the pavement, forgetting how unstable her legs were. She swayed uneasily and Cole rushed around the car to lend her his arm.

"Oops! I think the moonbeam is slipping." She smiled up at him.

Cole held her gaze for a second before his eyes dropped to the hand clinging to his arm. She looked so fragile, yet so determined as she struggled to retain her dignity.

She accepted his help up the steps and into the apartment building. Pausing on the landing she asked, "Where's Stacey? She has my keys."

"Here she is now." Stacey came down the hallway looking somewhat sheepish and exchanged a guarded look with Cole.

"Go on in, Mom," Stacey said, unlocking the door. "I think I'm going to go over to KiKi's party."

"But you haven't had any dinner," Rachel protested. "Let me make you something to eat first."

Cole led Rachel over to the sofa. "Your mother should have something to eat, too." He spoke to Stacey, casting her a glance that dared her to disagree. He didn't doubt for a moment that she had thought it was a humorous prank to spike her mother's drink, and the thought angered him. "Why don't you go into the kitchen and see what you can do."

Stacey tossed her purse onto a chair and stood with her hands on her hips. "I think maybe Mom should just go to bed. But I'd be happy to fix you something to eat." She looked at Cole, her eyes brimming with anticipation.

"I can do it," Rachel declared, about to rise from the sofa until Cole's arm halted her.

"You stay put. I'm sure Stacey can manage," Cole ordered, watching a smiling Stacey glide into the kitchen.

"How about an omelet?" she suggested eagerly when Cole appeared beside her. She was unprepared for his furious accusation.

"I want you to tell me why you would want to do that to your mother," he demanded angrily.

"Do what?"

Her dovelike response had him clenching his fists. "You know damn well what. You're the one who put the vodka in her soft drink."

"It was only a little bit."

"Well for someone who hasn't eaten all day it only takes a little bit to become intoxicated."

"I can't believe you're reacting this way. What's wrong with Mom having a little fun? Everyone drinks at parties."

"Not everyone, Stacey."

"You seem to enjoy your Scotch. Besides, Mom's always so uptight. I just wanted her to relax a little bit. I thought maybe if she started having a good time she'd quit worrying about me. She follows my every move."

"With good reason, it would seem."

"Why? What has she been saying to you about me?"

"She doesn't need to tell me anything, Stacey." Cole put his hands over hers, releasing a long, impatient sigh. "It would seem that alcohol has affected all three of us. You wouldn't have allowed a total stranger to pick you up in that bar if you hadn't been drinking, nor would I be standing here in your kitchen if your mother hadn't been drinking."

"You're wrong, Cole," Stacey objected. The conversation was not going at all the way she had anticipated. Tilting her head appealingly, she moved closer to him. "We were destined to meet. You're doing business with Annalise, and I know that after Mom gets to know you, she won't disapprove of our relationship."

Cole frowned. "Look, Stacey, I think you're a very attractive girl, but we have no relationship." He extricated his hands from hers.

"It's because of Mom, isn't it?"

"No, but your mother is right. You need a boyfriend who has the same interests as you, not someone old enough to be your father. But that doesn't mean we can't be friends." He paused, then added in a softer tone, "Your mother only wants what's best for you."

"God, I'm so sick of her thinking she knows what's best for me." Stacey barreled into the living room, ready to have it out with her mother. But Rachel was fast asleep on the sofa, her tiny feet tucked underneath her. Stacey picked up her purse and removed a cigarette, lighting it with a strike of a match.

"You know, everyone thinks that she's some kind of saintly widow. She doesn't drink, she doesn't smoke. I wonder what everyone would say if they knew that she's never had a husband." She exhaled a long stream of gray smoke.

Cole couldn't have been more astounded, but he didn't bat an eyelash. "I don't think that's anyone's business but your mother's, do you?" he said in a menacingly quiet tone. "After what you pulled this evening I think the least you can do is help her to bed." He wanted desperately to leave, but before he could cross the room, Stacey had rushed past him and opened the door.

"Where are you going?" Cole demanded.

"*That* is none of your business." And with a swing of her tawny hair, she walked out the door.

Cole sank down on the Queen Anne chair. How had he gotten into such a predicament? He looked over at Rachel and was struck once again by her vulnerable appearance. While she slept, he was able to study her features without her throwing nasty looks at him. The other times he had tried to look at her she had made him feel like he was ogling her.

Cole noted how incredibly thick her eyelashes were as they lay close against her cheeks. And instead of being pressed together tightly, her lips were slightly parted. With her hair drawn back away from her face she almost reminded him of a princess, sleep bestowing a patrician quality upon her delicate features. Her slender neck was going to end up with a terrible crick in it if she slept in that position all night long. Maybe he should carry her into her bedroom.

God, he was tired. It was thirty-six hours since he had had any sleep, and his body was beginning to protest. He had just returned from an all-night flight when Robert had announced his intention of flying to

Chicago. So what had he done? He had told himself he had to come too, to please his grandfather. Now here, he was dead on his feet, wondering if he should put this woman to bed, stay and wait for her spoiled daughter to return or simply wash his hands of the whole mess.

Rachel stirred, stretching her leg in a manner that caused her skirt to ride up over her left thigh. A very delicate, attractive thigh, Cole thought, as an unfamiliar sensation prompted him to cross the room and lift her into his arms.

He was surprised at how little she weighed as he carried her down the hallway, her cheek falling against his neck in a warm, familiar manner. Two doors were open, and a quick glance told him which room was Rachel's. He gently deposited her on the satin comforter atop the brass canopy bed, then turned on the small ginger-jar lamp on the nightstand. His eyes made a quick survey of the room, noting the tiny print wallpaper and the frilly priscilla curtains covering the window. Over the bed hung a watercolor Cole could only guess had been created by a younger Stacey, and in the corner of the room stood an exercise bicycle.

He looked once more at Rachel. The front of her dress had come partially open, exposing a lacy teddy and a voluptuous bosom that Rachel, up to this point, had successfully hidden. A deep sigh whistled through his teeth. She ought to be designing undergarments; she's a pro at minimizing the bust, Cole said to himself. A man could get distracted by those breasts. She had to have a housecoat or something he could cover her up with. He walked over to the closet and swung the door open, immediately taken aback by the life-size photo that confronted him. For a minute he just stood and stared at the worn picture, and wondered why it should bother him that Rachel had a soldier's picture on her closet door. Feeling a bit guilty, as though he had invaded her privacy, he quickly pulled out the robe and closed the closet door.

Focusing on her feet, he spread the robe over her exposed curves. He could see through the nylon stockings that her toenails were painted a bright red. Would he ever understand women? Rachel wore no lipstick but she painted her toenails! As he reached over to turn off the lamp, he noticed a small brass picture frame with three oval photographs in it. One he recognized as the soldier on the closet door. The other was Stacey, and the third was a woman with two small children.

Back in the living room, he loosened his bow tie and undid the top few buttons of his silk shirt. He stretched out on the sofa, lifting his feet onto the ottoman as he reached for the phone. No wonder Rachel had fallen asleep so quickly. It was a very comfortable sofa. Julian had insisted that he and Robert stay at his place, but right now all he wanted was a quiet room; after the past two days he needed silence. Glancing at his watch he knew that the party at Julian's would still be in full swing. He could catch a couple of hours now and then return to the Forrest place after Stacey had returned safely.

He was going soft in his old age, he thought. First there was his gallant attempt to save the impudent teenage girl from the local Lotharios at the bar, and then tonight he had played the knight in shining armor in order to spare that girl's mother embarrassment. Cole Braxton, gentleman extraordinaire. What a laugh his friends would have if they ever knew. Well, tomorrow he would wash his hands of the whole mess. He didn't need his protective instincts resurrected. He had buried them with Melinda Sue. "Uh-uh," he mumbled aloud. The sooner he was away from these two unpredictable females the better. Maybe he should simply leave right now. Why should he waste any energy worrying about a seventeen-year-old he barely knew? Because he, too, having been a parent, knew the anxiety a child's absence could cause. It wasn't for Stacey's sake that he waited, but for Rachel's. And before he could give it any more thought, he fell asleep.

RACHEL OPENED HER EYES, then closed them again, her head protesting even the slightest movement. Something wasn't right. She was on top of the rose satin comforter and her nightgown was twisted uncomfortably around her midriff. She opened her eyes again and saw that it wasn't her nightgown but her cocktail dress from last night. And with that discovery came the memories of Julian's party—and her abrupt exodus.

The last thing she remembered was sitting on the sofa while Cole and Stacey were... were what? Her brain ignored her efforts to think lucidly. Propping herself up on one elbow, she waited for her head to quit swimming before forcing herself out of bed. With slow, deliberate movements, she stepped out of the dress and into her blue robe. Then, she sank down onto the bed to peel off her panty hose. She would have loved to climb back under the covers and pretend that last night hadn't happened. It was only with a great effort that she made it into the bathroom, washed her face and brushed the vile taste from her mouth. She frowned at the way her once neat chignon now hung lopsided over her left ear, then pulled the remaining pins from her hair. As each long stroke of the hairbrush pulled on her already aching head, she grimaced and she abandoned her effort to give order to the unruly waves after only a couple of minutes. With small, indecisive steps, she walked across to Stacey's room and was puzzled by her daughter's absence.

Stacey had come home with her last night . . . she remembered her and Cole going into the kitchen. A feeling of unease crept under her skin.

"Stacey," she called out and made her way into the living room, hoping to find her lounging around.

The last thing she expected to see was a man's long, lean body sprawled out on her sofa. Her sudden, startled gasp had Cole shifting, as though he was trying to get comfortable.

"Where's Stacey and what are you doing on my couch?" Rachel demanded in a weak voice, her head splitting with pain.

Cole opened his eyes, then sat up with a jerk. He stretched his shoulders and ran a hand across the back of his neck before rising to confront Rachel. He was just as surprised as she that he had spent the night on her sofa, but right now he was stiff and sore and not in the mood to be assaulted verbally. Especially after the trouble he had gone to for her.

"In case you've forgotten, I brought you home last night."

Rachel flushed with embarrassment and clutched the lapels of her robe closer together. Was it her imagination or had his gaze lingered just a little too long? Suddenly conscious of her appearance, she remembered the image that had stared at her from the mirror only minutes earlier and wished she could disappear. Was Cole always going to witness her most embarrassing moments? She knew she had made a fool of herself last night and now it was obvious that she was suffering from a hangover. If only she had taken a few more minutes with her hair, she wouldn't look as though she had put her finger in an electrical outlet.

"But didn't Stacey come home, too?" she asked, trying to casually smooth down her undisciplined hair.

"She did but she left after you fell asleep."

"Did she tell you where she was going?"

"She isn't the sweetest-dispositioned teenager I've ever met," he said sarcastically, then, regretting his orneriness, added, "She said something about going to KiKi's."

Rachel opened the telephone book on the desk. "I'd better call and make sure she's there."

Cole watched her make the call and saw the relief spread across her tense features.

"She was in the shower but she's going to call back," Rachel said stiffly as she replaced the receiver.

Once again Cole was angry at the delinquent Stacey. He had been a parent and he could sympathize with Rachel. Stacey could at least have left a note for her mother.

"Why do you always jump to conclusions about me, Rachel?" he found himself asking, then wondered why the hell it should matter.

"I don't," she denied.

"Yes, you do. The minute you found Stacey missing you figured it was my fault."

"No, you're wrong. I was simply startled to find you on my couch."

Cole eyed her suspiciously, flexing his stiff muscles.

"Thank you for bringing me home last night," Rachel said to fill the awkward silence.

"You're welcome." He could see the pain in her eyes and guessed the reason. He had felt that horrible many times in the past five years. He knew he drank too much, but his suffering was self-induced. Rachel's wasn't. He could make her the Braxton cure-all, then leave. "I would imagine you've got a bit of a sore head this morning?" he said with a knowing half smile.

"Just a bit," she confirmed.

"If you show me your kitchen I'll make you an old cure my grandfather taught me," he offered.

All Rachel wanted was to be allowed to suffer in peace. "Look, Mr. Braxton..."

"Don't you think it's time you called me Cole, Rachel?" he interrupted her.

"Cole, then." Rachel drew her palm across her forehead. "Considering everything that's happened, I'd feel a lot better if you would just go." She was certain that if he didn't leave soon she would end up disgracing herself in front of him.

He looked at her in disbelief. God, she wasn't just an independent little thing but stubborn as well! "Why feel rotten all morning when I can fix you a remedy that'll work in ten minutes?" He walked past her into the kitchen, ignoring her sounds of protest as she feebly traipsed behind him.

"Are you always so overbearing?" she asked, clutching the back of a kitchen chair before sitting down on the vinyl seat.

"Ninety percent of the time."

Rachel watched as he opened cupboard doors, delved into the refrigerator, and then dumped unmeasured quantities of various food items into her blender. Soon, he was pouring red liquid into a tall glass.

"It's important that you drink it all at once," he advised, setting the glass in front of her.

Rachel eyed the liquid distastefully. The appearance was enough to cause her stomach to protest and Cole said sternly, "Don't smell it...just drink it...and fast!"

With eyes closed, Rachel downed the entire glass, her lips puckering from the aftertaste. "Oh, God! That was awful!"

"Just sit for about fifteen minutes and I promise you you'll feel terrific." He sat in the chair opposite her.

"Now I know why I don't drink on an empty stomach."

"I was as surprised by what happened as you were." His voice was low and reassuring.

"I know I should feel embarrassed, but right now I feel too rotten to even care." She dropped her face into her hands, her hair catching the sunlight as it fell forward. Cole had to fight the impulse to bury his hands in the gentle tresses draped around her arms.

After a few minutes of silence, when the only sound that could be heard was the low hum of the refrigerator motor, she lifted her head off her arms and said, "Cole, I want you to tell me how bad I was . . . what I mean is, I'm not sure I remember everything that happened last night."

He looked at the long lashes fanning her high, rounded cheekbones and felt the strangest need to tell her that no one had noticed a thing. "You were fortunate, Rachel, that Katie discovered your soda had been spiked before you did anything other than become a little silly." He almost added that he had never seen a more charming tipsy female in his life, but stopped himself in time.

"You wouldn't just be saying that to try to make me feel better?" she questioned, then saw him raise his eyebrows and added, "No, you wouldn't . . ." Her voice trailed off, remembering their previous confrontations.

"How are you feeling now?" He neatly avoided her question and glanced at his watch. "Your fifteen minutes are nearly up."

Rachel stood up gingerly and took a deep breath. "I think I'm hungry. It worked!" she exclaimed with an incredulous smile. "You ought to package it and sell it."

"Nothing but the best from Braxton's." He hummed a few bars of the advertising jingle synonymous with the department store chain.

"Now if only I could make those memories of last night disappear with a magic potion."

"To be perfectly honest with you Rachel, most of Julian's guests were already half lit when you arrived and even if they hadn't been, I doubt that your behavior would have raised an eyebrow. Everyone at Annalise has a great deal of respect for you and your work. No one is going to censure you." He smiled at her and she experienced a strange, unfamiliar sensation in her chest. It was easier to parry his pointed barbs than to accept his praise. She quickly changed the subject.

"I just realized the reason I'm so hungry is because we missed dinner. You must be famished." She eyed his large frame, remembering that he, too, had missed dinner at Julian's. "Would you like some breakfast . . . it's the least I can do . . . to return the favor."

What harm was there in having breakfast? Cole looked at her soft eyes and forgot his resolve to have nothing to do with the Kincaid females. "Would you mind if I washed up first?"

"No, not at all. The bathroom's at the end of the hallway and there are fresh towels in the linen closet just inside the door."

Rachel had hoped that he would refuse her offer. She did feel a hundred percent better, but she couldn't help but be disturbed by his presence. While Cole freshened up she quickly changed into a pair of twill slacks and a chambray shirt, grateful that at least the sickly green pallor was gone from her skin. Instead of taking the time to secure her hair into a chignon, she left it hanging around her shoulders.

The only reaction from Cole was a slight raising of one eyebrow. She looked slightly nervous, her movements jerky as she whisked the eggs and poured them into the omelet pan. Was it he or would any man have made her ill at ease? Once again he thought about the men's shoes that had been resting next to the doorway and the photo poster on her closet door. When he realized that he was staring at her, he turned his attention to the diamond-studded cuff links he had removed from his silk shirt.

"I'm sorry about crashing on your sofa like that. I hope I haven't put you in an awkward position." God, why had he said that? It sounded as if he thought she was some Victorian female whom he had tried to compromise.

Rachel avoided his face when she spoke, concentrating on buttering the toast that had popped up out of the toaster. She wanted to scream *awkward? Everything that has happened between the two of us has been awkward,* but instead she said softly, "I'm the one who should be apologizing for taking you away from Julian's party and dinner. You didn't have to bring me home. Stacey could have driven me."

He hadn't trusted Stacey with her own mother. And then that . . . feeling had surfaced and it had seemed only natural that he see she get home safely.

"Actually, I was grateful for the excuse to leave. Yesterday I had just returned from Hong Kong and I was suffering from jet lag. When I sat down on that comfortable sofa of yours, I had the intention of catching forty winks, not eight hours." She reminded him of a windup doll, systematically preparing breakfast. Everything about her was delicate, from the way she wrapped the cloth napkins around the silverware and placed the bundles on the crocheted lace place mats, to the manner in which she tossed the cracked eggshells into the garbage can. Her loose hair lent a wanton quality to her aristocratic features. He didn't know how he could ever have thought her plain.

Rachel glanced quickly at Cole as she set the plate in front of him. The dark shadow along his jawline enhanced her initial image of him as a ladies' man. As she sat across from him, she wondered how many other women had cooked breakfast for him and had seen him in his wrinkled clothes, the silk shirt open at the neck and the sleeves rolled back. A man's presence at breakfast was an uncommon situation for her, but she was certain that he was no stranger to spending the night in a woman's home.

She poured him a cup of coffee and was annoyed to see her hands tremble ever so slightly. "Do you take sugar or cream?" she asked.

"No, that's fine." He raised his hand off the table. She seemed slightly breathless, and Cole wasn't sure if it was because of his presence or because of the work she had done. He had to admit she was the only woman he knew who could serve up breakfast without a trace of having been in the kitchen. And it was a good meal, too. It was nice seeing a woman eat a normal breakfast for a change. Most of his companions rarely ate breakfast...and wouldn't make it even if he requested it.

To Rachel's surprise, breakfast was enjoyable. While they ate, Cole spoke of the fashions he had seen in Hong Kong and asked her opinion on several recent trends in the fashion industry. He told her of Braxton's golden anniversary celebration, which would be a tribute to his grandfather, as well as the premiere of the Mr. B's Boutique. They talked for an hour and Rachel was surprised that the time passed so quickly.

"Can I get you anything else?" she asked.

"No, I'm fine. Thank you, Rachel. I eat at restaurants so often it's nice having a home-cooked meal." He smiled and for a brief moment there was more than warmth in his eyes.

Rachel cleared away the dishes, then refilled his cup. "I don't often have the chance to cook breakfast. Stacey seldom eats any."

He felt like saying, *She doesn't deserve any,* but held his tongue and said, "From what I understand, that's typical of most teenagers." He picked up his cup and looked at her over its rim.

The mention of Stacey seemed to change the tone of the conversation, so she was surprised by his next words.

"Rachel, can you spend the day with me?"

She snapped her head around and looked at him in confusion.

"Julian, Robert and I are meeting to go over some of the details for the Mr. B's Boutique. I thought you should be there," he said quickly.

"I can't. Saturday is the one day of the week Stacey and I spend together." As if on cue, the phone rang and it was Stacey.

Cole had moved discreetly out of Rachel's vision, but he could still hear her end of the conversation, and he had no trouble guessing what Stacey was saying on the other end. Having already made plans for the day, she had no intention of spending this Saturday afternoon with her mother.

"Everything okay?" Cole asked as Rachel walked into the living room, her hands clamped together. It was obvious she had been crying.

"Fine," Rachel said, biting down on her lower lip in an attempt to stem the falling tears. "Can I get you more coffee?" She wished Cole would leave. How much more humiliation did he have to witness?

Cole should have said, *No, thank you, goodbye,* and left. But it irritated him to think of Stacey out running around and having a good time while Rachel sat home worrying about whether she had made a fool of herself. He could still hear the pride in her voice as she had recounted memorable events from Stacey's childhood. And then he recalled Stacey's bratty voice announcing to him, a near-stranger, that she was illegitimate, hoping to discredit her mother. So instead of leaving he found himself saying, "Just one more cup."

## *CHAPTER SIX*

RACHEL SET the silver-plated serving tray on the glass-topped coffee table. As Cole sat down, he caught a glimpse of the men's shoes out of the corner of his eye.

"I would imagine it's quite difficult as a single parent raising a teenager," he commented.

"Yes, it is. I guess I spoke a little too much last night, didn't I?"

"The alcohol loosened your tongue, but at least you said nice things."

"She is nice, Cole," Rachel said with a proud gleam in her eye. "She hasn't had it easy, growing up without a father."

"What happened to him, Rachel?" he asked gently.

She walked over to the desk and ran the tip of her finger across the silver photo frame around Floyd's picture. "He hasn't come back from Vietnam yet," she said simply, lifting the photo for Cole's perusal. "His name is Floyd Andrews. He was caught in a jungle ambush and listed as Class Two—probably captured."

Cole did not miss the fact that she hadn't said he never came back, but that he hadn't come back *yet*. Suddenly the soldier's picture on the closet door made sense. "How long has it been?"

"Eighteen years, four months and sixteen days," she said soberly, returning the silver frame to the desk.

"Rachel, I'm sorry. It must have been terribly difficult for you."

"Stacey's the one who has suffered. She's never seen her father, never had the chance to get to know his humor, his goodness. All she has is a piece of blue velvet with a Purple Heart and a Bronze Star on it. At least I have the memories of our short time together to cling to."

"Haven't you ever thought of remarrying?"

"I said he was missing in action, Cole, not dead."

"But Rachel, didn't the President declare almost all the MIA soldiers dead?" His voice was gently persuasive.

"Yes, and for a year I almost gave up hope. But then the boat people started arriving in the United States with reports of Americans alive in Southeast Asia, being held captive in brutal conditions. And I thought, what if Floyd's alive in some slave-labor camp, crippled by disease." Her voice was quietly steady. "I can't help but wonder if he ever thinks about the child he's never seen, or if he's even withstood the mental torture to be able to remember that we're back here for him."

"It would seem to me that the chances are almost next to none that this is the case, Rachel."

"But don't you see, Cole? There have been conflicting government reports from armed forces personnel that indicate it is a possibility. And then there's my book of poetry."

"Your book of poetry?" Cole raised an eyebrow.

"Here. I'll show you." She pulled open the desk drawer, removed a worn copy of Elizabeth Barrett Browning's poems and handed it to Cole. "I gave this to Floyd when he left for Vietnam."

"And it wasn't sent home with his personal belongings?"

"No. It came by mail, wrapped in brown paper, almost two years after he was reported missing. There was no return address, only a postmark from Hong Kong."

"And you think Floyd sent it to you?"

"I think it was his way of telling me he's still alive."

Cole sighed. "But anyone could have found it and simply returned it to you." He opened the cover and read the inscription. "Your name and address are in the front."

"In my heart I know he's alive," Rachel said simply.

"And how does Stacey feel about a father she's never even seen?"

"She hasn't lost her hope that he'll someday return. It seems to have become easier for her as she's grown older. Small children can't comprehend what war is, let alone that some fathers never return from it. As a child she would always ask, 'Is my daddy coming home tomorrow, Mommy?' and all I could ever answer was, 'I hope so, but we won't know for sure until he walks through the door.'

"Probably the hardest part has been dealing with the apathy. Few people seem to care that more than two thousand soldiers have never been accounted for. That's more than two thousand families that have gone through the anguish of not knowing what has happened to loved ones. Many have become so emotionally drained that they've simply given up. Floyd's mother has. We don't see her much anymore. Her husband died several years ago and he was the one who shared our hope. Now there's just me and Stacey left to wait."

"I'm sorry, Rachel." He wanted to hold her close to him, but she moved back slightly as he moved forward, and he knew that she didn't want his comfort. After eighteen years she needed no sympathy.

"It's what my heart knows that's important."

There was silence in the room and Cole felt like an intruder as he watched the play of emotions across her face. She was lost in her memories, and he wanted to bring her back to the present, make her smile again.

"Rachel, spend the day with me."

The temptation to step toward him alarmed her. She was grateful for the ringing of the phone, which forced her to look away from his intense gaze.

"It's Julian looking for you," Rachel mouthed, holding her hand over the receiver. She seemed embarrassed and Cole guessed that she was uncomfortable at Julian's having found him at her apartment.

"Yes, Julian." Cole said, watching Rachel cross the room to clear away the coffee cups and return the silver tray to the kitchen. "No, no problem. Uh-huh. I see." She was sneaking glances at him when she thought he wasn't looking.

"I told Julian not to expect either of us this afternoon," Cole explained as he hung up the phone.

"But what about your meeting?"

"Robert can handle any details that need to be ironed out. If I know Julian and Robert, they'll spend half the day reminiscing about their alma mater. Besides, it's Saturday. No one should have to work six days a week. Where's your favorite place to go when you have a free day?"

"I suppose it would either be the art institute or the museum of natural history."

"Then we'll do both."

"I'm not sure that's such a good idea." Thick lashes guarded her expression.

"That we do both or that we spend the day together?"

She didn't need to answer; her crimson cheeks said it all.

"Look, Rachel, we started off on the wrong foot. But I've just spent the night on your sofa, you've cooked me breakfast, and I think since we're going to be working together, we should make the effort to get to know each other a little better." His eyes were the deepest brown she had ever seen, his expression kind. "What do you think? Shall we start over?"

Against her will, she felt herself giving in. "All right."

Cole sensed the words had come from deep within her and he was oddly pleased at her response.

RACHEL SHOWERED in half her normal time. She chose a yellow shirtwaist dress with care and topped it with a white blazer. Authoritative, yet feminine, she thought as she pivoted in front of the mirror. After all, this was to be a professional as well as a friendly occasion. Instead of fashioning her hair into the usual chignon, she tied it back with a navy scarf splattered with yellow and white flowers, then dabbed a touch of musk scent behind her ears. Yes, professionalism was the key to dealing with Cole Braxton, she told herself, recalling the irrational feeling of joy she had experienced when he had complimented her cooking.

She thought about how every time she was with him she found his presence disturbing. At first she had attributed her uneasiness to the incident with Stacey. But now she knew exactly what it was about him that unnerved her: in his presence she felt alive and aware of herself as a woman. No man had been able to make her feel that way in a long, long time. But she refused to let her mind dwell on that point. As if it were some sort of protective device, she slipped the diamond engagement ring on her finger.

Reason and feelings were often light-years apart, Rachel discovered when she opened the door to Cole's appraising look and his deep, "Hello, Rachel." He had changed into a pair of dark slacks and a sport shirt, which he left open at the neck. His sport coat was slung over his shoulder and the subtle scent of soap wafted in the air.

"Er, come in," Rachel said when she realized that she had been staring. Her stomach had begun to flutter at the sight of him. It had only reacted like that once before, when she had first met Floyd. But this was crazy—this was the man her daughter was attracted to. She was determined to win her silent battle with the strange emotions she felt in his presence. She was just about to tell him she had changed her mind about going out when he smiled, and she couldn't help but warm to the overture.

"All set?" he asked, feeling a strong urge to reach out and loosen her hair, to let it cascade down around her neck and shoulders. He followed her into the foyer and watched her slip her dainty feet into a pair of open-toed pumps.

"Yes. I'm just going to leave a note for Stacey in case she returns before I do." She put her glasses on to write the message.

When she didn't remove them as they walked out of the apartment, Cole asked, "Do you need those things all the time?"

"What? My glasses?"

"I noticed you take them off to see distances."

"Yes, I'm farsighted. Actually, I only need them for detailed work."

"Then why do you wear them constantly?"

"Habit, I guess."

"You've got beautiful eyes, Rachel. You shouldn't hide them."

His tone was sincere, and again she felt that same irrational feeling of joy at his compliment. What in the world was the matter with her? If she didn't quit blushing he was bound to think she was starved for flattery.

As they stepped out into the sunshine, Rachel lifted her face to the sky and exclaimed, "Oh, it's so good to see the sun. What would you like to see of Chicago?"

"Generally, when I've been here it's been on business, so I haven't had much time for sight-seeing."

"Seeing that it's such a glorious day, maybe we should head over toward Grant Park. Once we're there we can decide if we want to go to the Field Museum, the Adler Planetarium or the Shedd Aquarium."

In the car, Rachel gave him directions and thought how strange it was that they were actually going somewhere together because they both wanted to...at least she hoped that Cole wanted to.

"Julian tells me you're originally from Wisconsin."

"Yes. I grew up in a town called Colby in the heart of dairy farming country."

"Did you know back in Colby that you wanted to be a fashion designer?"

"Oh, no!" she denied. "That was the farthest thing from my mind. My father was a minister and he had very strict ideas about what a girl should and should not do. Mama and I had to make all our own clothing and I always swore that I'd never sew another stitch once I turned eighteen and got myself a job. Little did I know that by then I would have to earn a living for two. Being a dressmaker was the only thing I knew how to do, and even though I never would have admitted it to my father, I enjoyed creating my own clothes. But I have to tell you, I would have given my left arm to be able to shop at Braxton's as a teenager."

"And now you'll be one of the people responsible for Braxton's exclusive label. What does your father think now?"

"He doesn't know." Rachel quickly changed the subject. "What about you? I suppose you grew up knowing that you would take your place in the department store business?"

"Actually, my father wanted me to be a lawyer, my mother wanted me to be a doctor and I wanted to be a marine biologist."

"So what happened?"

"My grandfather wanted me to be a department store executive."

"And have you regretted that decision?" she asked, hearing the slight tone of discontent in his voice.

Cole merely shrugged. "Not really. My grandfather is a very tenacious and wise man. He had to fight his way to the top without money or connections, only an intense ambition to create a family business that he could pass down to his heirs."

"What about your father? Does he work for Braxton's, too?"

"He's in charge of one of our subsidiaries in the Phoenix area. Actually, I think he's hoping that either Robert or I will succeed Grandfather when he retires. If it hadn't been for Robert's parents being killed when Robert was only three, I think Dad would probably have taught school all his life. He has a degree in education and loves children."

"Do you come from a big family?"

"I have three younger sisters—none are married and one's still at college. That's what disappoints Dad most of all. He figures we should all be married and reproducing like rabbits."

From the tone of his voice Rachel couldn't discern if he approved or disapproved of his father's view. She was tempted to ask him why he wasn't married and whether or not he ever wanted children, but the sight of the rose gardens in Grant Park precluded any further discussion and Rachel had to give Cole directions. "Why don't you park over there?" she said, pointing to a ramp on the corner ahead.

The April air was brisk off the lake and Rachel wished she had brought her raincoat as they climbed out of the car and began to walk to the park. "It's too early in the year yet for the flowers to be in bloom, but during the summer this is one of my favorite places to come," she told him as they strolled past statues and carefully manicured flower beds not quite alive with the colors of spring. By the time they reached the large marble building that housed the Field Museum of Natural History, her cheeks were flushed and wisps of curls had escaped the scarf's knot.

"What would you like to see first? Primitive arts? The cultures of the American Indian? Civilization of China?" Her petite size was emphasized by two stuffed African elephants in the entrance hall. "You probably don't want to miss the Chinese jade collection, do you?" Cole was becoming used to her tendency to end statements with questions.

"I'll leave it up to you. I'm in your hands."

So Rachel played tour guide to Cole, first taking him through the Hall of Dinosaurs in the museum, and then to the coral reef exhibit in the John Shedd Aquarium. They stopped to get ice cream cones from a vendor before finally ending up at the Adler Planetarium to watch the sky show.

Rachel discovered that with Cole she felt special. He had an infectious vitality about him and over the course of the afternoon they discovered many mutual interests, including a love of history. As they walked back across the causeway connecting the aquarium and the planetarium, they admired the spectacular view of the Chicago shoreline.

"Do you know how nice it is to see a beautifully manicured lakefront and not a series of docks and warehouses?" Cole asked.

"Umm. I thought I would have a hard time adjusting to the city, coming from Wisconsin where everything is so green and quiet. But I was pleasantly surprised. I love to come down here in the summertime. Over there—" she pointed to the park "—the Grant Park Symphony Orchestra gives free summer concerts. You can see the band shell through those trees. After the concerts there are computer-programmed light-and-colored-water-displays in the Buckingham Fountain."

While they had been indoors, gray clouds had been accumulating, and by now the sun was no longer visible. "It's getting cold. Maybe we should head back," Cole suggested.

A strong gust of wind tugged at Rachel's skirt and Cole's arm came around her protectively. "Now I know why they call this the windy city."

"Actually, that name came to be in an election year; the Eastern papers claimed one candidate in Chicago was full of hot air!"

Cole laughed, a deep, melodious laugh that set Rachel's heart racing. It started to rain, and Cole took off his sport coat and held it over their heads as they ran the remaining distance to the parking lot.

"Will you have dinner with me, Rachel?" Cole asked, once they had reached the shelter of the car.

"Thank you, but I really should get home in case Stacey's back." It was beginning to get dark.

"How about if we pick up some take-out food? Chinese?"

"I'm sure you'd much rather have a decent meal with Julian and Robert."

"No, I'd prefer to eat with you," he said quietly.

"All right. There's a place called Kwan's that isn't far from my place, but first I'd like to stop at home."

But when they arrived at the apartment, Stacey was nowhere to be seen. Rachel found a note on the kitchen table that put a frown on her face.

"Dinner for two or three?" Cole asked.

"Better make it two."

"One question, Rachel."

"Yes?"

"Whose shoes are those?" He pointed to the black wing tips in the entryway.

"Aunt Catherine's."

"*Aunt* Catherine's?" he repeated.

"She insisted I have them. She thinks that intruders are less likely to enter an apartment if they think a man is at home."

"Has it always been just the two of you?"

"Of course, except for when Stacey was a baby. We lived with Aunt Catherine until I had graduated from the school of design and had built up a small clientele."

While Cole was out getting the food, Rachel made a pot of coffee, then set the table with her Dresden China and silverware. She placed her silver candlesticks hesitantly beside the bowl of fresh flowers she always bought for the weekends. She stood back from the table, closing one eye. Did it look as if she thought he intended a romantic dinner for two instead of a get-acquainted topper to their day? She pulled the candlesticks off the table and put them back on the bookshelf, just as the doorbell sounded.

"I hope you're hungry because everything on the menu looked so good I decided to sample the lot. You're not on a diet, are you?"

"Cole, I don't think there's a woman over thirty who isn't on a diet."

"Well, you certainly don't need one."

"I think I'm beginning to like you, Cole Braxton," she teased.

"That's a giant step forward." His response was soft as he sat down at the table. The easy camaraderie they had shared while sightseeing continued on through dinner. As she reached across the table to remove his plate, his hand caught hers. He lifted the ringed finger and studied it in the light.

"I didn't know you were engaged, Rachel." He held her gaze for a moment before his eyes dropped to the hand held captive in his.

She attempted to maintain a casual tone while she became more and more troubled by the warmth of his hand on hers. "Floyd gave me this ring."

"Don't you ever get lonely, Rachel?"

She snatched her hand away from him. "No," she lied. "I have Stacey and my work."

"I mean lonely for a man's company."

"I have male friends, Cole Braxton. Is that why you took me out today? You think I'm so starved for male companionship that I need your pity?" She jumped up from the table and began to clear away the dishes.

"Pity is one emotion I don't feel for you, Rachel."

There was something in his voice that Rachel wasn't ready to acknowledge. The only sound in the room was the clanging of cutlery and plates, until after several minutes, Cole rose and came to stand beside her. He stilled her two, tiny efficient hands by placing his large one over them, then reached out to touch her face, his fingertips gently tracing her jawline.

"I spent the day with you because I wanted to be with you." Their eyes met and Rachel found herself wanting to touch him. Neither of them had heard the front door open and didn't realize that Stacey was leaning up against the doorjamb until she spoke.

"Isn't this a cozy scene!" Without saying hello, she walked past the two of them and slammed the door to her bedroom, ignoring her mother's greeting.

"What do you suppose is her problem?" Rachel wondered aloud, moving away from Cole.

Cole reached out and took her wrist. "Leave her be, Rachel."

"I can't, Cole. It's obvious she's upset. Please excuse me."

"Stacey?" She knocked on the bedroom door, but received no response. "Stacey, open up."

"What is it, Mother? I'm really tired." Stacey was sprawled across her bed, her head resting on her folded arms when Rachel entered the room.

"What's bothering you? Did something happen at KiKi's?"

"What's bothering me, Mother, is that man standing in the kitchen. What is he doing here? I thought you hated him!"

"Stacey, he's a colleague. We just had dinner."

"Fine. Then you entertain him. Don't ask me to. I'm really tired, Mom. I'd like to go to bed."

"Stacey, you're acting very immature, not to mention rude. Last night you couldn't get close enough to Cole. . . ."

"Please, Mother. I don't want to talk about it." She started undressing.

"That's fine for now, but we are not through discussing this," Rachel warned before leaving.

She returned to the living room to find Cole slipping on his sport coat. "It's probably better if I leave."

"I'm sorry about her rudeness, Cole. She's such a temperamental teenager these days."

"Not only did I enjoy spending the day with you; I discovered that I like Chicago. But I haven't changed my opinion of Stacey. I still think she's spoiled and she needs to stand up on her own two feet. You've got to let go of the reins, Rachel."

Rachel's mouth tightened. There were some truths a mother didn't like to hear, and she was not receptive to advice from Cole Braxton. "We may be business associates, but just because we spend the day together and you buy me dinner doesn't give you the right to criticize me or my daughter. I don't think you know either of us well enough for that."

Cole looked at her and thought he knew her much better than she realized. And that daughter of hers as well. But unless he wanted to lose the ground he had made today, he had to leave.

"Thanks for spending the day with me, Rachel." He bent down and placed an unsuspecting kiss upon her lips, then left.

ON HIS RETURN FLIGHT to Minneapolis, Cole listened to Robert extol the virtues of Julian and his creative ideas for Braxton's, until finally he had to speak up.

"Julian is a wonderful designer, but I have the feeling that Rachel Kincaid is the creative force at Annalise." His statement quieted Robert, who promptly dug into his own work and forgot all about conversing with his cousin on the short flight, which was fine with Cole. He was lost in thoughts of a petite female who was allergic to cigar smoke and carried a torch for a missing soldier. What kind of love inspired eighteen years of devotion? And what kind of woman had that kind of loyalty to a man? His ex-wife had had trouble remaining faithful when he had been away for a week.

He recalled how cute Rachel had looked when she was tipsy and a smile tugged at his lips. And then he remembered the curve of her breasts and the sexy lacy teddy that had been exposed when he had carried her to bed. He leaned back and closed his eyes. He could see the warm, soft look that had entered her eyes at the mention of her long-lost soldier and he imagined her looking at him in that same way. She would walk up to him and press those magnificent breasts up against him. How could such a tiny creature have such sumptuous breasts? Then she would press her delicate thighs close to his and he would discover what was underneath the lacy black teddy.

Cole shook his head to end the fantasy. God, what was he thinking? She was not the kind of woman he wanted. He pulled out a cigar and lit the tip, then savored the taste with several quick puffs. He couldn't even smoke his cigars around her. The smell bothered her. Well, her smell bothered him, too, but in a different way. He remembered the elusive scent that was barely discernible . . . just enough to tempt his senses.

What a contrast she was to the type of woman he normally dated. Dated? They had only spent one afternoon together...for professional reasons. Rachel was not exactly naive but pretty damned close to it. Yet her freshness had a certain appeal. She was different and she was attractive. He imagined her skin would be satiny smooth all over, especially under the teddy; sleek and supple under a man's hands. He found himself becoming aroused at the images and could feel the blood rushing through his veins. God, he felt like an adolescent fantasizing over a picture in a men's magazine. All right, so she had a certain sex appeal, but it was also obvious that she was the kind of woman a man who didn't want any ties should avoid. And it would be wise for him to remember that. Lonely women were often like clinging vines.

LONELY? Rachel recalled Cole's words. She had adjusted to missing Floyd. She really wasn't lonely. And what did Cole understand about love, anyway? He probably put women in the same category as his Scotch and his cigars.

"Did he leave?" Stacey's voice interrupted her musings.

Rachel nodded. "I just don't understand you. You were extremely rude."

"You don't know what happened last night after you fell asleep."

Rachel had been washing the dishes, but Stacey's tone made her stop with a jerk. "What do you mean?" she asked warily.

"You were right when you said Cole was crass. You fell asleep and I offered to make him an omelet."

"And?" Rachel prodded, her heart suddenly anxious.

"He told me he was too old for me, but that we could still be friends. It was humiliating." There was a break in Stacey's voice.

Rachel's heart contracted in sympathy for her daughter, but relief spread through her at the same time. "Sometimes the truth is painful, but I'm sure he didn't intentionally try to humiliate you."

"Just what were you doing with him today?" Stacey asked.

"Stacey! It's part of my job!"

"To eat Chinese food on Saturday night?"

"No, to develop a working relationship with a client."

"Well, just as long as you don't forget that that client tried to seduce your daughter."

"But he didn't!" My God, Rachel thought to herself, how ironic that the roles were reversed. Last month she had been the one saying those things and now she was defending Cole.

"Look, Mom, let's not argue over Cole Braxton anymore. You probably won't have to work with him after today anyway. Julian said Robert Braxton was in charge of the project."

"Yes. He is." Rachel found herself sadly disappointed by Stacey's logic.

Later, as she lay dead tired but wide awake in the brass bed, she couldn't help but think of Cole. She had almost forgotten what it was like to feel desires stirring—desires she didn't want to feel for Cole. She groaned silently and closed her eyes. She didn't need a man the way he had implied she did. But the warm, throbbing sensation that blazed through her at the thought of him contradicted her thoughts.

## *CHAPTER SEVEN*

"I HOPE THIS ISN'T GOING to be a rough trip," Julian said to Rachel, leaning across the aisle of the 727 jet after the plane had hit an air pocket and upset his cocktail.

"Me too," Rachel agreed, knowing she wasn't thinking of the same aspect of the journey. She could deal with a turbulent flight, but would she be able to handle the commotion Cole caused inside of her whenever he looked at her? It was more than two weeks since he had gone back to Minneapolis and she'd thought she had successfully pushed thoughts of him out of her mind. But all it had taken was Julian's mentioning this business trip and her imagination had begun to work overtime. Some of her anxiety must have shown on her face.

"You're not worrying about leaving Stacey, are you?" Julian asked.

"No, Aunt Catherine is staying with her." She didn't mention that Stacey had begged to come along. "You did say that this trip to Minneapolis would only be for a couple of days?"

"Yes. In that time we should be able to meet with Braxton's buyers and the staff working on the Mr. B's Boutique. Robert felt it would be best for us to see what concepts they were using and also meet his grandfather, who is really the one being honored by this golden anniversary celebration. Robert's invited us to dinner this evening."

"I have to admit I am nervous about that. Meeting with the Braxtons professionally is one thing, but socially is quite another."

"Just be yourself, darling. They are nice, ordinary people like us. Trust me."

Nice and ordinary were definitely not the adjectives Rachel would have used to describe the Braxton estate. It was not the average person who had an indoor swimming pool in his home and a stable of horses in the backyard. But then Owen Braxton, Sr. was not an average fellow, either. Cole had said his grandfather was eighty years old, and Rachel had expected an elderly, white-haired gentleman with bifocals and baggy pants. She was quite unprepared for the debonair, energetic man who greeted her with a kiss on her hand. On any other octogenarian, a hot-pink shirt and black suspenders under a white suit would have looked flamboyant, but on the stately figure of the Braxton patriarch, they looked as distinguished as the gray hair that only sprinkled his dark hair. He was as tall as Cole, and Rachel could see the resemblance in the dark brown eyes and the lean features. Her first thought was to wonder if Cole would be as handsome as his grandfather when he was eighty.

After only a few minutes in his presence, Rachel knew that although Owen Braxton, Sr. might have delegated most of his authority to his grandsons, he was still the moving force behind Braxton's.

"I've heard a lot about your work. Why don't you open that portfolio and let me take a look at your ideas?'' He made a motion for Julian to take a seat beside him.

''Isn't that just like you, Grandfather, to be conducting business before your dinner guests are even offered a drink?''

There was no mistaking the deep, melodious voice and Rachel felt a rush of warmth spread through her body.

''The sooner we take care of business, the sooner we can play,'' the older man replied. ''What brings you around this afternoon? I thought you were meeting with that Turner fellow?''

''Postponed,'' Cole replied, turning his attention to Rachel. ''Hello, Rachel.''

Rachel's pulse quickened. He was even more attractive than she remembered. All the mixed emotions she had managed to suppress resurfaced at his closeness. She didn't want to be near him, to have to deal with the feelings his presence aroused.

''You're staying for dinner, Cole?'' Owen asked, removing a thick brown cigar from a carved wooden box before offering one to Cole and the others.

''Can't tonight, Grandfather.'' Cole slipped a cigar into his breast pocket.

''What's her name? Do I know her?'' he said in an aside, not intended for Rachel's ears. He was about to put a flame to the cigar when Cole's hand stopped him.

''Rachel's allergic to cigar smoke, Grandfather.''

''Is that so?'' He turned to cast an accusing look at Rachel.

"It's all right, Mr. Braxton... really. It's only in close, confined quarters that I have a problem," Rachel explained.

"They taste better after dinner anyway," he said, returning the cigar to the box. "Now let me get a look at those designs."

"I thought this was a social occasion," Cole reminded him.

"It is. It is," he repeated. "This is just a sneak preview for my sake." He wiggled his pointer finger in a command that signaled he wanted to see Julian's portfolio. "Come sit down next to me, Cole, if you want to see. You know I dislike anyone looking over my shoulder."

"I'll wait until tomorrow. I have to get going."

"That special tonight, eh?" His grandfather shot a knowing look at Cole, then slapped him on the back, a chuckle accompanying the friendly gesture. "Well, have a good time."

After he had gone, Rachel thought about the upcoming visit to Braxton's Department Store. Would Cole be the one showing them around or would he now be content to let Robert handle the entire project? He hadn't seemed too eager to look at the preliminary designs that Julian had brought along. But then he had other things on his mind... like his date. She didn't want to question which bothered her more: the fact that he didn't want to see their designs, or the fact that he had a date....

THE NEXT MORNING Rachel dressed in a navy-blue gaberdine suit and white tailored blouse; her dress-for-success suit, as Stacey called it. She wished that she had brought along some makeup. If nothing else, it would have helped to camouflage the circles under her eyes. Today they would be meeting the people responsible for Braxton's success and she needed all the confidence she could muster. After slipping into navy-blue pumps and pinning her hair into a chignon, she went to meet Julian in the hotel lobby.

Julian had chosen the Marquette Inn because it was located in the IDS Center, which was where the Braxton corporate offices were. After breakfast, they were met in the courtyard by Robert, who took them into an elevator that whisked them up to the thirty-fifth floor. Rachel and Julian were introduced to a group of employees from sales, advertising and marketing, who explained their various roles in the fiftieth-anniversary celebration. It was clearly Robert's project, as Cole was not present, and Rachel wondered if she was even going to see him today. No one commented on his absence, and Rachel didn't want to ask about him.

Next they crossed the street via a skyway over to Braxton's downtown department store. After a tour of the store and an explanation of where and how the Mr. B's Boutique would fit in, they were escorted to the Skyroom Restaurant on the top floor of the building where lunch was served. The room was lined with plate-glass windows that permitted a lovely view of the Minneapolis skyline. Still, there was no sign of Cole...until they were nearly finished and he came in with a tall brunette on his arm. A strange sensation shot through Rachel at the sight of the unknown female clinging to Cole's sleeve. Was this the woman from last night?

"Hey look, there's Cole," someone in the group exclaimed. "And Patsy's back."

Patsy was gorgeous, Rachel had to admit to herself, noting that she was able to afford a Paris designer original. One glance told Rachel that she was a woman who had it all: good looks, a career and probably Cole, too.

"Welcome back, Patsy." All the men at the table rose to greet the elegant brunette. Even Julian seemed to know her, planting a kiss on her cheek and fawning over her with the rest.

When Patsy caught sight of Rachel, she turned to Cole questioningly.

"Patsy, this is Julian's assistant, Rachel Kincaid. Rachel, this is Patsy Burke. Patsy's head of the buying department," Cole said, "a job she obtained, I might add, by her connections."

"How do you do, Ms Burke." Rachel offered her hand, wondering about Cole's last comment.

"Please, call me Patsy. I've heard so much about you I feel as if I already know you, Rachel," Patsy said, smiling.

*The lonely frump from Chicago, no doubt,* Rachel speculated.

"Julian has promised me the afternoon with you." She turned toward Rachel's boss. "So you be good and keep your nose out!" she said teasingly, tapping Julian's nose with her beautifully manicured fingertip, a gesture only someone as gorgeous as Patsy could get away with, Rachel reflected.

"That will be nice." She didn't know what else to say and thought to herself that she had seen a number of impressive women on the Braxton staff, but none in Patsy's class.

After lunch, however, Patsy's cutesy personality disappeared and she was all business. And Rachel knew that Cole had only been joking when he'd said she had gotten her job through connections. She undoubtedly had connections with the Braxtons—just what those connections were, Rachel didn't think she wanted to know—but it was obvious she was also a very hard worker. Cheeks aglow and hands gesticulating, Patsy was all enthusiasm for Rachel's work, and Rachel felt confident that the two of them would work well together.

By the end of the afternoon, she was tired. Julian had disappeared with Robert and she wasn't sure if she was expected to go back to the hotel, which was only across the street from the department store, or to wait for Julian. She knew Robert had included the two of them in his plans to host a dinner party at the Chanhassen Dinner Theater. If she didn't leave soon, she wouldn't have time to change; they were meeting at the Braxtons' for cocktails prior to the dinner.

"How did it go?" Cole caught her off guard as she sat waiting for Patsy, who had excused herself to make a phone call.

"Fine." Rachel's heart began to pound like a jackhammer.

"Robert left me a note asking me to give you a lift back to Grandfather's." He waved a pink slip in his hand.

Rachel groaned inwardly. Did that mean she wasn't going to be able to change her clothes before they left? When Patsy returned looking as fresh as a morning daisy, makeup perfectly applied and not a hair out of place, Rachel was certain that there were dark bags under her eyes and wrinkles on her suit.

"I think you and Robert made the right choice, Cole," Patsy drawled, sweeping a cloud of scent into the room with her. "I like Rachel's ideas very much."

"I had a feeling you would," he returned. "Are you about ready to leave? Robert wants us at Grandfather's by six."

"Are you escorting Rachel and me?" Patsy asked.

Rachel felt panic setting in. She would have to go in her suit . . . and crash their date.

"Julian's already left with Robert," Cole explained. "I'll bring the car around and meet you downstairs." And before Rachel knew it, she was seated in the front seat of a silver Mercedes-Benz while Patsy sat elegantly in the back, one slim leg crossed over the other.

"I hope you have your briefcase handy, Patsy," Cole said with a quick glance over his shoulder. "You know the minute you walk in the front door Grandfather's going to expect a progress report." Then he said to Rachel, "Patsy just returned from a buying trip in Paris. At least it was supposed to be company business, but judging by the number of suitcases she brought home, I'd say she spent some of that time shopping."

Rachel knew that Cole had to be exaggerating. Just from the short time she had worked with Patsy, she knew that she put business first, pleasure second. The drive to the Braxtons' home wasn't as uncomfortable as Rachel had expected, but she didn't look forward to the prospect of dinner.

It was a balmy May evening and the Braxtons chose to serve cocktails outdoors in their beautifully terraced yard, which Rachel figured had to be maintained by several full-time gardeners. The scent of lilacs combined with freshly mowed grass was a balm to her nerves, as was the realization that all the faces looked familiar. She joined the other guests on the patio; Patsy quickly disappeared, but Cole remained at her side.

"What can I get you to drink? White wine, soda?" he asked.

"A glass of spring water would be fine, thank you," replied Rachel, nervously clasping her hands together.

He led her over to the bar, and though his hand barely touched her elbow, tiny electric currents went through her, which she tried desperately to ignore.

"I like your suit. It's a very effective combination of power and femininity. It's hard to achieve both." His fingers brushed hers as he handed her a glass and smiled. "One sparkling water on the rocks."

"Thank you." Rachel blushed and wondered why she had such difficulty accepting his compliments gracefully. She felt even more gauche when she went to take a sip of the water and felt ice cubes nudge her nose.

His smile lingered in his eyes. "You made quite an impression on Patsy, which isn't an easy thing to do. My sister can be as tough as Grandfather."

*Sister. Patsy's his sister.* Rachel's eyes flew to where the other woman sat straddling the bench of a picnic table, managing to look as regal as Princess Di, and immediately noticed the similarities between brother and sister. They had the same strong chin, only Patsy's was a bit softer, the same straight nose, even the same manner of tilting their heads when they were listening intently.

"I think Patsy and I will be able to work well together," she finally said.

"So do I." He finished his Scotch just as they were joined by Julian and Patsy.

"Rachel, you aren't rushing back to Chicago tomorrow, are you?" Cole's sister asked, her animated features expressing her disappointment.

"Julian said we'd be finished in the morning." Rachel could feel Cole's eyes on her.

"Yes, but I had hoped you'd stay through the weekend. Cole's racing Saturday morning and we thought you might like to come watch. Have you ever seen a hot air balloon race?" Patsy asked.

"No, and I'd love to, but I'm not sure it's such a good idea leaving my aunt for too long a time with my daughter. She's elderly, and a teenager can be a handful for anyone."

"There's no need to worry, Rachel." It was Julian who spoke up. "Stacey is a good kid. She wouldn't cause trouble for anyone, especially not Catherine. She adores her."

Rachel's eyes flew to Cole's but she quickly forced her attention back to Patsy, who was pleading for her to call home and see what Aunt Catherine thought of the idea.

"We can change our reservations and fly back on Saturday afternoon," Julian suggested. "I've always been fascinated by hot air balloons. I think we'd have a marvelous time, Rachel."

She could still feel Cole's eyes, intent upon her face. When she met his gaze she saw more than a challenge in them. They were actually caressing her, and for the first time in a long time Rachel thought of herself before her daughter and said, "I'll stay." She felt a thrill of excitement at the sultry gleam in Cole's eyes.

"Oh good! It's all set then. You can ride down with me." Patsy was all animation once more. "It's only about thirty minutes from here. Cole will be leaving with his crew before sunrise."

"Before sunrise?" Rachel questioned.

"That's the best time of day, weather-wise, for a flight. The morning air is usually still and cool, and allows the balloon to rise more easily," Cole explained.

"It really is quite a sight, all the different colored balloons dotting the sky," Patsy told her. "I should tell you, too, that it's best if you wear jeans. The launch takes place in the country."

"I'm afraid I didn't bring any jeans along," Rachel said.

"That's not a problem. Just stop by the store tomorrow and I'll provide you with a pair!"

WHEN SATURDAY MORNING dawned, Rachel was up in a flash. She put on the exclusive designer jeans Patsy had insisted she have and a white cotton-knit sweater, the scooped front of which showed off the delicate curve of her neck. The soft denim jeans clung like a second skin, emphasizing her curves in a way she was unaccustomed to. Doubt furrowed her brow as she stared in the mirror. How could she be comfortable in an outfit she might have purchased for Stacey? Patsy had just laughed when Rachel had hinted that the styles she was showing her were too juvenile.

Rachel's apprehension increased as they got closer to the launching site. Neither Julian nor Robert had commented on her appearance, but then it wasn't their comments she was worried about. As they turned off the main highway onto a dirt road that cut through a farmer's field, Rachel's heart rate accelerated. In the distance were dozens of pickup trucks and cars, one of them Cole's. She was surprised by the number of people present. They pulled up alongside a white four-wheel drive truck, and she saw Cole and two other men unfold a huge rainbow-colored piece of nylon fabric across the plowed ground. Cole wore a striped shirt that matched his balloon, the color of which corresponded to the Braxton's Department Store logo. Rachel could see his arm muscles stretch tautly as he attached the balloon to a basket of steel wires. He turned as Patsy called to him.

"Fill it up, John," he directed one of the other two men, walking toward them. "So Patsy did manage to wake you up this early," he said as a greeting to Rachel.

"It's actually the prettiest time of day. It's a shame most people never get to see it." Rachel could feel his eyes lingering on her sweater.

"Cole, explain to Rachel what John is doing," Patsy instructed.

"This part here is called the bag, or the envelope. It's made of the same material as parachutes." Cole took Rachel by the elbow and steered her closer to the balloon. "My buddy, John here, is going to get the balloon up on its side first. That's what the fan is for.

It blows cold air into the balloon to fill it up. Since cold air doesn't rise, the balloon stays on its side on the ground."

As the balloon began to inflate like a giant piece of bubble gum, Rachel could see the name Melinda Sue stenciled vertically on one side.

"Once the bag is full, I'll light the propane burner on top of the basket so the air inside will warm just enough to tip the basket right side up. That's when things get a little tricky."

"And Cole makes us work for our money," John called out.

"What he means is once I climb inside the basket, they have to help hold it in place until I've run through the safety checklist. And there's a delicate balance between the point of just enough heat to hold the balloon upright and not enough so that it falls back down."

"When does the race begin?" Rachel asked, noting the many balloons that looked as though they were about ready to take off.

"Actually, it's not a race, but a game of hare and hound. One balloon is chosen to be the hare. He takes off and lands, then the rest of the balloons, the hounds, follow him and the winner is the one that can throw a marker closest to the hare."

"Just about ready, Cole," John shouted, as the wicker basket tipped upright.

Cole climbed into the basket while the other two men held it steady. "Are you going solo, Cole?" Patsy asked.

"I was hoping one of you might like to accompany me." He looked directly at Rachel.

"Good heavens, not me," Julian exclaimed. "I get nosebleeds on stepladders."

"Take Rachel. She's never been before," Patsy suggested.

"Oh, no, I couldn't," Rachel protested.

"Sure you could." And before she could think about it, Cole had hoisted her into the balloon alongside him. "God, you're a lightweight," he said for her ears only.

"Looks like the others are just about ready, Cole," John informed him.

There was a lot of technical communication and Rachel heard Cole shout, "Hands off!" right before the crew members let go of the basket. Then the earth seemed to sink from underneath them and hands were waving below them. Rachel felt a sense of detachment, as though she and Cole weren't rising but the ground was moving away, and the countryside rolled slowly by while the balloon silently whisked upward. The sky was a brilliant azure with only a scattering of cumulus clouds.

Cole could see the fascination on Rachel's face. "What do you think?"

"It's wonderful!" Rachel's eyes danced with excitement. "It's such an odd sensation, watching everything move away from us. And it seems strange that we don't feel the wind pulling at us."

"That's because it isn't. The wind and the balloon are traveling together; this is too big an object for the wind to blow against. But right now it is pretty calm."

Rachel's face glowed with exhilaration. "Don't the balloons down on the ground look like giant colored mushrooms? How high up are we going?"

"Oh, between five hundred and a thousand feet." The sound of static radio communication had Cole reaching for the two-way radio for a short message to his crew. "The crew is in the chase vehicle. John is driving and Ray is watching the balloon so that they'll be able to meet us when we land." He pointed downward. "Look! See that red-and-white balloon on the ground over there? That's the hare. We want to get as close to it as possible."

Rachel could share in Cole's excitement as they descended closer and closer to the hare. Just when she thought he had waited too long to toss his marker overboard, he released the disk and she saw it land closer than any of the others.

"That was almost perfect," Rachel enthused, clapping her hands.

"We'll have to wait for the rally to be completed until we know for sure. In the meantime, I'll show you some of the beautiful Minnesota farmland."

Rachel had thought they would land after they had descended to throw the marker, but she heard him radio his crew to tell them he was going to remain in flight for a while longer, and the gleam in his eye told her he was truly in his element up in the sky. They rose again and Rachel was entranced by the neatly plowed fields that looked like a patchwork quilt.

Cole glanced at her. Normally he would be experiencing those same sensations, but right now he couldn't take his eyes off Rachel's tight-fitting jeans. There was nothing like smooth denim to show a man what a skirt usually hid. He had tried to tell himself that he had imagined the sexual pull he had experienced in Chicago, but now he knew that it was real, and he knew that he needed to touch her, to feel that smooth denim beneath his hands.

"Oh, Cole, this is glorious. To be able to leave behind all the noise and worries of the earth and just float. Thank you for bringing me along."

"I'm glad you like it. I often wonder if other people feel the same things I do when they're up here." He moved closer to her, and bent his head down next to hers. He put his arm around her shoulder as he pointed in front of them. "See that tiny little church nestled between that copse of trees? That's where my grandparents were married." His face was only inches from hers, and Rachel could smell the aroma of cigar on his breath. And just as gently as the wind carried the balloon, Cole kissed her.

"I've been wanting to do that ever since I saw you strutting toward me with those clinging things on. Is that your first pair of jeans?" His hand held her close at her back, and Rachel could feel his eyes intent upon her figure.

"No. Of course not," she said with quiet indignation. Then she added, "I owned a pair when I was in the tenth grade. I bought them with my baby-sitting money specifically to spite my father."

"Well, if they fit you as well as those do I can understand why your father was reluctant to have you wear them." Her sweater was low cut, permitting him a glance at her generous cleavage and he had to force his eyes back up to her face. "You've got such a beautiful figure; why do you hide it?" Rachel was about to deny his accusation, but he didn't give her time. He cupped her chin in his hand and ran his thumb over her jawline before claiming her mouth once again, but this time his lips were urgent and moved with a hunger against hers. His tongue thrust deep, leaving Rachel trembling with pent-up passion.

"Cole, we shouldn't..." she said, gasping.

He captured her mouth again, his hands sliding down her back, pressing her loins into his. He felt her breasts crushed against his chest, and the feel of her made him wild with longing. He kissed her intimately, and Rachel, flinging her arms about his neck, kissed him back, moving her lips with a hunger that surprised even Cole. He could feel the pulse in her throat throbbing in time to his own rapid heartbeat.

A moan escaped Rachel's mouth as his hand slipped inside the scooped front of her sweater and cupped her breast. Exquisite erotic sensations shot through her as he gently fondled her nipple between two fingers.

A slight jerk on the basket and a radio signal had Cole reluctantly withdrawing from her, but his eyes held hers for several moments before he picked up the two-way transmitter. A few minutes later he said, "Looks like we'll have to land. The wind's starting to pick up."

"So how do we get down?" Rachel asked when she finally felt able to speak.

"We'll just float for a ways. As the air cools inside the envelope, we'll gradually descend, but if the wind is too brisk, I can pull on this cord here." His hand pointed to a rope attached to the balloon. "It's hooked to a valve on the top that will open and release the hot air. That will prevent us from bouncing across the countryside when we set down."

Rachel watched Cole maneuver the balloon, the descent steady until finally they met the land. She noticed that the white chase vehicle was only a short distance away and she began to climb out, but Cole stopped her with a hand on her shoulder.

"If we get out now, the balloon will rise again. That's why we have the crew."

Rachel appreciated the importance of Cole's crew as they worked to dismantle the balloon. After all the air was out of the envelope and the nylon fabric folded, the bag and basket were loaded onto the truck. Because the pickup only had seating for three people in its cab, Rachel found herself sitting on Cole's lap as they made their way out of the field.

She leaned forward slightly and clung to the dashboard with one hand so as not to fall against Cole as the truck bobbed and swayed. He had one arm casually draped around her waist, but it was his other hand that disturbed her. The longer it remained across her thigh, the more difficult it was for her to ignore what it was doing to every sensual nerve ending in her body. Her skin burned at the memory of his embrace, and she wondered how Cole could carry on a conversation so casually with the other two men. He could have been holding a child on his lap!

In reality, it was costing Cole a great effort to keep the hand on her thigh from caressing the inner softness of her legs. It was only the presence of his crew that stopped him from pulling her into the crook of his arm and kissing her senseless. He could smell the musky scent she wore and it reminded him of the soft spots his lips had kissed.

They hadn't driven far when the truck pulled into a roadside restaurant. Rachel saw Patsy's car parked in the lot amid other trucks carrying balloons and breathed a sigh of relief.

"Hungry?" Cole misinterpreted her sigh.

"A little," Rachel responded, carefully shifting her position to get out of the truck, but he was quick to lift her down.

"This is sort of a hangout for balloon enthusiasts."

When she entered the country-style café, Rachel knew why he'd warned her. There was a large room at the back of the restaurant filled with strange people. Her eyes skimmed the crowd, searching for Julian's or Patsy's face. Cole was waylaid by several people, and she felt like a fish out of water, until she located his sister.

Patsy introduced her to several members of the balloon club, but Rachel wished she could go home. It turned out that Cole had come in second in the rally, which qualified him for a future national competition, and the attention of most of the people in the room. Although the food was delicious and the people friendly, Rachel was relieved when Patsy offered to take her back to the hotel. When Julian informed her he was going to stay over for several more days, Rachel decided she would go back to Chicago alone.

It was Cole who ended up taking her to the airport. As the Mercedes-Benz pulled into the terminal, he asked her, "Are you sure you want to leave at this stage of the game?" He didn't want her to go, especially since they hadn't had any time alone since the balloon flight.

"Our business has finished here; Julian is staying on for personal reasons," she said softly.

"You know, Rachel, if Robert had his way Julian would be designing the collection exclusively."

"You mean you wanted me on this project? I thought..." Her voice trailed off.

"You thought Julian had insisted?"

"He's been so supportive of my work."

"You're an excellent designer, but your apprenticeship is over, Rachel. You should have your own collections...and not just some lingerie that Julian takes the credit for."

"Julian and I worked together on those collections and he doesn't take all the credit for them. I don't think you're being fair to him. He's a genius."

"I'm not saying he isn't. But there is an intrinsic quality in your work that sets you apart from other designers. And I think it's time you got the recognition you deserve. Have you ever thought about branching out on your own?"

"Of course not!" she exclaimed.

"I don't understand you. Why of course not?"

"Because I don't need the pressures and the headaches of that kind of move. I like working at Annalise. I make enough money to provide a good home for Stacey and I'm happy."

"That's always been just enough for you, hasn't it? Where's your ambition, your drive? I can't believe you ever made the move from being a dressmaker in Milwaukee to a design apprentice in Chicago. You're so determined to keep things the same as they were eighteen years ago. Everything is so neat and ordered in your little world; you don't want to plan for your future because you're too wrapped up in preserving the past. Are you afraid that if you get on with your life you'd be admitting that Floyd will never be coming home? Rachel, look around you. You've a daughter who's nearly an adult. You've got a promising career ahead of you. You shouldn't be hiding yourself away from society, and you shouldn't have waited eighteen years for a man who hasn't come home."

"Don't say that. He is coming home. He is." Rachel covered her ears with her hands.

Cole wrapped his arms around her trembling frame. "Shhh. It's all right, Rachel. I'm sorry. I shouldn't have said all those things. It's just that I care about you."

"Well, I don't want you to care about me," she cried, pushing his arms away. "Everything was just fine until you came into our lives," she said, glaring at him.

"Was it?" he asked coldly.

"Yes, yes, yes!" Her voice was muffled and she scrambled out of the car.

"Rachel, wait!" He jumped out of the car and called after her, but she was already going inside, her one large suitcase in hand as her slender legs pushed past porters and luggage-toting tourists. He started running after her, then stopped himself with the sudden realization that she would be back. Business was *not* concluded.

ONCE SHE WAS SEATED on the plane, Rachel thought about the past three days and how much she had learned about Cole. She had thought when they first met that he lacked scruples, yet his associates and coworkers held him in the highest esteem. It was obvious he drank more than he should and that he didn't lack for female admirers. He had money, success, power, yet she sensed an uneasiness about him, a restlessness that only seemed to abate when he was in his balloon, high up and far away from the world. Had it not been for his grandfather, she wondered, would he be an executive vice president at Braxton's? Probably. There was a strong sense of family pride in him and she couldn't see Cole turning his back on his family's heritage.

Rachel leaned her head back against the seat and closed her eyes. She could still feel his body contoured against hers, his chest pressed against her breasts, his thighs touching hers...his arousal. She had wanted to be kissed, held, loved. Why now, after eighteen years, did she feel such an urgent need for a man? Her previous relationships with men hadn't elicited half the passion she felt now. Why Cole Braxton made her feel this way was beyond her comprehension. Oh God, it just wasn't fair! How could she be drawn to the same man as her daughter?

## *CHAPTER EIGHT*

"SO COME ON, Mom. You've been home over an hour and you still haven't told us what it was like."

"What what was like?" Rachel asked innocently.

"Owen Braxton's house. I mean, here you were off visiting one of the wealthiest families in the Midwest and you haven't even told us how the rich people live."

"Stacey, they're only human. They eat, sleep and have problems just like everybody else."

"God, Mom, I swear, Bruce Springsteen could walk through the front door tomorrow and you'd say, 'He eats, sleeps and has problems just like everybody else.' Just tell me what his house was like and if there were scads of servants. Was it terribly decadent?"

"Decadent? Stacey, you have such a vivid imagination." Rachel took a sip of her coffee. "Although they did have an indoor pool."

"Oh, how fantastic! I wish I could have been there. What about a hot tub?"

"Stacey, Owen Braxton, Sr. is eighty years old."

"But what about his grandson, Robert? I thought you said he lived there, too."

"He does, but he has his own wing and it's separate from the rest of the house."

"How many servants are there?"

"I didn't count them," her mother replied dryly.

"Give your mother a rest." Catherine spoke softly but firmly, patting Stacey's hand affectionately. "She's probably tired; it's quite late."

"No. I'm not tired at all," Rachel assured her. "I like the three of us sitting here talking. It's like old times, isn't it?" She glanced fondly at the white-haired woman whose round rosy cheeks and dimpled chin were dearly familiar.

"Yes, it is, but I'm afraid you two will have to do without me. I'm off to bed."

"Good night, Auntie Kay." Stacey reached over to hug her great-aunt. "Sleep well, because we're going to the flower show tomorrow."

"Flower show?" Rachel questioned after Catherine had disappeared.

"Yes. Auntie Kay saw it advertised in the paper. It's at the First National Bank building. Since she's leaving on Tuesday I suggested we go tomorrow. Do you want to come along?"

"Sounds like fun. So tell me. Have you enjoyed her visit?"

"She's just like a little kid in the city, Mom. And I can't believe how much energy she has for someone her age. I mean we walked up and down the miracle mile, stopping at every window. Friday night we went to a crafts fair and last night I took her to play bingo... and she won a turkey. It's in the freezer. She wants to cook it for us before she goes home."

"I'm glad you two had a good time."

"We did, but Mom, I'm kind of worried about her." Stacey leaned forward and rested her elbows on the table. "She's getting old, isn't she?" she said, lowering her voice.

"Of course she's growing older; we all do."

"It's too bad she won't move here with us. Then we could keep an eye on her. She's getting forgetful, you know."

"Is she? I didn't realize that." Rachel's brows drew closer together.

"Mom, couldn't you talk her into moving? There must be an efficiency apartment in the building that she could move into."

"I couldn't think of anything nicer, but I'm not sure she would want to. She has friends in Milwaukee, not to mention the senior citizens group she belongs to, as well as her bridge club and sewing circle. If you remember, I did ask her to come with us when we moved, but she refused." Rachel recalled how difficult emotionally it had been for her to leave her aunt behind. Catherine had been like a mother to her and a grandmother to Stacey.

"I suppose you're right. But would you talk to her about it?" she pleaded.

"Yes. But if she says no, we'll just have to see to it that we visit her more often." Stacey's concern over the older woman's welfare tugged at Rachel's heartstrings. Maybe she hadn't failed as a mother, after all.

"Do you think you'll have to be making many trips to Minneapolis?"

"I hope not." Rachel sighed.

"Why? Didn't you have a good time?"

"It was interesting enough, but I prefer to have Julian handle the public relations end. By the way, I brought you back something. It's in my suitcase."

Rachel cleared away the dishes while Stacey jumped up and ran into the other room. Within seconds, she was back, holding Rachel's designer jeans up to her long slender legs.

"They're cute, Mom, but I don't think they're big enough. How come you only got me a size five?"

"Those are mine."

"Yours?" Stacey asked in disbelief. "You never wear jeans."

"You and I know that but Patsy doesn't. She's the head buyer for Braxton's and she insisted I have the jeans and that white sweater that's in my suitcase. I put your gift in my travel bag."

Rachel followed Stacey into her bedroom, wondering if she should mention the reason Patsy had given her the clothing. She disliked the twinge of guilt the intentional omission of the balloon ride stirred, but she also recalled Stacey's emphatic request that night of Julian's party for a ride in *Melinda Sue*. And she couldn't help but worry that if Stacey knew she had been with Cole, it would create more tension between the two of them. She was loath to disrupt the harmony that had greeted her after her four-day absence.

"Oh, it's adorable," Stacey crooned, hugging the stuffed bird close to her cheek. "What is it?"

"It's a loon. That's the Minnesota state bird. Everywhere you go you see its picture—on mugs, T-shirts, sweatshirts—all over."

"Thanks, Mom. He'll fit right in with the rest of my menagerie." She hugged Rachel tightly. "I'd better get to sleep. You know Auntie Kay. She gets up with the roosters and I promised to bring her breakfast in bed." She paused at the doorway to her room. "I'm glad you're back, Mom. I missed you."

"I missed you, too. Good night." For the first time in a long while, Rachel went to bed with a happy heart. So many times in the past few months she and Stacey had been at odds over one thing or another. But tonight the old Stacey was back; the rebellious, temperamental stranger who had been taking her place had disappeared. Was it Aunt Catherine's gentle touch? Or had they simply needed some time away from each other? Cole's words echoed through her mind. "You have to let go, Rachel." Had she been trying to hold on too tightly, to protect her daughter rather than let her learn as she matured?

Whatever it was, the tranquility continued for several weeks. Aunt Catherine returned to Milwaukee, but Stacey remained in a good frame of mind. Rachel often thought of Cole, but each time she did she reminded herself that he was a professional associate; and with the delicate situation between mother and daughter, it was for the best that she forget about him. Her relationship with Stacey was far more important than a friendship with Cole. But she couldn't deny that he had affected her in a way no man had in a long time. She wondered if she would have been more receptive to Bud if she hadn't met Cole.

Bud had invited her to dinner one night shortly after Catherine's departure. He had taken her to an elegant Italian restaurant with crystal chandeliers and a palatial decor. Rachel enjoyed his company; he had an offbeat sense of humor that always caught her off guard. They had eaten fettuccine, drunk smooth wine and laughed a lot. After dinner they had watched television at her place, and it had been comfortable.

*But not exciting,* a tiny voice in her subconscious had nagged.

Stacey's graduation was followed by an overnight party at the school, which Rachel allowed her to attend since it was parent supervised and the students weren't permitted to leave the building until six a.m. Stacey had worked hard on her schoolwork of late; she and Rachel had spent many nights working in companionable silence, Rachel on her Braxton designs, Stacey on her studies.

Julian worked at a frenetic pace, and Rachel wasn't sure she would be able to keep up with his inexhaustible supply of energy. Stacey, meanwhile, was unable to find a summer job, and Rachel was unsuccessful in her attempts to interest her in summer school. By midseason she had a gorgeous tan, but no money, and Rachel was grateful when Julian found her a small modeling job, which at least gave her something to do.

One night when Rachel arrived home later than usual, Stacey informed her that Cole Braxton had phoned.

"Why would he be calling you at home?" she asked.

"Maybe he couldn't reach me at Annalise. I was in and out all day running errands for Julian." Her tone was deliberately casual.

"He could have left a message for you there."

"I suppose he could have. *Did* he leave any message?"

"Only that it was important that he talk to you this evening. He said he would call back at nine."

"Have you had any dinner?" Rachel dismissed the phone call intentionally.

Stacey nodded. "Mother, did you see Cole when you were in Minneapolis?"

"Of course. He's an executive at Braxton's, and as I told you, Julian and I met with the whole board of directors. So what kind of day did you have?" She quickly changed the subject.

"It was okay. Chelsea was over and she wanted to know if I wanted to drive up to Milwaukee with her tomorrow. Well, actually her mother is driving. They're going to visit Marquette University."

Rachel's interest was captured at the mention of the school. "Do you want to go see what it's like?"

Stacey shrugged. "I suppose I could. I think I'd rather get a full-time job than go to college, though."

Rachel swallowed her disappointment. "You haven't had much luck finding one since you graduated," she reminded her.

"That's because it's summer and all the college kids are home, too."

"It might not hurt to go with Chelsea and see what the school has to offer. Are they just going for the day?" At Stacey's nod, she added, "Maybe you'd like to visit Auntie Kay for a few days. She doesn't live far from the campus." Stacey's expressive face told Rachel that she was contemplating the idea.

"That might not be such a bad idea. I could probably look up my old friends from junior high, too."

"I'm sure Auntie Kay would love to have you. I could either drive up to get you or you could fly home."

"I'm going to call her right now." Stacey scrambled off the couch.

The remainder of the evening was spent in a flurry of activity as Stacey packed and made several phone calls. Rachel was happy upon speaking to Chelsea's mother and hearing her enthusiasm for the trip. Stacey had scored well on her college entrance exams, but it seemed the harder Rachel tried to get her to decide on a school, the more uninterested she became. It was with a sense of hope that Rachel kissed her goodbye the next morning.

Rachel stayed late at Annalise the next day. When she arrived home, the phone was ringing.

"Hello." Her voice was breathless from hurrying.

"Rachel, is that you?"

"Yes." Immediately she recognized Cole's voice.

"I've been trying to reach you for two days. It seems we've been missing each other."

"I've been working long hours. I just got home."

"It's past nine o'clock," he stated emphatically.

"Yes, well, I've been working hard," she said defensively. "The Braxton designs are due next week."

"Well, you don't need to kill yourself over them."

"I'm not. I enjoy the work."

"That's what I'm calling you about. I need to see the sketches you've completed. We'd like to construct several pieces right away so we can get going on the promotional photos. Could you fly out tomorrow to meet with the director of the advertising agency?"

"I'd have to talk to Julian first and I don't know if there's a flight available."

"I just spoke to Julian and I've reserved a ticket for you. All you have to do is get to the airport by seven-thirty tomorrow morning."

"And what if it isn't convenient for me?" If she hadn't been tired she wouldn't have snapped at him.

"Rachel, Julian knew the date of the photo session several weeks ago," he replied.

"I wish he had told me. All right, I'll be there tomorrow," she conceded, biting her lip.

"Terrific. I'll see you in the morning."

"Yes. Good night." At the sound of the dial tone, she placed a call to Aunt Catherine and was relieved to learn that Stacey was out with friends. Would Stacey suspect that she had bundled her off to Auntie Kay's so she could fly to Minneapolis alone? Rachel carefully explained the situation to Catherine and trusted her aunt's ability to handle the explanation.

COLE WATCHED closely as a throng of briefcase-toting businessmen dressed in gray and blue business suits disembarked at gate twenty-three on the blue concourse of the Charles A. Lindbergh International Airport. Rachel was so tiny she could easily be hidden from view. But although several women passed through the gate, Rachel was not among them. He hoped that her misplaced loyalty to Stacey hadn't caused her to alter her plans. He rubbed the back of his neck with his palm. Was he letting his emotions rule his head? His grandfather had put him on the project because of his stoic nature. What would his grandfather say if he knew Cole Braxton III was acting like a little kid waiting for a double scoop of chocolate ice cream?

Then he saw her, her portfolio clutched under one arm, her shoulder bag weighing down the other. She had her glasses on and the chignon tightly in place, but at least she had come. He felt as though a heavy weight had been lifted off his chest and he rushed over to greet her.

Rachel's stomach did its own landing pattern when she caught sight of Cole's dark face smiling at her. She almost missed her footing coming up the ramp into the concourse, then blushed as his eyes caught her slight stumble.

"Here, let me help you with your things," he said, taking the flight bag from her shoulder. "I'm glad you came, Rachel."

He talked of mundane things as they retrieved her luggage from the revolving carousel, such as the heat wave that was hitting the Twin Cities at the moment. As he escorted her across the terminal, it struck her that she hadn't inquired as to where she was going to be staying in Minneapolis. Maybe he hadn't even intended for her to stay overnight! And here she had packed a suitcase! A gust of warm, humid air struck her as they walked from the air-conditioned terminal out into the parking lot, and she realized how unwise it had been to wear the long-sleeved suit jacket over her dirndl skirt. She had wanted to look professional and instead she was going to look tacky.

In the car, however, the air-conditioning soothed her flushed cheeks, and she could only hope that she didn't look as flustered as she felt. When Cole pulled into a town house development not far from the airport, apprehension swamped Rachel. Was he taking her to his home?

"I'm afraid it's the Aquatennial Celebration here in the Twin Cities and all the decent hotels are booked. Patsy insisted that I offer you her hospitality."

"That's very sweet of her," Rachel said calmly.

"It's also very private and we'll be able to discuss the project without any interruptions."

Patsy's town house was just as Rachel would have expected it—sleek, sophisticated and ultramodern. The tubular furnishings were very avant-garde as were the paintings on the walls, splashes of color.

"Did you speak with Julian before you left?"

"I tried, but his answering machine was on, so I left him a message."

"I figured you would. Do you want to show me what you have in there?" he asked, pointing to her portfolio.

"I just want you to know that some of these are results of joint effort—Julian's and mine."

Cole carefully looked them over, his face not revealing his emotions. When he glanced up and recognized the anxiety on Rachel's face, he said, "They're perfect . . . especially these." He pulled out her activewear designs. "These are yours alone, aren't they?"

"Yes. But you do like them all?"

"Very much."

Rachel smiled and let out a pent-up breath of air.

"We've got to show these to Patsy and Robert."

The smile disappeared from her face. She had completely forgotten about the Braxton staff. She had only been worried about what he thought of her designs. It had been so important that he approve her work, she hadn't given a second thought to Robert, who was the person in charge.

"You don't need to look as though I'm leading you to the lions."

She smiled weakly. How could she tell him that it didn't matter to her whether the others liked the designs? That all she had been working for was to prove to him that she was an excellent designer?

"I'm so unprepared for the business world," she admitted. "It's been so easy sitting back in my little cubicle following Julian's instructions, not having to deal with the problems."

"Rachel, Annalise was given the contract because of your work. Julian is a great designer, but we wanted your ideas as well. Now, I'm going to take you over to the store and you can see for yourself the progress we've made on the Mr. B's Boutique." He showed her to Patsy's guest room and waited in the living room while she freshened up.

Rachel couldn't help but get caught up in Cole's enthusiasm for the Mr. B's Boutique and the Braxton's golden-anniversary celebration. After a brief meeting during which he showed her designs to the staff, he left her with Patsy who took her to meet the director of the advertising agency. When they met with the photographer he suggested that she visit the Braxton hair salon, and Rachel soon found herself turned over to Mr. David, the exclusive salon's top stylist.

Mr. David confirmed the photographer's diagnosis. Rachel did, indeed, have beautiful hair, too lovely to be hidden in a chignon. With the skillful use of scissors, he layered her fair tresses in such a flattering fashion that when she emerged from the salon, she felt wonderful. While she waited in Patsy's office for her, she couldn't resist opening the cabinet door that hid a full-length mirror. She had been worried when she first entered the exclusive salon that she might walk out with one of the latest extreme hairdos, but while Mr. David had given her a more youthful style, she was satisfied with the result.

Patsy's secretary knocked on the open door and announced, "You have a call on line one, Ms Kincaid."

Rachel sat down behind the mahogany desk and punched the blinking button. It was Cole's warm voice that greeted her.

"Patsy's not here," she explained.

"You're the one I wanted to speak to. I hear they're shooting some promotional photos tomorrow?"

"Yes. I understand it will only take an afternoon." She tried to sound casual and ignore her heartbeat, which had sped up at the sound of his voice.

"Are you anxious to go back to Chicago?"

"I do have quite a bit of work waiting for me."

"I was hoping you'd stay for a few days as Patsy's guest. It's Aquatennial time and I thought I could show you a few of the ways we celebrate summer in Minneapolis."

"It's very kind of you to offer to show me around, but—"

"Believe me, Rachel. I'm not doing it out of kindness," he interrupted. "I want to take you out on a date and this seems like an ideal time. Will you go with me?"

"I don't think that would be a good idea." She clutched the telephone closer to her ear.

"Why not? Stacey is with your aunt, isn't she?"

"It isn't that."

"Then what is it?"

How could she tell him that she, a grown woman, was afraid of the feelings he stirred within her, feelings only one other person had ever aroused? Feelings that seemed wrong when she thought about her daughter and her fascination with the same man.

"Why don't we take it one step at a time? There's a special music celebration called Sommerfest going on. It brings a taste of Vienna to the Twin Cities. Will you go with me to a concert at Orchestra Hall tonight?"

"But I didn't bring anything appropriate for a symphony."

"You know as well as I do *that* excuse won't work. You have a whole department store at your disposal."

"What time would I have to be ready?" Rachel could feel excitement invading her senses.

"I'll be there at seven." And without giving her the opportunity to change her mind, he hung up.

A date. That changed their relationship. A glance at her watch told her she didn't have much time to find a dress. She left a message with Patsy's secretary and headed toward the dress department.

Her eye was caught by a beautifully made-up face behind the cosmetic counter when she stepped off the escalator. A small sign indicated the saleswoman was trained in applying the skin care products she was selling. The next thing Rachel knew she was sitting on a velveteen stool and the woman was showing her how to cleanse and moisturize her skin. Then she helped her choose the right shades of foundation and eye makeup. Rachel hardly recognized the beautiful face that stared back at her in the gilt-plated mirror when she was finished. It was like the before and after pictures she had seen in women's magazines.

As she crossed the carpet of the exclusive dress department Rachel felt buoyant. When she told the clerk that she needed something appropriate for Sommerfest, she was shown the top of the evening line. Much to Rachel's delight, among the garments was one of her very own creations. It was a tea-length dress in white, with a double ruffle at the bodice that could be worn either on or off her shoulders. The underskirt was flounced, giving the dress a fullness that made the overskirt, trimmed with delicate lilac rosettes, feminine and romantic.

"I'll take it." She beamed brightly at the sales clerk, holding back a chuckle at the thought that she was buying one of her own pieces!

"Don't you want to try it on first?"

"Oh no, it's an Annalise. I know it will fit."

"Yes, they are wonderful dresses, aren't they? So stylish, yet so feminine. With your coloring it will look quite lovely." The saleswoman glanced enviously at Rachel's blond hair and bronzed skin.

Rachel made only one more stop before she went back to Patsy's office and that was to purchase a pair of Italian leather sandals with a high heel. To say that Patsy was surprised at Rachel's appearance was an understatement, but she was much too seasoned to call attention to Rachel's makeover.

"I like it, Rachel." Her keen eyes examined her closely. "I really do. Can I see the dress?"

Rachel opened the dress box. "What do you think? Is it suitable for Sommerfest?"

"Is that where my brother's taking you?"

"Yes. Isn't it appropriate?" Rachel's face fell.

"Yes, of course it is. In fact, it's perfect. But I just realized how late it is. I'd better get you home so you can get ready. I can't wait to see that dress on you."

The dress fit Rachel perfectly, making her petite figure look both dainty and sensual, only hinting at the generous cleavage beneath the ruffled bodice. When the doorbell rang, Rachel felt a moment of fear at the realization that Cole would be seeing the new Rachel for the first time. As he entered the room, she pretended to be looking at a piece of sculpture on Patsy's étagère.

"Hello, Rachel." The simple sound of his voice caused goose bumps to run up and down her arms.

"Hi." She turned around and hoped that he couldn't hear her sharp intake of breath at his appearance. Every time she saw him he seemed to become more attractive. She didn't miss the appreciation in his glance as his eyes roved over her.

"Do you two want a drink before you go?" Patsy inquired.

"No. We want to sample the Marketplatz before the concert, so I think we'll leave right away," Cole told her. Rachel felt his hand on her bare elbow guiding her out of the room and heard Patsy's voice calling, "Have fun."

Cole felt as though he were sixteen years old and on his first date. How he could ever have thought Rachel to be wrong for the Braxton's image was beyond him. She was beautiful, probably one of the most beautiful women he had ever known. So why for the first time in his adult life was he finding it so difficult to compliment a beautiful woman? And when he wanted to be talking about her, why was he chattering on about the Minnesota Orchestra and the Tchaikovsky Spectacular they were going to hear?

The first thing Rachel heard as they walked toward the Orchestra Hall was the exquisite sound of a string quartet. As they crossed the street, Cole took her hand in his and led her to the colorful tents on Peavey Plaza, adjacent to the hall.

"It's like a little bit of Vienna right here in downtown Minneapolis," he told her, as gaily costumed folk dancers swirled around them. "What would you like to sample? A little wurst with mustard? Bratwurst? Viennese pastry and *kaffee mit schlag*? I'm going to have a glass of Austrian beer with a bratwurst."

"I think I'll try the coffee, please, and a pastry."

"No white wine?"

"No, thank you." She smiled demurely.

Before long, it was time to enter the concert hall. She hated to go inside. The soft strains of a Strauss waltz created a fairy-tale setting as she and Cole strolled hand in hand across the plaza. When they entered the concert hall, he did not relinquish her hand, but kept it tightly enfolded within his as they listened to the Tchaikovsky program. When it was over, the stars were out, and although the air had cooled, it was a perfect summer evening.

"Come." Cole led her back onto the plaza, where couples were dancing under the stars to the music of the string quartet.

She stopped in midstep. "Cole, I can't dance." The words tumbled out awkwardly.

"Why not? Are you tired?"

"No. It's just that I never learned how."

He had seen the dancing as an opportunity to hold her close in his arms. It had never crossed his mind that she wouldn't know how to dance.

"I'll show you. It's easy. All you have to do is follow me."

"I couldn't. Not in front of all those people."

"I've a better idea," he said, and they returned to the car.

He drove until they came to a deserted parking lot next to a small lake. The moon was reflected across the water and it cast an iridescent sheen on its surface. Cole left the key in the ignition and inserted a tape into his tape player, then climbed out and came around to her side of the car.

"Come." He offered her his hand. "It's easy. Now all you have to do is follow my lead. We'll start with a slow song." He leaned into the car and punched a button, filling the still air with Lionel Richie's voice.

"First, we do this." He pulled the ruffles at her neckline down onto her shoulders. "There. I've been wanting to do that all night." Without giving her time to protest, he took her right hand in his left and placed his right hand around her waist. "Now look at my feet." He was moving and counting softly, but Rachel was having difficulty ignoring the sensations his hand was creating as it clung to her waist.

"Just relax. You're not going to hurt me if you step on my toes." He smiled charmingly. "You've got to listen to the music, get into its rhythm."

Rachel heard the words of one of her favorite love songs. Hesitantly, she slid her feet according to his directions, and soon she was matching Cole's steps.

"That's it. Didn't I tell you there was nothing to it?" They moved slowly around the asphalt parking lot and the doors of the Mercedes stayed wide open as the music played on. When the song ended, Cole didn't release her, but slipped his other hand behind her waist and clasped his fingers together.

"You look lovely tonight, Rachel."

"Thank you, but it was Braxton's hair salon and cosmetics counter that created all of this." She waved her arm around her face.

"They just highlighted what was already there. With or without the trimmings, Rachel, I like the way you look." He bent his head and brushed her lips lightly with his. It was a soft, exquisite kiss that had her parting her lips in an unconscious invitation. With an urgent moan, Cole covered her mouth with his and moved his lips hungrily against hers.

Rachel wanted Cole's kiss. She opened her lips, hesitantly at first, but once she felt his tongue teasing hers, she responded passionately. It felt so right, so good, so inviting. She wrapped her arms around his broad shoulders and pressed closer to him, as their mouths hungrily sought each other's. She could feel his fingers move across her bare back to her shoulders and then down the hollows of her neck until they came to rest on the burgeoning flesh revealed by the dress. Feather-light touches grew stronger until she felt his fingers curve around her swollen breasts. Had Cole's other arm not held her so tightly she might have dropped to the ground, such was the sensation charging through her.

It was the bright beam of a searchlight that had them pulling apart. Cole snapped his hand up as though he could shield them from the glaring light.

"You folks will have to move along; there's no parking here after two a.m.," the police officer called out his open window, turning off the high-powered beam when he realized the ages of the two people embracing.

"We were just admiring the beautiful view of the lake," Cole returned, holding Rachel protectively with his left arm.

"It is a beautiful night for being outdoors, isn't it?" The car slowly pulled away. "Drive safely now."

Cole looked at Rachel; and the two of them started to giggle. "He probably thought we were a couple of teenagers," Rachel suggested.

"Right now I feel like one." His eyes were serious, intent on her face.

"Me, too," she admitted shyly.

"How is it that you never learned how to dance?" Cole asked as he began the drive back to Patsy's.

"My father never allowed it. He was a minister—a very strict minister. If he had suspected that I had even danced with my girlfriends in my bedroom at home, he would have had me doing penance."

"And after you moved away from home?"

"By then I had Stacey, and after Floyd disappeared I didn't feel much like partying. I guess there just wasn't an occasion for me to learn."

"Do you see your parents very often?"

"My mother died when Stacey was only six. My father never forgave me for getting pregnant. He expected me to go live with Aunt Catherine until

Stacey came, then coldly turn her over to an adoption agency. No scandal, no reflection on his position in the church."

"But certainly after he saw his granddaughter, he felt differently, especially considering what had happened to Floyd."

"It was because of Floyd he could never forgive me. When I heard that Floyd was missing in action, I became very emotional. My father, as I said, was a conservative man. Every Sunday he would get up on his throne and preach how the Lord was watching over our fighting men in Vietnam and that good would triumph over evil. One Sunday something inside of me snapped. I couldn't stand to hear one more word about the Lord punishing the enemy and protecting our fighting boys. Right in the middle of his sermon, I stood up and screamed at him. I called him a liar; I told him the Lord wasn't protecting the father of my baby, that He had gone and forgotten about him completely. I humiliated him publicly, announcing to the whole congregation that I was pregnant. Reverend Kincaid's daughter, an unwed mother. I left for Aunt Catherine's the next day and I haven't been home since."

"And your mother?"

"She was forced to choose between husband and child. She chose her husband. I tried to explain to her what had happened, but she wouldn't listen. Finally, I gave up trying. Which is why my relationship with Stacey is so important to me. I could never alienate my daughter for anyone."

Cole was hoping that she wasn't insinuating what he thought she was. When he walked her to Patsy's door, he grabbed hold of her chin and placed a kiss on her lips. "Thanks for a wonderful night, Rachel. I'd better say good-night or neither one of us will make the marketing meeting tomorrow morning."

## *CHAPTER NINE*

RACHEL COULD FEEL Cole's eyes on her during the entire meeting the next morning, and she dared not look at him for fear he'd see the desire in her eyes. She had wanted his caresses; even now parts of her were warm with longing as she remembered the way he had slipped his hands under her breasts, his fingers moving in an erotic rhythm. She could feel her nipples harden at the memory and purposely crossed her arms over her chest. She forced her attention to what the director of marketing was saying about the diagrams on the overhead projector, but still her mind flashed images of Cole making love to her.

"Didn't I tell you they would love your ideas?" Cole was beside her the minute the meeting was adjourned, bending his head to speak close to her ear.

"Everything is going perfectly, Rachel," Patsy agreed. "Granddad is going to be thrilled."

Cole turned to his sister. "Would you see that Rachel gets to the photo studio? Something's come up and I'm going to be tied up this afternoon."

Rachel breathed a sigh of relief. Having Cole present during the photo session would only have added to her nervousness.

"Will you be joining us for dinner, Cole?" Patsy asked.

"No, and Rachel won't be, either. From now on she's on vacation." He handed Rachel's portfolio to Patsy. "Put this someplace safe."

"Cole, I'm not completely finished with the designs. I can't just say I'm on vacation," she protested.

"We're ahead of schedule at this point," Cole argued.

"Listen, I've got to make a long distance phone call," Patsy cut in. "Why don't I meet you back at my office, Rachel. You can let me know what you've decided then." And with a wave, she was gone.

"*Now* what do you suppose she's thinking?" A warm flush spread over Rachel's face.

"She's thinking I want to spend some time with you...and she's right." He spoke quietly, fighting the urge to take her in his arms and show her why he needed her to stay.

"But I should get back to Chicago," she insisted, feeling her resolve weakening at the same time.

"You told me Stacey was staying with your aunt until next week; and Julian knows where you are. All I'm asking is for you to extend your weekend. Surely you're not working weekends, too?"

She didn't want to admit to him that she had been, but her face was very expressive.

"You *have* been working weekends," he accused, clicking his tongue disapprovingly. "Look, Rachel, we've both been working hard. A couple of days of relaxation would be good for both of us. And what better opportunity than the Aquatennial celebration." He held her hand, gently massaging her palm. "Think of it as a working vacation. If it makes you feel any better, we'll schedule a few appointments between the festivities."

But other than a few progress reports on the Mr. B's Boutique, the next few days were filled with anything but business. Rachel ended up expanding her present wardrobe as Cole announced plans that included a paddleboat ride down the Mississippi River, bicycling around the city of lakes, watching the milk boat carton races and judging a sand castle sculpture competition.

On the last night of her stay, he took her to the Aquatennial torchlight parade. They sat in Parade Stadium munching on popcorn and peanuts and watching marching bands, colorful floats and beauty queen candidates go by.

"You need a souvenir," Cole said, watching kids file past with monkeys on sticks, inflatable toy animals and pennants.

"How about one of those pink balloons?" she suggested, as the vendor paused in front of them.

Cole bought her two—a pink one and a blue one. "There. Just in case you break one." He smiled at her.

"They're perfect." She beamed, watching the two helium-filled balloons bob in the slight summer breeze. "I can remember when a small traveling circus came to Colby one summer and my brother Dave and I begged Dad to let us have a balloon. He thought they were frivolous."

"And you didn't get one?"

"I was lucky that we were able to attend the circus. Oh, look!" She pointed to where the clown unit was cavorting down the street, their antics drawing laughs and guffaws from the crowd.

Rachel was sorry to see the parade end. It was her last evening with Cole and she was already regretting having to return home tomorrow. Cole was different from other men she had dated, and it wasn't just the sexual attraction between them, which seemed to grow stronger every time she was with him. She found herself telling him things she normally didn't tell even her closest friends. He had been able to elicit all sorts of information from her about herself, yet he still remained somewhat of a mystery to her.

Rachel didn't question where they were going as the Mercedes headed out of downtown Minneapolis and onto the freeway, in the opposite direction from Patsy's place. She watched the city lights disappear and then he turned off the highway and drove down what Rachel thought had to be the darkest road she had ever traveled. After several miles he turned again, this time onto a gravel road that led to a brick archway marking the entrance of private property. Nestled in the woods was a rustic home, contemporary in design but made out of logs. Cole brought the car to a stop in front of the attached garage and came around to help her out of the car.

"Want to come in and see my etchings?" He raised his eyebrows in a sinister manner.

"This is your place?"

"Home, sweet home," he declared.

Rachel had forgotten about the helium-filled balloons in the car, which floated out the open door and ascended into the moonlit night. "Oh no, my balloons! They're gone forever," she cried, watching them disappear into the blackness.

"Melinda Sue would have said they're halfway to heaven," Cole said solemnly.

"Melinda Sue?" Rachel probed, aware of the sober expression that had chased away Cole's mischievous grin.

"Let's go inside."

From the side of the place, Rachel hadn't realized the size or the location of the house. Full walls of glass provided a spectacular view of a small lake, the dark surface as smooth as glass. Just as Patsy's decor was ultramodern, Cole's was refined rustic. Although the furniture had formal lines, the earth-toned upholstery lent an informal accent and complemented the rich, handcrafted details of the house. A deerskin rug covered the hardwood floor in front of the massive stone and wood-beam fireplace. Cole opened the sliding glass door and led her out onto a redwood deck that ran the length of the house.

"Cole's landing," he murmured, pointing to a wooden dock where a small fishing boat rested alongside the remains of two bald tires.

"You have your very own private lake?" Rachel asked.

"Pond would be a better description," he replied. "And I do have a neighbor across the way. But it's a good little fishing spot, and quiet. Do you like to fish?"

Rachel shrugged. "I've never tried it."

"Tomorrow I'll take you out and show you what panfish look like."

"I'm going back to Chicago tomorrow," she reminded him, her heart catching at the thought.

"Then the next time you come," he promised. "Come inside and look around while I get us something to drink. If we stay out here too long the mosquitoes will attack." His mood seemed to have changed, and Rachel couldn't help but believe the mention of Melinda Sue was responsible.

Rachel admired the extraordinary workmanship displayed throughout the house as she peeked into the simply decorated bedrooms and bathrooms. One could easily tell Cole was a bachelor; the house lacked a woman's touch. She paused in the doorway to what she knew had to be his room. She could smell his after-shave and the faint scent of cigars. A pair of slacks and a polo shirt lay crumpled across the bed, as though he had changed clothes in a hurry. But it was the oil portrait on the wall opposite the bed that caught her eye. It was of a child, a young girl with raven-black curls and deep brown eyes, posed with a bouquet of daisies in her hands.

"That's Melinda Sue," Cole said from behind her, causing Rachel to jump slightly. "My daughter."

"She's lovely, Cole."

"Yes, she was the most beautiful thing in my life." He stood staring at the picture, momentarily forgetting about the two glasses in his hands.

"Is one of them for me?" she asked.

He handed her a glass. "Try this. It's a mixture of wine and fruit juice. Not very potent, but interesting. Just enough to give you a little glow inside."

Rachel wanted to tell him that he did that to her without any wine. "Umm. It's good." She sipped it slowly. "Cole, will you tell me about Melinda Sue?"

"She died when she was only ten years old."

"Oh, Cole. I'm sorry."

"She had kidney disease. We were fortunate enough to locate a replacement for her, but she died during the transplant surgery." He crossed the room and cranked open the windows facing the lake, and the sound of crickets broke the silence.

"What was she like, Cole?" Rachel had to ask the question.

"She was perfect. I know every father says that about his daughter, but she really was an exceptional child. One of her teachers once told me that she wished she could bottle Melinda's special talent for making others feel good. That no matter what happened during the school day, she knew that Melinda would have a smile for her. She was gifted both intellectually and musically. She was so inquisitive. I tried to have all the answers for her, but I couldn't find the answer to her illness. Neither her mother nor I were compatible donors, and by the time an organ transplant was arranged, it was too late."

Rachel could see that time had not eased the pain of losing his daughter and the effort it took for him to talk about her.

"I remember the first time she lost a helium-filled balloon in the wind. 'Is it halfway to heaven yet, Daddy?' she asked, tilting her delicate little neck way back to watch its progress."

Rachel could see the tenderness in his eyes as Cole spoke, a delicate mixture of pain and pride.

"Then it became a game with her. She'd giggle as she watched her balloons ascend into the sky. 'Someday I'll get to see all those balloons when I get to heaven, won't I, Daddy?' she even questioned once.

And I, in all my wisdom, merely laughed and said, 'Not for a long, long time, Pumpkin. You'll be old and gray and a grandma by then.'" His voice broke. "She never even made it past childhood."

"It must have been a very painful time for you. You and your wife never thought about having another child?"

"My marriage to Elaine was over before Melinda Sue died. We were as mismatched as two left feet. But Melinda had a bonding effect on us. After she was gone, there was nothing to keep us together. We had grown so far apart, it would have been preposterous to even consider having another child. We didn't share anything—not even our grief. There were simply no feelings left to deal with. We sold the house, I built this place and she moved back East where she had come from originally. That was five years ago. We finally divorced last year when she decided to remarry." He paused. "You're a very soothing person, Rachel. I've never been able to open up to anyone like this before." It warmed him to think of her in that light.

"Is it because of Melinda that you took up hot air ballooning?"

"Melinda's always with me up there. Actually, I went through a rather reckless period after she died. I suppose it's not uncommon when people are faced with death, especially that of a child. I left Braxton's and became a recluse. I lost interest in everything, preferring to hide away up here and drink myself into oblivion. Then I took up skydiving, which had my family a bit nervous."

"So what brought you back to Braxton's?"

"My grandfather had a stroke. But I'm afraid many of the bad habits stuck. I drink more than I should; I'm cynical—which you have already experienced—and I'm often too blunt or insensitive to the feelings of others, as Patsy accuses me of regularly. What you see standing before you is a thirty-eight-year-old man who has nothing to show for his life but a secluded home and his work."

It was as though his discontent was a tangible thing and Rachel wanted to reach out and push it away. Now that she knew about his past, everything made so much more sense.

He swallowed the remainder of his drink. "Let's go into the other room. Tonight we progress to lesson two in the 'Learn to Dance the Cole Braxton Way.'" He led her by her hand into the living room, then shoved the sofa and chair back against the wall.

"First, the right music." He placed a record on the stereo system hidden in the rustic bookshelves. "The polka." He held up his arms, pretending she was in them, and circled around the room, counting aloud. "Ready?"

Rachel was surprised at how quickly she caught on. "This is wonderful, but when am I ever going to dance the polka in Chicago?" she asked as he complimented her on her success.

"The polka? Why, at all those formal society events you're so fond of," he teased. "Or weddings... it's very popular at wedding dances."

After several dances, Rachel was out of breath. "Are you sure people our age do this regularly?" she asked, sinking down onto the sofa.

"You should have seen my grandparents before grandfather had his stroke. More sangria?"

"Is it safe?"

"It's very diluted wine."

"Why not then?" She handed him her glass.

When he returned he replaced the polka music with the soft sounds of Neil Diamond. "Let's see what you remember from your first lesson."

Rachel glided into his arms. This time she didn't have the advantage of her high heels and Cole's chin rested near her forehead. Gathering her closer, he pulled both her arms up around his neck and placed his own arms around her waist, bending slightly to dance cheek-to-cheek.

"I'm minus my heels."

"That just means we get to dance closer."

Although the tempo of the music had slowed, Rachel's heartbeat had picked up the minute she felt Cole's warm body next to hers. She was experiencing sensations she had forgotten she was able to feel, and admitted to herself that she felt a strong sexual attraction to him. But these feelings were monumental compared to what she remembered feeling for Floyd. And for just a second, thinking of Floyd, she stiffened.

But Cole was not about to ease his hold on her. "We're getting quite good at this, aren't we?" he murmured huskily into her ear, his breath warm against her cheek. And Rachel knew once more the power a woman could exert over a man, for his desire for her was obvious, and it gave her a feeling of importance to know that she could arouse him.

Everything about him seduced her emotionally. How could anything that felt so good be wrong? His arms were a haven for her, strong and protective. She had thought him a cold and insensitive man, but she'd been wrong. He was warm and caring, though the pain he had suffered over the loss of his daughter had taken its toll. It was a pain that she could identify with, knowing the power children had over their parents. Their steps became barely noticeable as their bodies swayed with the rhythm of the music.

Rachel could feel her breasts strain against her bra, and without any conscious effort, her body rubbed closer to his. Just when the dancing stopped and the caressing began, Rachel didn't know. Had she actually started to kiss his neck? Desire seemed to blur rational thinking, and all that mattered was this aching hunger running through her, begging to be assuaged.

Rachel's warm, delicate lips on his neck was all the invitation Cole needed. When he had brought her back to his house he'd thought he would be able to take things slowly. But she was so damned soft and inviting, and he could feel her nipples pressing through the silky shirt she wore. What had started out as a series of tiny kisses along her neck turned into a trail across her cheek until he found her mouth, soft and inviting beneath his.

He kept telling his body to go slowly, but she met his kisses with such ardor, he couldn't stop the hands that eased their way up over the silky smooth fabric of her shirt to teasingly touch her breasts. Cole felt her weaken and he gracefully eased her down onto the sofa.

When he pulled back from her to look at her flushed cheeks, she released an involuntary husky objection. Cole glazed her cheek with a finger, lifting her chin toward him. "You are one hell of a woman, Rachel Kincaid," he growled before kissing her intimately. This time he didn't hold back, his passion stronger than his reason.

Rachel was swamped with feelings, both emotional and sensual. Nothing mattered except that she be in Cole's arms and that the wonderful sensations he stirred in her never stop. His hands were torturing her with ecstasy as they caressed her silken-clad torso, and her breasts ached with the need of his touch. Had he not unbuttoned her blouse then, she would have done it for him.

Cole's eyes were mesmerized by Rachel's loveliness. Under the silken shirt she wore a transparent nylon bra that barely concealed the golden breasts he had only been able to fantasize about. His fingers nearly trembled as he reached for the front clasp that would free the sensuous mounds. Rachel caught the look of admiration in his eyes and a ripple of pleasure shot through her as the nylon fabric slid to the floor. Cole's fingers worked magic on her breasts while his tongue explored her mouth. Rachel reached up to lock her hands around his neck while his lips turned her bones to molten lava.

She found herself on her back, with Cole on one elbow leaning over her. Undoing his shirt, she touched the mat of dark hair with tentative fingers, his swift intake of breath exulting her. Then he kissed her again, a deep, long probing kiss that had Rachel quivering with eagerness. Turning on his side, Cole stroked her breasts, his hands setting the satiny smooth flesh afire, his fingers drawing feathery circles around each nipple. When his mouth replaced his fingers, Rachel groaned, certain that his tongue would drive her mad. Never had she felt this way, so alive, so impatient, so willing to lose herself in pure sensation. She wanted the pleasure she was feeling to last forever.

With the skill of a well-practiced lover, he wiggled his arms out of his sleeves and tossed his shirt aside without taking his lips from her hot flesh. Rachel's hands found the naked skin and she marveled that the feel of rippling muscles under her hands could be so delightful.

When his hand found the zipper on her slacks, Rachel made little sounds of satisfaction in the back of her throat. As Cole's fingers worked their way under the elastic of her bikini briefs, he gave a low moan of pleasure and feverishly brought his mouth back to hers.

"Rachel, do you know what you're doing to me?" he murmured against her lips.

"The same thing you're doing to me," she returned throatily.

Cole swept her up into his arms and started carrying her across the wooden plank flooring down the hallway.

"What are you doing?" she said, her eyes glazed with passion.

"I want you in my bed," he said huskily, in between kisses.

The meaning of his words took a moment to register, but by the time Cole was lowering her onto the king-size bed, Rachel realized that if she didn't say something now, there would be no stopping their passion. When he straightened to remove his jeans, she rolled off the other side of the bed.

"I can't do this, Cole. It's not right," she managed to get out in a small voice.

He stopped in midair, one leg out of the denims, one leg in. "It is right, Rachel. We're good together. You know it and I know it." He stuffed his leg back in the jeans and came around to her side of the bed. He wanted to take her in his arms and kiss some sense into her but she eluded his touch and rushed out into the living room.

An uneasy silence enveloped them. Rachel fumbled with her clothes as Cole watched her tuck her large breasts back into the bra. He could have kicked himself for his mistake. He should have taken her right there on the couch. He moved over to the patio door, taking several deep breaths as he raked his fingers through his hair.

Rachel was disgusted with herself for her childish reaction. Compared to the women he usually dated she must have seemed like a frightened virgin. How could she tell him that she, a thirty-four-year-old mother, hadn't taken any precautions against getting pregnant? She wanted to explain to him that she was frightened; not only of her feelings for him, but about making love to a man. How could she explain that she was afraid she wouldn't meet his expectations as a lover, that she had only been intimate with one other man and that had led to Stacey?

Stacey! My God, she had nearly made the mistake that could alienate her from her daughter. How would

Stacey react to the knowledge that the mother who had chastised her for her behavior had turned around and gone to bed with the very same man?

She couldn't tell Cole any of these things, but she needed to try to make him understand.

"Cole, I . . ." she began, but she couldn't find the words.

Cole didn't want to be angry, but looking at her he couldn't help feel frustrated. "I'd better take you home," he said abruptly.

The ride back to Patsy's was silent except for the music from the tape player. On the way to Cole's house, romantic lyrics had foreshadowed their emotions; now, the soulful sounds of rhythm and blues seemed to cry out in sympathy.

When they arrived at the town house, Cole's hand reached across to prevent Rachel's from opening the door.

"I need to see you again, Rachel."

"Why?" The question was spontaneous.

"Because you know we're right for each other."

His lips crushed hers and his tongue thrust into her mouth, as though to compensate for that part of her he couldn't enter. Rachel was suddenly weak with desire and arching her body toward his.

"Tell me you don't want this as much as I do," he challenged.

"I do want you," she admitted. What good would it do to deny him when her body would only betray her? "But that still doesn't make it right."

"Right?" A low laugh escaped his throat. "Rachel, we're two grown adults, not a couple of teenagers. I want you in my bed, not in a car."

"Cole, I'm sorry. It's just that I'm not used to... I mean, it's been so long I..." she stammered.

Suddenly he realized that she was trying to tell him she hadn't been to bed with a man since Floyd left. "My God, Rachel. No one should be without love for that long a time!"

"If you're thinking I'm some sex-starved widow, you're wrong. I don't need sex." She closed her eyes to shut out the memories of all the lonely nights she had lain awake, fighting her desires. "I haven't been without love, even though that love has meant sacrifices."

Cole put his finger to her lips. "Shhh. You don't need to explain. I've rushed you." He held her close to his chest and Rachel could feel the comforting rhythm of his heart. He had forgotten that she wasn't like most women he knew. "We'll work something out. I'll come to Chicago on Saturday and we'll go to dinner," he assured her. Then he pulled her into his arms and covered her lips with a kiss that left Rachel with no doubts about their being able to work it out.

But on the plane heading back to Chicago the next morning, Rachel wondered how she and Cole would ever work anything out. There were simply too many hurdles to leap. She lived in Chicago; he lived in Minneapolis. She thought of the women who smiled at him on the street, eyed him from passing cars and peered over their shoulders with inviting smiles. How could she compete with all that temptation? And then there was still the problem of Stacey. The past few weeks had finally brought about a strengthening in their mother-daughter relationship. Would all that ground be lost if Stacey discovered that Cole was interested in her mother?

Cole Braxton was not the type of man to want only friendship from a woman. But then neither did he want only physical possession. So what exactly did he want from her, Rachel wondered. He had pushed his way into her life and had caused her to question the three other relationships that were most important to her. That first night he had made her question her daughter's trustworthiness. Then he started in on Julian and had tried to make her feel as though she were being taken advantage of by him. And now it was his face she saw when she closed her eyes, not Floyd's. He was forcing her to face up to problems she didn't want to deal with.

Julian was waiting for her at the airport, much to Rachel's surprise. As she stepped out into the terminal, he rushed over to hug her.

"We did it! They loved the collection! Did I not tell you we would make a fantastic team?"

Rachel's smile was forced. "Yes."

Julian talked effusively all the way back to Annalise while Rachel sat thinking about Cole's suggestion that she open her own studio. Was she ready to make that type of a career move?

Rachel was tired when she made her way home that night. She had been unsuccessful in her attempts to push thoughts of Cole Braxton out of her head. When she opened the door to her apartment, she caught her breath. Clinging to the ceiling in the living room were balloons—hundreds of them: pink, blue, yellow and green. Dropping her suitcase in the hallway, she rushed across the carpet, pulled the bunch down and detached the note suspended from the common string.

I'll see you at 8:00 Saturday night. Cole.

Rachel took the balloons into her room where she released them under the canopy top. That night before she went to sleep it wasn't Floyd's poster that stared at her, but Cole's balloons.

## *CHAPTER TEN*

SEVERAL TIMES during the next few days Rachel picked up the phone to call Cole and tell him she couldn't go out with him on Saturday night, and several times she replaced the handset without completing the call. She could think of a hundred reasons why she shouldn't see him again, but none of them could make her pick up that phone and actually tell him. Instead, she found herself visiting the doctor about birth control. When Stacey phoned to announce she would be flying home Sunday evening, Rachel was filled with relief. She knew that if she was going to continue to see Cole, Stacey would have to know, but right now she wanted just one more night with him without her daughter knowing.

Rachel didn't want to question her relationship with Cole—what he wanted from her, what she wanted from him—nor was she prepared to face her feelings for him. She only knew that she didn't want to deny herself his company. At thirty-four years of age she knew it would be a mistake to think that going to bed meant commitment. In fact, it would be a mistake to think seriously of Cole at all. He was divorced, handsome, virile. No, it would be silly to think of this as anything other than an affair.

But when Saturday came, Rachel wasn't sure if there would even be an affair. Other than the flock of balloons that had greeted her upon her return, she hadn't heard so much as a word from him. At seven o'clock on Saturday evening she debated as to whether she should get dressed up or stay in her jeans. At eight-thirty she sat curled up in her favorite chair staring at the clock in a pink organza sundress. Anxiety had turned to anger at the thought that he hadn't intended coming and after another half hour she marched into the bedroom, took off the sundress and slipped into a pair of raspberry silk pajamas. Returning to the kitchen, she opened the bread drawer and withdrew two slices. Grimacing at the choice of spreads in the refrigerator, she finally took out a jar of mustard and nearly dropped it at the sound of the doorbell.

She didn't need to look in the peephole to know it was Cole; she could feel his presence in her heart. Opening the door, she was greeted with a "Hello, Rachel," and the lazy smile she was coming to expect from him.

"You came!" she blurted out unexpectedly.

"Yes," he said, his eyes sweeping over her. "You didn't doubt that I would?"

"But why didn't you call?" she asked, forgetting that he was still standing in the hallway.

"We were late getting out of New York. Can I come in?"

She blushed, then ushered him in, suddenly conscious of the fact that she was in her pajamas.

Cole eyed the open button on the silk pajama top and felt an irresistible urge to undo the other two buttons. The raspberry silk clung to her breasts, outlining the protruding points that refused to be ignored.

Rachel, aware of the direction of Cole's glance, felt the sudden tautness of her nipples under her top. She wanted to say, "Don't look at me that way," but the silence was packed with erotic messages. When he lifted his eyes to meet hers, she could feel her body melt at the message there.

Cole drew her into his arms, his lips tender as they claimed hers. His kiss became passionate as her arms went around his neck and she pressed herself closer to him. All of the obstacles Rachel had thought about the past few days disintegrated with his touch. Gone were the doubts, the questions, the worries. He kissed the edges of her mouth, tracing the outline of her lips with his tongue, and Rachel's lips parted, inviting him to twine his tongue with hers in a deep, probing kiss.

"I could have damn well hijacked the plane and flown it here myself when they announced we were going to be late," he murmured huskily into her ear, nibbling at her soft flesh. "God, I've missed you."

"It's only been three days," Rachel responded, attempting to regain her equilibrium.

"Three days too many. I didn't want to let you go in the first place."

Rachel felt a yearning such as she never believed possible. To break the tension, she said, "Why don't you sit down and I'll get you something to drink."

Cole watched her walk from the room, the slight sway of her bottom tantalizing him. He wondered if she wore anything under the lounging pajamas. It had taken every bit of his self-restraint to stop himself from dragging her into the bedroom when he had first arrived, especially when he knew she would offer little resistance.

She returned with two short glasses and Cole patted the sofa cushion beside him invitingly.

"Maybe I should get dressed."

"Just sit for a few minutes." He smiled appreciatively as Rachel handed him the Scotch before sinking down beside him. She expected him to casually place his arm around her shoulder, draw her close and kiss her intimately. But much to her surprise, he leaned back and began to talk about his hurried business trip overseas that had prevented him from calling her.

For the past seventy-two hours she had been alone and his presence was comforting. They talked like long-lost friends, sending out for pizza when they both realized they hadn't eaten any dinner.

Cole had forgotten how nice it was to have someone to come home to after a stressful day, and he realized how empty his life had been before he met Rachel. With the type of women he usually associated with there was no time for quiet, intimate conversation. But Rachel was different. There was something about her, something besides sex, that attracted him, and he found himself reluctant to see the evening end.

"Could I fix you a cup of coffee?" she asked, as though she were able to read his thoughts.

Cole glanced at his watch and shook his head. "I should be getting to my hotel. I came directly from the airport."

Now would be the time for her to tell him she wanted him to stay with her. She had rehearsed in her mind dozens of times what she would say to him. But modesty held her captive. He hadn't so much as made an attempt to kiss her after their passionate greeting, and she was wondering if perhaps he wouldn't prefer to stay at the hotel. She hadn't been intimate with a man in such a long time; she couldn't make the first move—even if she had fantasized that they were lovers for the past three days!

The apartment was completely silent as their gazes met and locked for several minutes. Cole hated leaving. He knew she was alone and that worried him. He almost wished he had fallen asleep on her sofa, so he could at least know that she was protected. She wasn't the kind of woman who should go through life without a man, he thought, yet that was just what she had done, out of some misplaced loyalty to a childhood sweetheart. He caught sight of the picture of Floyd Andrews out of the corner of his eye and felt an overwhelming stab of jealousy. Rachel had so much to give a man, yet she kept it hidden in a safety deposit box inside her heart. Would he ever get the key?

"You know it bothers me that you're here alone."

"It does? Why?" she asked innocently.

"That's exactly what I mean. You don't realize how unsafe it is for a woman living alone with her teenage daughter in a city like Chicago."

"Why, Cole, I do believe you're a bit of a chauvinist. Women don't need men to take care of them. There are millions of us living without men and raising children as well."

Her flippancy irritated him. "And do you know how many of them are assaulted and raped every day?"

When she saw how serious he was, she said, "Cole, I've had no choice but to live alone with Stacey."

Cole rubbed the back of his neck with his hand. "I know. I'm sorry for snapping at you like that." He pulled her into his arms. "You're such a trusting soul and I can't help but worry about you." His fingers were massaging her scalp, gathering silken strands of blond hair between them. How could he explain this irrepressible urge to protect her? "I especially don't like the fact that Stacey isn't here."

"Would you like to sleep in the guest room?" Rachel found herself saying in a soft voice. "Actually, it's my sewing room, but we keep a bed in there for when Aunt Catherine visits."

"I'll get my suitcase," he said with a smile.

Rachel found that there was an exciting intimacy about sharing an apartment with a man. Her imagination went wild with visions of Cole as she heard the shower running. She waited for the sound of a hair dryer, but none came. She pictured him toweling his hair dry.

He gave her a chaste kiss on the lips before saying good-night, which left her strangely disappointed. After an hour of tossing and turning, she tiptoed out into the kitchen for a glass of milk. On her return, she couldn't resist peeking into Cole's room.

"Looking for someone?" he drawled in a husky voice as she spun around and met his hard chest, a tiny screech escaping from her throat.

"How come you're not sleeping?" she demanded, pointing toward the empty bed, then turning her back to him upon discovering that he was only wearing a pair of briefs. The night-light from the bathroom cast just enough illumination to allow her to see him clearly.

"The same reason you're not," he answered, placing his hands on her shoulders and turning her back around. He couldn't tell her that he had been coming to her room, that he had ached for her so badly his good sense had been overruled by his desire and his need to be with her.

Rachel was grateful for the darkness, for she was certain her cheeks were scarlet as her eyes saw the reason for his insomnia, the knit fabric of his briefs unable to hide his physical need. She could feel her nipples harden beneath the silky softness of her nightgown and saw Cole's gaze slip to the spot where the fabric seductively clung to her breasts.

"You don't have any pajamas on," she squeaked, then felt ridiculously naive.

"I never wear them," he said huskily, trailing his fingertip across the piped edging of the square cut bodice of her gown.

"Cole..."

His mouth silenced her protest with a kiss that left her in little doubt that he wanted her, or that he had been waiting for her. It was a kiss that brought a long, shuddering sigh from Rachel as her body quivered with eagerness. She loved the feel of his naked torso.

"Do you want me to stop?" he demanded in a hoarse whisper, his hands gliding softly over her hips.

For an answer she pulled his mouth back to hers. Cole swung her off her feet and carried her into her bedroom, where the soft glow from the bedside lamp gave a warm intimacy to the room. Rachel felt the coolness of the satin sheets beneath her, but when she expected Cole to sink into her embrace, he stepped back away from the bed and looked over his shoulder. With deliberate movements, he crossed the room and closed the closet door, which Rachel had left open after years of habit. When he returned to her bedside, he hesitated, until Rachel raised her arms, reaching for him. "Don't go!" she whispered.

He lowered himself beside her on the bed, gazing at her for a long moment before he exclaimed in a low voice, "Do you think I could leave you now?"

Rachel saw the passion in his eyes and felt a momentary sense of panic. He was obviously experienced in sexual intimacy, whereas she had little confidence in her ability to please a man like him. But then he pulled her into his arms and his mouth claimed hers in a seductive kiss that drew every ounce of passion from her. Her fears were banished, as were all the doubts she had about their relationship, as she gave willingly of herself, wrapping her arms tightly around his neck. He lifted the ivory nightgown over her head, pausing to place delicious kisses on each breast.

"You are so beautiful," he averred, lowering her back against the pillows. In one swift movement, he had slipped off his briefs and stretched out beside her, one leg insinuating itself between hers, his rigid maleness insisting itself up against her.

His fingers traced erotic patterns across her nipples while his mouth moved on a sensuous journey down her slender throat, nibbling at her tender flesh until it reached her full breasts. His tongue fluttered over them, teasing and exciting her, bringing Rachel to the brink of ecstasy. His hands found the softness of her buttocks and pulled her close so that she could feel the pulsating pressure against her stomach.

Instinctively, Rachel's body moved rhythmically against his. The sweet ache between her legs needed to be satisfied, but she thought her heart would stop beating when his fingers found the secret moistness between her thighs. Just when she thought she would go mad with wanting, his leg parted hers and she felt him enter. Rachel stiffened momentarily in anticipation of the pain she thought might accompany his possession. Had it been possible, Cole would have withdrawn at her obvious hesitation, but he wanted her more than he had ever wanted any other woman, and he needed to know the fulfillment only she could bring.

"You feel so good," he said huskily in between passion drugged kisses. The more deeply he drove into her, the more pleasurable the sensations became, until Rachel found herself gasping in delight. With a groan of satisfaction, Cole gave up trying to hold back, and met her passion with a shattering climax that left both of them clinging in a feverish embrace.

After a few moments, Cole brushed a silken strand from Rachel's damp brow to place a soft kiss on her forehead. He smiled, a tender smile of satisfaction and intimacy that nearly brought a rush of tears to Rachel's eyes.

"God, what you do to me, woman," he said, breathing a sigh of contentment and tracing her lips with the tip of his finger before tucking her into the crook of his arm.

Rachel, lying in his arms, thought she had never felt such bliss. She didn't want to question why it had happened or think about tomorrow. She only wanted to luxuriate in the euphoria and, pressing her lips to his throat, she whispered drowsily. "I've never felt this good."

A low chuckle of smug pleasure tumbled out of Cole. "Don't fall asleep on me, sweetheart."

"Hmm?" Rachel moaned sleepily.

But when Cole's mouth found hers, she came awake. Pressing his palms against her buttocks, he drew her closer so that she could feel his arousal.

"Again?" she whispered.

"We can sleep tomorrow." And before Rachel knew it, she was underneath him meeting his passion with an even greater fervor.

RACHEL WAS the first one to awaken the next morning, feeling unusually relaxed and comfortable in the strong arms that were wound around her possessively. She had never slept in a man's arms before, and after the initial surprise at finding herself pinned beneath a muscular leg, she took the opportunity to study Cole's naked form. He had such a fine body: broad chested, narrow hipped, lean yet muscular. She could see the line at his waist where the smooth brown skin met the pale area that had been covered by his swimming trunks. She felt an uncontrollable desire to lift the corner of the satin sheet draped across his midsection and run her fingers through the dark thatch of curly hair she knew lay hidden there.

As though Cole's sleeping body knew the direction of her thoughts, a hand slid intimately over her hip to rest on the most sensitive area of her stomach, creating disturbing sensations that told Rachel the night before had not been a dream. He had shown her what a devastating experience lovemaking could be, and now, when her body knew the delights of intimacy, she craved more. She didn't want to leave the bed; she wanted to arouse Cole from his sleep and rekindle the passion they had shared last night.

She lifted her hand tentatively; wanting, yet unsure as to whether or not she should explore his body.

"Did you want something?" Cole asked. His hand was seeking the rounded swell of her breast before his eyes lazily flicked open.

"Just wondering if you slept better in this bed than in the spare single?" Rachel asked coyly.

"This bed is much softer," he replied. "Plus I always did fancy pink satin sheets... as well as pink flesh." His lips replaced the hand at her breast and Rachel felt the familiar tightening in her stomach and the ache his touch brought. She was about to make another journey into euphoria...

IT WAS THE INCESSANT RINGING of the telephone that woke Rachel. A possessive hand came to rest on her derriere, and Rachel was tempted to turn over and let the fingers explore. But the phone kept ringing and she silently cursed herself for not having taken it off the hook.

"Hello?" Her voice had a breathless quality that betrayed her.

"Mom! Where were you? The phone must have run ten times." Stacey's voice was like a splash of cold water on her face. The euphoria vanished.

"I was sleeping," Rachel said, trying to tug the sheet up over her body.

"Sleeping? Mother, it's nearly noon!"

"Yes... well, I've been keeping late hours." She glanced at the digital clock and saw that Stacey was right. "How's everything?"

"Pretty good. I just called to tell you I'll be landing in Chicago at eight-forty tonight."

"You're coming home today?" Rachel's eyes flew to the sleeping man beside her.

"Of course I'm coming home today. It *is* Sunday. Mother, are you all right?" Stacey sounded suspicious.

"I'm fine. Don't worry, darling, I'll be at the airport to meet you."

Replacing the phone, Rachel attempted to escape from Cole's arms. "Where are you going?" he drawled, his voice muffled by the pillow.

"It's almost noon," Rachel said huskily, unable to ignore the sensations his fingers were arousing as they fondled her nipples, yet angry that she couldn't prevent the traitorous sensations. Rachel grabbed the covers up close to herself.

"What are you trying to cover up? I'm never going to forget one inch of that delectable body," he said softly. He reached out to grab her as she tried to get up from the bed. "Just because your daughter calls and tells you it's noon doesn't mean you have to go getting prudish on me."

"I am not prudish," she denied. But hearing Stacey's voice had brought back all the thoughts she hadn't wanted to admit to last night. She didn't know the rules of the game Cole played by. Was it simply a matter of lust? It just didn't seem right that she found such ecstasy in the arms of a man her daughter had wanted for herself.

"You can't leave me like this, Rachel," Cole pleaded with a mock look of torture.

Rachel couldn't prevent a smile. She purposely turned her back to him.

"Listen, Rachel, last night was wonderful. Why are you so embarrassed? There's nothing wrong with admitting you want me as much as I want you."

His words were more erotic than his caresses. Rachel shut her eyes, hoping to close her senses to his presence and the look of possession she knew was in his eyes. She felt his fingers lightly touch her arms and trace a pattern upward across her shoulders. His lips interrupted the exploration with feather-light kisses.

"Cole..."

"Umm...you taste even sweeter after you've been sleeping." He continued to kiss the back of her neck, pushing the gold curtain of hair aside. Rachel felt a trembling reverberate over the entire length of her body. When Cole's hands reached under her arms to encompass her breasts, she was lost. Instinctively she yielded to the warm lips that found hers. Nibbling and sucking gently, they sent a blast of hot pleasure deep into her groin.

She felt the faint bristle of his beard against her lips as she moved her mouth across his face. If she had any reason to doubt the reality of last night, his long, hard legs against her were familiar evidence of the passion they had shared.

"How can you deny that you need this?"

"I don't..." Excitement took her breath away.

His hand was massaging her inner thighs, tantalizing the moist entrance to her body. Rachel found her legs parting of their own accord, and she gave a low groan of pleasure. Fleetingly, she thought of Stacey; then, caught up in her own mounting sensual excitement, she felt the beginning of ecstasy, and met Cole's passion with equal force.

"Oh, Cole, yes..."

LATER, PASSION SPENT, they talked. They chose not to spend their one day together in the heat of the July sun, but to remain in Rachel's air-conditioned apartment, eating scrambled eggs and toast for dinner, drinking wine cooler and talking about his dream—to balloon someday over the Alps, and hers—to see her fashions make the cover of *Vogue*. They didn't talk about the past or the future, but carefully avoided any mention of what would happen after he went back to Minneapolis. When Rachel told Cole what time Stacey would be arriving at the airport, he made reservations on a flight that coincided with Stacey's arrival. Before he boarded his plane, he made Rachel promise to fly to Minneapolis the next weekend. Then he kissed her passionately, ignoring the crowd of people surrounding them.

The minute he was out of sight, apprehension began to infiltrate Rachel's brain cells. As she walked across the concourse to the gate where Stacey's plane was expected, she considered her choices. She could treat her affair with Cole as just that: something private that Stacey didn't need to know about. After all, she herself didn't know what it would lead to. Or she could tell Stacey that she had been seeing Cole on a professional basis. But that smacked of duplicity, and if there was one thing she had insisted upon in her relationship with her daughter, it was straightforwardness. Or she could tell Stacey the truth: that she and Cole were dating; that the man her daughter had fantasized about was now her mother's boyfriend. No wonder she felt so miserable. Her choices were such that she could be either secretive, dishonest or insensitive with her daughter. Rachel wished she had more time; there had to be a solution she was overlooking.

But Stacey was coming toward her, looking tired but happy, and Rachel could only think of how good it felt to have her arms around her.

"Hi. Did you have a good visit?" Rachel asked, relieving her daughter of her overnight case. "Did you like the university?"

"It was fine. Mom, what have you done to yourself?" Stacey's voice held censure.

Guilt had Rachel blushing and wondering if Stacey could tell that she had spent the day making love. She smoothed the blond curls down self-consciously. "I had a make-over in Minneapolis. This is what the advertising people thought Rachel the fashion designer should look like. What do you think?" She stood back for inspection.

"Why would you want to change your image?"

"You're the one who's always telling me I'm old-fashioned," Rachel reminded her. "Don't you like it?"

"You look great," Stacey admitted reluctantly.

"But?" Rachel could tell by the tone there was a "but" in there.

"But you're my mother, not my sister."

As they crossed over to the baggage claim area, Rachel explained to her about the promotional photographs for the Mr. B's Boutique. When a good-looking, muscular man offered to lift Stacey's suitcase off the luggage conveyor belt for Rachel, she smiled appreciatively, sparking a brief, casual conversation that didn't include Stacey.

"*Mother*," Stacey said pointedly, only to be disappointed; for her revelation didn't seem to discourage the young man.

By the time they had reached the car, Stacey was tired and ready to tell her mother just what she thought of her new look. "See what I mean? That guy couldn't have been more than twenty-five and he was flirting with you, and all because of your appearance."

"He wasn't flirting," Rachel denied. "He was simply being polite and making conversation. You have to admit, it was awfully nice of him to retrieve your suitcase."

"But that's just the point. He didn't offer for me. What does Braxton's want? For you to look like you're eighteen?"

"I'm only thirty-four, not fifty-four," Rachel reminded her.

"What has Bud said about your new look?"

"I haven't seen him since I've been back," Rachel admitted. "And just what do you expect him to say? That I look like my daughter? Look closely, dear. I have crow's feet around my eyes and dishpan hands."

"How come you aren't wearing your glasses?" Stacey asked as her mother drove the car out of the airport parking lot.

"Contacts. I never realized what a nuisance those things were until I bought these."

"Mom, I just can't believe you've changed so much."

"Darling, I haven't done anything I shouldn't have done years ago. You were right. I was old-fashioned. My hair was nice, but outdated; my clothes were nice, but plain; and I didn't really need the glasses. But let's not talk about me: I want to hear all about Milwaukee and how Aunt Catherine is doing."

By the time they reached home, Stacey had quit casting strange looks in Rachel's direction. The enigmatic stares had changed to enthusiastic expressions as she spoke about her great-aunt. When she inquired about her mother's trip to Minneapolis, Rachel went into great detail about her sessions with the advertising people, reluctant to divulge that she had stayed on a few extra days to be with Cole. But since she didn't really know what plans Cole had for seeing her again, she felt almost justified in not telling Stacey the truth. Why put any undue stress on the slender thread of trust that had developed between them? And anyway, Cole was in Minneapolis and she was in Chicago. Could there possibly be a future for the two of them?

Rachel was changing into her nightgown when Stacey came storming out of the bathroom. "What is *this* doing in the bathroom?" She held a black leather shaving kit in her hand that Rachel recognized as Cole's.

"I had a houseguest." She was furious at herself for blushing. She felt as though she were breaking out in hives. She grabbed the black case away from Stacey.

"A *male* houseguest? I can't believe it, Mother. How could you?"

"How could I what? This is my home and we do have a spare room."

"Do you expect me to believe that? Now it all makes sense: the makeup, the new hairdo, the juvenile clothes. That was all for the benefit of some man." Stacey sounded outraged.

Rachel sighed. "So what if it was? And it's no crime to have a male houseguest." She realized how odd it was that she was defending herself to a seventeen-year-old.

"All these years I thought you were being faithful to Dad!" she exclaimed emotionally.

"I have been faithful to your father," Rachel protested.

"Ha! I bet every time I've been away overnight you had Bud stay over."

Giving herself a few moments to control the angry beat of her heart, Rachel finished hanging up her clothes, then turned toward her daughter. "I do not have to account to you for my actions," Rachel said firmly. "Bud has never slept here, and I'd appreciate you not attacking him on the subject when you next see him."

"Do you expect me to believe that some guy stayed here and slept in the guest room when you look like love in bloom? And what's this?" She picked up the puckered remains of a deflated balloon off Rachel's vanity glass.

"It is not your place to question my personal relationships, Stacey. Now I suggest that you go to bed before we both say things we'll only regret. We're both tired.''

Stacey left without a word.

AS RACHEL PULLED BACK the covers, she smelled Cole's presence there. She closed her eyes, trying to blot out the images that haunted her. Cole lying naked, his body firm and solid, entwined with hers. And then, as though her thoughts had reached him, the phone rang and it was Cole.

''I just wanted to make sure you got home safely.'' His voice was soothing, familiar.

''Yes, I'm fine.'' Her voice was barely a whisper.

''Good. Then you'll let me know what time you'll be coming next Friday?''

A long pause followed. Rachel finally said, ''Yes.''

After he had said goodbye, Cole tried to reassure himself that he had only imagined the slightly distant tone in her voice. Why was it that the only time he was sure of Rachel's feelings was when he was with her?

WHEN RACHEL ARRIVED home from work the next day she found a note from Stacey saying she had gone job hunting but she would be home for dinner. At least she left a note, Rachel thought happily. She fixed Stacey's favorite dish, a casserole that tasted of pizza and spaghetti, hoping that today Stacey would be in a more receptive frame of mind. But when Rachel saw her face as she came through the front door, she knew it was going to be difficult.

''How'd the job search go?''

''Terrible,'' Stacey grudgingly admitted. ''Everyone's already hired their summer help and about the only place that needs anybody is that awful burger place on Third Avenue.''

''Before you left for Auntie Kay's, that awful burger place was where you wanted to work,'' Rachel gently reminded her.

Stacey sat down on a kitchen chair and watched her mother set the table. ''That was when I thought Chelsea was going to be working there.''

''She's not?''

''No. Her mother got her in at that new drugstore in the Westbrook Mall. Besides, all my friends are only working to pick up extra money for college. I could use a good full-time job. I want to get a car.''

''Does that mean you haven't changed your mind about going to college?''

Stacey shrugged. ''Auntie Kay thinks I should. But I don't know yet.''

Bless your heart, Catherine, Rachel said silently. ''You never told me how you liked Marquette University.''

''Actually, I did like the campus . . . especially since it's so close to Auntie Kay's. A lot of my old friends have already been accepted and Chelsea's asked me to be her roommate if I decide to attend.''

''Academically, it's a fine school,'' Rachel added.

''I guess, but I'm just not sure if it's what I want. I wish you wouldn't keep harping on it.''

''All right. I'll try not to mention it for a while, but I want for us to be able to talk openly with each other, Stacey.''

''If you're referring to last night, Mother, you're right. I'm sorry I overreacted. But you looked so different...sort of sexy. Whenever you dated men in the past I knew you only looked at them as friends and I never expected any of them to try to take the place of my dad."

"No one can ever take his place in my heart, Stacey. Don't you know that a day doesn't pass when I don't think about him and wish he was back here with us?"

"I do know that. But I guess I don't understand why now, all of a sudden, you want to act single. Have they identified remains found in Vietnam as Dad's and you just haven't told me?" she asked.

"I'd never keep that information from you," Rachel assured her seriously.

"Then why now? And why Bud?"

"Bud?"

"Wasn't it Bud who stayed here?" At the confusion on her mother's face she added, "Just who is this new man in your life?"

Rachel was saved from having to answer by the sound of the doorbell.

With a suspicious glance at her mother, Stacey said, "I'll get it."

Rachel fought the urge to follow her to the doorway. After a few moments, Stacey returned, bearing a huge bouquet of roses.

"They're for you." Her tone was accusatory as she set them down on the kitchen table.

Rachel grabbed the card before Stacey could get a look at it and tucked it into her skirt pocket.

"Umm. I've never seen such a gorgeous shade of red." Stacey sniffed the flowers appreciatively. "Well, Mom? Who are they from?"

Rachel knew it was useless to believe she could keep her relationship with Cole a secret from her daughter.

"It's not what you think. Cole Braxton was here on business and we had dinner together."

"You and Cole Braxton?" Stacey's mouth flew open. "I don't believe it! My own mother with one of my boyfriends?"

"He was never your boyfriend, Stacey, except in your imagination." Rachel didn't want to sound harsh, but Stacey was making it sound as though she had seduced a seventeen-year-old.

"No wonder you didn't want him paying any attention to me. You wanted him all to yourself!"

"You're wrong, Stacey. Listen to me." She tried to grab her by the shoulders but she shrugged away, tears welling up in her pain-filled eyes.

"And you denied that you thought he was attractive. You told me you hated him," she cried. "When all along you wanted him for yourself. And then you expect me to believe that you love me and are only thinking of my own good?" Sobbing, she ran from the room and into her bedroom, slamming the door.

Rachel wasn't sure what to do. Her heart felt as though it was lacerated with pain. How could she make Stacey understand that she loved her and that what had happened with Cole had been out of her control? She was a normal, healthy, adult woman with physical needs. How could she tell her daughter that for the first time in eighteen years she didn't feel as though her life was slowly dissolving away? That for eighteen years she had only been going through the motions of being a woman, that her loyalty to Floyd Andrews had suffocated her to the point where she'd subconsciously picked the Buds of this world to date because they would offer no challenge to her heart.

As she lay in bed that night she played the "what if" game. What if Stacey hadn't gone to that bar? What if Cole hadn't been in that bar? What if she hadn't gone to Minneapolis alone? She buried her face in the pillow as though she could bury all the self-recriminations. Then she remembered the florist's card in the pocket of her skirt. She scrambled out of bed to the closet and extracted the tiny envelope.

She held it beneath the ginger-jar lamp and read the bold, strong signature: *I do believe in magic. Cole.*

Rachel fell asleep with it tucked in her hand.

# *CHAPTER ELEVEN*

RACHEL HADN'T BEEN ABLE to concentrate on work all morning. In the three hours she had been sitting at her drawing table she had not had one vision of a dress, a coat, lingerie... nothing. The only visions whirling around in her head were of Cole. Cole with his tie loosened as he sat on her sofa and confided his anxieties about a business deal; Cole with his hair windblown as he had carried her up and away in his balloon; and Cole lying naked next to her, satiated with love. She ached to hold him, to feel his caress.

"You must be having a very pleasant daydream. You look like the cat that ate the cream."

Blushing, Rachel glanced up to see Katie standing in front of her. She crumpled a sheet of paper and tossed it into the wastebasket.

"Creative juices not flowing?" Katie asked.

"Today they're positively stagnant." She moved a few papers around on her easel while Katie slid her slender figure down onto an office chair.

"I need you to take pity on me. There isn't a single soul in this place who will join me for lunch at The Mexican Hat."

"That's because the last time you went everyone you dragged along had to chew antacid tablets for three days," Rachel said dryly.

"You're not going to chicken out on me, too?"

Rachel heaved a long sigh. "I'll come, but not for the food. I need to get away from this for a bit." She stood and stretched her arms above her head.

"You've caught the bug, Rachel. Can't work, day-dreaming half the day, and walking around with that starry look in your eyes. I'd say you have a good case of man trouble."

Her perception caught Rachel off balance. "Is it that obvious?"

"Only to someone who's suffered the same symptoms," she replied sympathetically. "Rachel, there's nothing wrong with falling in love. You look radiant. And I think I can guess his name." That brought Rachel's head up with a jerk. "Cole Braxton."

Rachel looked at her with startled eyes.

"Relax. No one else at Annalise knows. I wish you'd talk to me about it, Rachel," Katie gently pleaded, noting the troubled look on her friend's face.

Rachel hesitated. The urge to pour it all out to Katie was tempting. Maybe it would help to put things in perspective. After the past few days, the need to talk to someone had become too great for her to ignore.

"I don't know what's wrong with me, Katie. I've spent the past eighteen years trying to be strong, determined not to become emotionally dependent on a man. It's not as though I haven't had relationships with men, but I've always been able to put Stacey's interests ahead of my own personal feelings."

"Stacey's the problem," Katie stated categorically. "Why is that, Rachel? It isn't as if you haven't gone out with men before. Bud's never mentioned trouble with her."

"That's because she's never wanted to date Bud," Rachel said quietly.

"Do you mean she actually thought of Cole as a prospective boyfriend? I remember her flirting with him at Julian's party, but..." Katie looked thoughtful. "Wait a minute! That would explain why she spiked your cola. She could see that he was attracted to you back then."

"Katie, do you mean to tell me that it was Stacey who put the vodka in my drink? Why didn't you tell me?" she demanded, rising from her stool.

"Because I know how hard it is for you to open up to me and I didn't want to pry into the trouble the two of you were having. Would it have made any difference if I had?"

"No, you're right. It probably would have just widened the rift," Rachel reluctantly admitted. "It just seems that no matter how hard I try I can't get close to her, Katie. After my first trip to Minneapolis, I thought we had finally worked out all the kinks. We were sharing our feelings, being open with one another and really laughing together. Then she found out about Cole and me and poof! Everything is chaotic again."

"Rachel, you're not thinking about *not* seeing Cole because Stacey disapproves?"

"It isn't just Stacey's disapproval, Katie. For eighteen years I've only dated men who wouldn't make emotional demands on me. Stacey has always been my first consideration. I shied away from affairs because I didn't want her to get the wrong ideas about relationships."

"So it isn't just a case of the two of you being attracted to the same man. Stacey has to face the fact that her mother has physical needs just as she does. Don't you see, Rachel? If you deny those emotions, you aren't doing yourself or Stacey any good."

"Don't *you* see, Katie? Stacey is all I've got. For eighteen years it's been me and her. I've only known Cole a few months and I'm not even sure what he feels for me. I lost my mother over Floyd; I don't want to lose my daughter over someone else."

"Stacey is almost eighteen years old. You can't keep her if she wants to go. What's going to happen if she meets a guy you don't approve of? Will you sever your relationship with her?" Katie reasoned.

"No, of course not, but I'm a mother."

"But what about your feelings for Cole? Can you deny them?"

"I don't want to, but I can't help but feel that they're wrong."

"It's that restricted background of yours. You seem to think that if it feels good there must be something wrong about doing it."

Rachel smiled weakly at her friend's candor. "You talk as though I grew up in a convent."

"The possibility has crossed my mind," she teased. "Will you take some advice from a friend? If Cole makes you feel good, then let him make you feel good. Rachel, you're a warm and decent human being who for nearly all her adult life has managed to repress some very natural feelings because of loyalty to another person. I finally see you blossoming into the woman you should be. Your career is on the rise and you've got a fabulous guy interested in you. I'm happy that you're realizing at last that there's more to life than Annalise and Stacey. It's time you thought of what Rachel needs, and maybe Cole Braxton is it."

"You're not disappointed that it's not Bud?" Rachel queried.

"Not when I see the effect Cole has on you. Come." She waved her hand. "I'll spring for lunch."

They were about to leave when the phone rang. Upon hearing Cole's voice, Rachel smiled into the receiver.

"Hi, Cole," she said shyly, conscious of Katie's inquisitive stare.

"Do you know it's nearly eleven-thirty, Rachel, and I haven't done a bit of work because all I can see is that beautiful body of yours wrapped in those pink satin sheets."

She couldn't answer. She was certain that Katie could see the desire in her face. "That's nice," she managed to reply.

"Nice? It's painful. I ache for you, woman."

Rachel felt as though she were suffocating with warmth. Katie, seeing her flustered state, motioned that she would meet her out front and quietly excused herself.

"I miss you, too," she said softly.

"The proofs are back for the advertising campaign and they're wonderful. I have you laid out before me in glossies; I guess they'll have to do until I see you this weekend."

Weekend. Rachel knew she had to tell him she wouldn't be seeing him. "Cole, about this weekend..."

"Yes?" His voice was deep.

"Maybe it isn't such a good idea."

"Are you trying to tell me you aren't coming to Minneapolis?"

"It's not critical to the advertising campaign, is it?"

Cole's heart sank. Damn her. She knew that the campaign was only an excuse for them to be together.

"It's Stacey, isn't it?" He didn't need to ask.

"Not exactly. There's an MIA rally this weekend just south of Chicago. We usually try to attend the ones in this area."

"And let me guess. Stacey made arrangements for the two of you to go."

"I can't say that I really blame her, Cole. It's been hard enough for her discovering that I've been unfaithful to Floyd. Don't you see how it would look to her if I abandoned our hope that he could still be alive?"

"Unfaithful to Floyd?" Disbelief crept into his voice. "The man's been declared legally dead, not to mention the fact that you've given him eighteen years of your life!"

"That's easy for the rest of the world to say, Cole, but in Stacey's mind he's still alive."

"And what about in your mind, Rachel?"

The line was silent. How could she tell him that she was confused about her feelings for Floyd without revealing that she was falling in love with him? "Cole, please try to understand that Stacey and I need some time alone. She needs to know that I'm not going to desert her. Maybe we shouldn't see each other for a couple of weeks."

"A couple of weeks!" How could she even suggest such a thing after what they had shared? "What kind of blind-sided logic is that?"

The blind-sided logic stung. "You don't understand, Cole, and I'm not sure you ever will," Rachel said curtly.

"I understand perfectly well that that daughter of yours is manipulating your emotions, Rachel."

She sighed. "Cole, I have an appointment. I've really got to go."

"Rachel, please reconsider about this weekend."

"I can't. I'm sorry."

He groaned, then said, "I'll call you tomorrow."

But Cole didn't call Wednesday or Thursday or Friday. Rachel could only assume he had accepted the fact that she wouldn't be flying to Minneapolis for the weekend. *So much for his uncontrollable passion to be with me,* she thought cynically to herself as she climbed the steps to her apartment. By now he was probably ensconced in another woman's arms, one of those heavily lacquered beauties who wouldn't need to be told what to do with her hands. They were probably making love at this very minute in his balloon high above the clouds. She frowned at the thought of Cole in someone else's arms and was startled out of her reverie by a deep, "Hello, Rachel." Cole was leaning against the wall next to her door, giving her his most charming smile.

The sight of him sent her heart ticking like a metronome. "What are you doing here, Cole?"

"I came to invite you to dinner."

"I mean what are you doing in Chicago?"

"I told you. I came to ask you to dinner." He took the keys from her hand and opened the door for her.

"Are you sure you want to have dinner with someone who uses blind-sided logic?" she asked.

"I don't mind," he said with a sheepish grin. He followed her into the living room. "I've missed you, Rachel." He had wanted to stay away, but he couldn't.

Rachel looked away from his penetrating eyes. She wanted him so terribly. Why was she afraid to let him know how she felt about him? Was it because of Stacey? Or was Stacey just an excuse? How could their relationship possibly last? Everything seemed so complicated.

"Cole, I wish you hadn't come." She turned her back to him, but he quickly swung her around to face him.

"Rachel Kincaid, if I didn't have such an ache for you I'd walk out that door right this minute." He pulled her roughly into his arms.

Rachel felt her strength being sapped by desire. She knew that once he kissed her all her protests would disappear. "Cole, this is wrong. I don't want to be doing this." She tried to wriggle out of his hold.

But he drew her closer until his lips found hers, his tongue thrusting into her mouth, drawing every ounce of passion from it. Without hesitation, she wrapped her arms around his waist and met each of his long, searching kisses with all she had to give. She forgot about Stacey, forgot about Floyd and all the other reasons why she shouldn't continue seeing Cole. It was heaven in his arms.

"Mmm, I swear you were made for me," Cole murmured, nuzzling his nose under her ear, the scent of Scotch pleasantly teasing her nostrils. "I've missed you." Passion and desire were there in his eyes as he tilted her face back in a sensuous appraisal that had Rachel remembering the way he had looked at her in the aftermath of their lovemaking. He could arouse such urgent, powerful emotions in her with a single look, and make her forget all about the rights and the wrongs of their relationship. Unconsciously, she stiffened.

"What's bothering you about us, Rachel?" Cole asked, his eyes probing hers as he gently put a small distance between them, his finger outlining her cheek. He only had two days at the most to be with her. He didn't want to spend them arguing.

"I preach morality to Stacey, yet here I am having an affair myself and I expect her to understand. I feel guilty."

"Rachel, don't you see? Stacey is pulling all the right strings at this point. She's playing on your maternal feelings as well as your difficulty in letting go of the past. You're thirty-four years old. Look at yourself in the mirror. You've practically been living like a nun, worrying about doing what's best for Stacey. For once in your life think about what is best for you. You want me and I want you. It's as simple as that." He drew her back into his arms.

"Nothing is ever that simple," she returned, trembling beneath the probing intimacy of his hands.

"How about coming to dinner... now... before I feast on you?" He nibbled at her lower lip. Ignoring her logic, Rachel agreed and wrote a brief note to Stacey before leaving.

Cole took her to an intimate French restaurant where each booth was draped privately. He slid in beside her on the same side of the table and pressed his knee against hers. She could feel the warmth of his thigh, his muscles flexing, as he moved closer after the waiter had disappeared with their order.

When his hand captured hers and pulled it beneath the table, she could barely breathe, and then he placed her hand on his hardness. She turned away because she knew that she would see desire in his face.

But much to her surprise, during dinner he acted as though sex was the farthest thing from his mind. He spoke of the progress being made on the Mr. B's Boutique and the grand-opening celebration he wanted her to attend. But they both knew the inevitable topic had to be dealt with.

"Cole, it isn't going to work."

"What isn't?" he asked innocently.

"Avoiding the subject of Stacey."

"Is she always going to be between us?" Rachel shifted away from him uncomfortably, but he drew her closer. "What happened after I left last Sunday?"

"She found your shaving kit."

"Ah. Now I see the problem. And what did you tell her?"

"That I was an adult and I didn't need her permission to entertain a guest in my home."

Cole's eyes glimmered in admiration. He drew her fingertips to his lips and kissed them.

"Is everything okay between the two of you?" he asked.

"Everything hasn't been okay between Stacey and me since she was thirteen years old. Even as a child she was contrary. If I wanted her to take ballet lessons, she'd want to take jazz. If I suggested piano, she'd want guitar. I never felt we were rivals, though, until..."

"Until I entered the picture, right?"

"Cole, I wish you hadn't come to Chicago," she said on a sigh.

"You don't mean that, Rachel." He grabbed hold of her chin. "We're so good together."

Rachel blushed. "There's more to life than sex."

"Is that what you think I want from you...sex? Rachel, I haven't exactly been celibate the past twenty years. Don't you realize a man can get sex any time of the day if he looks for it? I don't want to be with any other woman, Rachel. I want to be with you. Come back to my hotel room with me."

Again she felt a rising sense of excitement, and she caught her breath at the unguarded passion sparkling in the depths of his eyes. Why did he want her? Why did she feel guilty about wanting him? What harm could there be in an affair? But she didn't want to search for answers. She wanted to be with him, and placed her hand in his outstretched one.

Rachel entered Cole's hotel suite with some apprehension. She knew they would make love. The want, the need and the longing were as strong as ever. Yet she couldn't dismiss the uneasy feeling. When he turned to shut the door behind him, she quickly moved into the living area, rather than the bedroom of the suite.

"Want to dance?" Cole's arms slid around her from behind.

It was all she needed. In a rush of joy, she turned and wrapped her arms around his neck, and his mouth claimed hers, tenderly at first, then with a deepening passion.

"I like the way you dance," he said, his lips brushing her throat while his hands undid the front of her blouse.

"I had a good teacher," she said huskily, as his hands cupped her breasts, a strong thumb massaging her nipple through the tricot bra. When he unfastened the front closure, he gazed at the white mounds and the rosy tips before stooping to kiss the exposed flesh, trailing a burning path of arousal across her skin before suckling the nipples to tautness. When his mouth returned to hers, she was breathless and clinging to him hungrily.

"Shouldn't we go into the bedroom?" she asked coyly, as Cole drew her toward the sofa and pulled her down onto his lap.

"If I get you into my bed I'm not going to be able to let you go home." He removed his shirt, then crushed his hard muscled chest against hers, covering her body with his as he lowered her onto the sofa underneath him. Then he rained a storm of kisses on her forehead, her cheeks and her throat before smothering her mouth with a sudden blaze of passion.

To Rachel, nothing mattered except that he was bringing every part of her body achingly alive. She ran her hands down his back, feeling the heated flesh beneath her fingers. When she slid her hands under the waistband of his jeans, he laughed, rolled to one side and impatiently unbuckled his belt, allowing her to be the initiator. Rachel loved the way his body trembled at the touch of her fingers as they slid inside the jeans to ease them off his hips. Knowing that he wanted her as much as she wanted him gave her the courage to be aggressive, and when he was completely naked and she was about to unbutton her own slacks, his hand stopped hers.

Gently, he did it for her, caressing the tender skin with fingers that stopped to sensuously probe the erotic zones. Undressed, they lay face-to-face, overwhelmed with excitement, caressing and kissing until Cole gently rolled back on top of her. She felt the wiry hairs of his chest rub her nipples as he moved inside her. She almost forgot to breathe, so wrapped up was she in the exquisite sensation of penetration. And once again she wondered how she could have lived for so long without knowing the unbearable happiness that this sharing, this oneness with Cole could bring. Sweet ecstasy swept them once more to the brink of fulfillment and engulfed her. With small, broken sounds of pleasure she met his surges until she felt him flood her with his warmth.

"God, you make me happy," Cole said, breathing hard, and when Rachel would have moved, he added, "Just stay here and let me hold you." He needed to savor the moment. Every time he was with her it got better, and he wondered if he would ever tire of her.

"Okay," she whispered softly. Winding her arms and legs around him, she basked in the heat of the aftermath of their passion, feeling the beat of his heart gradually return to a regular rhythm.

"Mmm, you smell like a woman who's been made love to. Your skin is so soft." His thumb caressed the side of her neck.

"Cole..." *Do you love me?* she wanted to ask.

"Hmm?" he murmured, kissing her forehead.

"Do you...?" she began, but found she couldn't bring herself to finish.

"Do I what, love?" he asked, breathing softly against her ear.

Love. He had called her love. But then it wasn't the same as an "I love you" spoken outside the heat of passion.

"Do you plan on staying the whole weekend?" she finally managed to say.

"Do you want me to?" He raised himself up on one elbow.

"Yes, but I still think it was a mistake for you to come to Chicago." She extracted herself from his arms. "I'd better get dressed." She sat up and reached for the clothes strewn on the carpeted floor.

With a groan, Cole got to his feet. "I'll drive you home," he said, stepping into his jeans.

"It might be better if I took a cab," Rachel suggested, buttoning her blouse with shaky fingers.

Cole faced her with his hands on his hips. "I'm not sending you home in a cab. God, Rachel, I feel like we're a couple of teenagers sneaking around and I don't like it."

"This is a problem Stacey and I have to work out on our own," she told him.

"It doesn't have to be that way. What if I accompanied you to the rally tomorrow?" he suggested. "Rachel, let me drive the two of you there. Maybe it'll help Stacey realize that I'm not a threat to her. I think she should get used to seeing the two of us together."

"Do you really think that's a good idea?" she asked, unsure whether her feelings for him were clouding her judgment.

"I'll come in and talk to her tonight. She needs to see that you can't be manipulated by her temperamental outbursts."

Rachel hesitated and finally said, "I'd like you to go with us to the rally, but I think I should talk to her alone tonight. Let me explain about tomorrow and then I promise we won't have to be secretive anymore."

"If that's what you want." Cole begrudgingly conceded against his better judgment. "But I'm going to drive you home."

Stacey was waiting up, watching television when Rachel got there.

"Where were you?" was how she greeted her mother.

"I left you a note. Didn't you see it?"

"'Went to dinner' doesn't tell me a whole lot, Mother. I called Bud and he said you weren't there."

Rachel felt like a child being reprimanded. "Actually, we had dinner at Chez Jacques—that new French restaurant. They have wonderful escargots."

"We?"

"Cole and I."

"Does that mean you've dumped Bud?" Silence filled the room and Stacey turned her attention back to the television. Rachel crossed the room and sat down beside her on the sofa. "Stacey, we need to talk about Cole."

"What's there to talk about? Obviously, he means more to you than I do...or Daddy. So go ahead.

Spend the whole weekend with him. I'll go to the rally by myself."

"Will you please let me finish what I have to say?" She pulled her around by the shoulders. "Just because I'm going out with Cole doesn't mean I've completely forgotten about your father nor have I given up the hope that he's alive. I simply wish you would try to understand that I have the same needs as you do. I enjoy being with a man."

"Fine. You be with Cole whenever you like; just don't bring him around me."

"He's taking us to the rally tomorrow."

"What?" she shrieked, leaping up off of the couch. "Mother, you've got to be joking!"

"No, I'm serious. What's wrong with his accompanying us to an MIA rally? He's a very compassionate person. He has feelings about such things as MIAs just as you and I."

"He's only doing it to be with you."

"No, he's doing it to be with you. He wants you to realize that he cares about your happiness. He knows all about your father being missing and he understands the problems you've had to deal with."

"You told him about Dad?"

"Yes."

"Why?"

"Because I care about him."

"More than you do about me, it seems," Stacey cut in sulkily.

"That's not true and you know it. Please try to at least meet him halfway in his attempts to be friendly."

The next morning Rachel was still dressing when Stacey opened her door and said, "Your boyfriend's here."

"Did you ask him to sit down?" Rachel inquired, pulling a cotton top over her shoulders.

"No."

"That wasn't very polite."

Stacey shrugged, then said. "I'll offer him a cup of coffee."

Rachel was tempted to rush out into the living room without applying her makeup, but decided against it. She had to trust Cole and give Stacey an opportunity to act in a mature way. When she entered the living room, she was surprised to find Cole seated next to Stacey on the sofa, a leather-bound photo album spread out on the glass-topped coffee table. Upon seeing Rachel, Cole stood up, his hands automatically reaching for her. Rachel didn't miss the way Stacey flinched as he placed a tender kiss on her lips.

"Stacey was showing me pictures of her father and explaining what's going to happen today," Cole remarked.

"I see," Rachel replied reflectively, then watched Stacey put the photo album away.

"I didn't realize that there was so much substantial evidence to support the theory that there are still U.S. servicemen alive in Vietnam."

"There are several impressive speakers scheduled today. I think you'll find it quite interesting," Rachel told him. "Are you ready, Stacey?"

Although Stacey was quieter than usual on the way down to Joliet, Rachel was relieved that at least she was being civil. Cole seemed eager to talk about the upcoming rally and she was grateful for his perspicacity. It was a topic Stacey warmed up to easily. She couldn't help but admire the sincere effort he made to ease the antagonism that occasionally bristled in the air.

The sun gradually disappeared and the sky grew dimmer as they got closer to Joliet. By the time they arrived at the park where the rally was scheduled to be held, a steady drizzle was falling, but Cole insisted they stay for the entire program. Rachel watched his face as he listened to a retired intelligence officer relate his personal account of a sighting of prisoners in Indochina. She realized that every time she looked at Cole she saw something new, something special. When the rain became a heavier downpour, he ignored Rachel's suggestion that they leave, recognizing Stacey's need to participate in the final candle-lighting ceremony and prayer service. Then, while they waited in the bus shelter, he went to get the car.

On the way back to Chicago they stopped for pizza and Rachel felt just maybe everything could work out all right. Stacey wasn't her usual bubbly self, but Rachel had caught her smiling a couple of times in response to Cole's humor, and a little ray of hope shot through her like lightning. But the ray of hope lasted about as long as a lightning bolt. When Cole suggested the three of them take in a movie, Stacey spit out a caustic comment that had Rachel's blood boiling. It was only Cole's persuasion that kept her from following Stacey into her room.

During the next few weeks Rachel felt her hopes waver from one minute to the next. Just when she thought her daughter was softening in her attitude toward Cole, Stacey would frustrate her with a sarcastic remark. Cole seemed to have the patience of a saint, though, and Rachel realized that she was becoming less tolerant with her daughter. But Cole insisted on the three of them doing things together, and one evening after they had attended a summer concert in Grant Park, Rachel questioned Cole about his equanimity.

"Why do you put up with us, Cole?" she asked reflectively.

"I thought you knew the answer to that by now, Rachel." His brown eyes held her blue ones, his large hands encompassing her tiny ones. "I love you."

## *CHAPTER TWELVE*

"HE LOVES ME."

The next two weeks found Rachel often speaking the words aloud. She went around with a constant smile on her lips and a softness in her eyes. There was a tenderness in her voice, even when she was forced to bear sarcastic comments from Stacey. For the first time in her life she felt like a complete woman. And she knew it was all because of Cole. He had aroused a part of her that had been sleeping, and she found she didn't want to go back to the stifling celibacy of the past. She had forgotten the pleasures of being a woman, and her recent awakening was both ecstatic and frightening.

She was thrilled with the attention she received from him. When she was with him her heart soared. He called her daily, and had even surprised her twice with unannounced visits during the middle of the week. It was during one of those visits that he told her about the grand-opening celebration of a new Braxton store. Despite Stacey's indifferent attitude toward the trip, Rachel made arrangements for both of them to attend the opening, which was in a suburb of Minneapolis. Rachel felt there wasn't a problem she couldn't handle, until the night before their scheduled departure when she arrived home from work to find a note on the kitchen table.

> Mom: I know you'll be relieved to know you won't have to drag me with you on your romantic tryst with your boyfriend. Don't bother looking for me. Steve will take care of me.
>
> Stacey

Rachel felt a nausea rising in her throat and swallowed it back. She ran into Stacey's room and opened the closet. Sure enough, the royal-blue overnight case and travel bag Stacey had supposedly packed for their trip to Minneapolis were missing. Her heart missed a beat.

Steve? Rachel racked her brain trying to recall a boy by that name. She didn't think Stacey had been dating anyone; she had recently found a job working evenings at an airport boutique. But of course, there hadn't been much time for the two of them to talk. Usually, Stacey had to leave for work before Rachel was home from Annalise. She certainly wouldn't have run off for the weekend with a boy she barely knew. Would she have? The thought occurred to Rachel that the "Steve" might have been put on her note for effect. She could be at Aunt Catherine's. Rachel placed a call to Wisconsin, but there was no answer. Then she dialed her aunt's best friend, Hilda Cooper.

"Catherine went on a bus tour up to Mackinaw Island with the senior citizens from church," the older woman informed her. "She should be back on Monday."

"Oh, that's right." Rachel sighed, as she recalled Stacey mentioning her aunt's proposed vacation plans.

She put down the receiver with an unsteady hand. So there probably really was a Steve and Stacey was probably with him. She took a deep breath before making the next phone call.

"Chelsea, it's Mrs. Kincaid. Do you know where Stacey is?"

"No, I'm sorry, Mrs. Kincaid, but Stacey got mad at me a couple of weeks ago and hasn't spoken to me since."

"I didn't know," Rachel said absently, realizing that she had been so wrapped up in her own life, she hadn't even been aware that her daughter and her best friend had had a falling-out. "Chelsea, do you know who Steve is?"

"Do you mean Steve Granger?"

"Yes, I suppose that must be the one," Rachel said pensively.

"He's a guy Stacey met at work. He's also the reason Stacey and I had the fight." Rachel was expecting Chelsea to tell her that they had both fallen for the same boy and was totally unprepared for her next words. "Actually, he's a pilot my sister used to date, but he's bad news. A real creep. Plus he's not legally divorced."

"And Stacey's going out with him?" Rachel's voice rose an octave.

"I know she's seen him a couple of times, but I'm not sure how serious she is about him," Chelsea answered.

"Chelsea, I need to find out where he might have taken her. Stacey's left me a note saying she's gone away for the weekend with him."

"Jeeez!" Chelsea shrieked. "The reason he's getting divorced is because he abused his wife. Maybe my sister would know where he is. I'll call her, then call you right back, Mrs. Kincaid."

Rachel's heart began to thud painfully in her chest. Stacey was in trouble, she just knew it. She made herself a cup of strong black coffee while she waited for Chelsea's call, which finally came after what seemed like an eternity to Rachel.

"Ginger said that Steve Granger has a summer cottage about sixty miles north of here on a lake in Wisconsin." Chelsea's voice was breathless.

"Does she have an address?"

"Not yet, but she's calling around. I'll call you as soon as I hear, okay?"

"Thank you, Chelsea." Rachel replaced the receiver, and started to pace the floor. When the phone rang again, she jumped.

"Yes?"

"Rachel, it's Cole."

"Oh, Cole. I'm so glad you called." Tears threatened her composure. "Stacey's gone and I don't know what I'm going to do. She's run off with some man who's a wife beater. Up to some lake cottage. It's all my fault." Her composure slipped.

"Rachel, listen to me. It's not your fault. I'm going to catch the next flight and help you find her. Just don't go looking for her without me, okay?"

"Oh, Cole, please hurry," she said, sobbing.

Cole called back and told her he was booked on the next commuter flight. He instructed her to pick him up at the airport. Waiting for Chelsea's call, she paced back and forth from the kitchen to the living room of her apartment. When Chelsea finally called with the information, Rachel grabbed her purse and headed for O'Hare Field. If she was going to pace, she thought, she might as well do it at the airport.

Watching the television monitor flash the arrival information, she silently berated herself for having come to the airport. If it weren't for her involvement with Cole, Stacey wouldn't have run off with this pilot. Here she was waiting for the man who had come between her and her daughter. Where were her priorities, that she would risk her daughter for a near-stranger? But when she saw Cole come walking through the terminal gate, the handsome stranger became the familiar man her heart knew intimately. She rushed into his arms, her mouth quivering, her eyes shimmering with unshed tears. He stroked her hair as she rested her chin on his shoulder, a smothered sob shuddering through her body.

"Oh, Rachel..." he said softly, pulling her away from the crush of passengers departing the aircraft. He was so relieved to see her. Throughout the flight he had worried that she would have gone looking for Stacey alone. He wanted to be all things for her—her friend, her lover, her protector. But would she let him? He led her to a secluded corner of the terminal and savored the feel of her against his side. He kissed her forehead and asked, "Did you get the address from Chelsea?"

Rachel nodded and told him about Steve Granger's reputation and his lakeside hideaway as they moved hurriedly through the airport.

"Rachel, I know you're blaming yourself, but you're wrong. Stacey is an adult." Cole knew that Rachel saw the logic of his point, but her eyes revealed some misgivings. Damn Stacey, he thought. She had known exactly how her mother would react. She was doing everything in her power to come between the two of them.

It was dark by the time Rachel's Honda Civic turned off the main highway onto the gravel road leading to Steve Granger's hideaway. Rachel was grateful that Cole was driving: the road had eroded due to the heavy summer rains, and the tiny car lurched from one pothole to the next. They were surrounded by darkness until a flicker of light in the distance gradually grew stronger. Rachel recognized a wood cabin through the density of the thick trees.

"This must be it," Cole said, bringing the car to a stop next to a Corvette that was parked alongside a small cottage. Just after they had slammed the car doors shut, the outside light came on and a T-shirt-clad man toting a can of beer appeared in the doorway. Cole placed his large frame in front of Rachel's protectively.

"We'd like to see Stacey Kincaid." It was more of an order than a request, and when the man stepped out onto the wooden steps Rachel could see that although he was dressed in a youthful way, he was actually a contemporary of hers and Cole's.

"No one here by that name. You must have the wrong place." His words were slightly slurred and he took a long swig of beer.

"You're not Steve Granger?"

"That's me." The words were spoken with a lazy vanity.

"But Stacey isn't with you?"

"Not this time," he said with a wicked grin.

"Well, where is she?" Rachel stepped forward, anxiety lacing her words. "She left me a note saying she was coming up here with you."

Suddenly a van pulled into the yard, rock music blaring from the tape system. Out climbed several boisterous men followed by two women, one of them Stacey. When she recognized her mother, she ran over to her and threw her arms around her.

"Mom! I'm so glad to see you. I wanted to go home, but Steve wouldn't take me." She began to cry, and Cole told Rachel to put her in the car.

Rachel hesitated, concerned that Cole might get into a fight with the inebriated Steve.

Sensing her concern, he said, "It's all right. I'm just going to make sure she didn't leave anything behind."

"My overnight case . . . is . . . in the . . . bedroom," Stacey stammered.

"Hey, Stacey! You aren't leaving already, are you?" Another drunken voice called out in the still of the night. "I thought you wanted to party?"

"I don't think she likes us," Steve Granger said in a mockingly sweet voice.

"Would you bring me Stacey's things?" Cole spoke to the lone woman who didn't seem to care if Stacey left or not.

"Sure," she replied, bestowing an interested glance on Cole. She swung her barely covered hips provocatively as she walked up the wood deck leading into the cabin. From the car Rachel watched Cole take the blue case from her, then say something to Steve Granger, which provoked an obscene gesture that Cole chose to ignore.

When she saw him turn and walk toward the car, all her nervousness and anxiety seemed to dissipate with the exhalation of a long breath. His handling of the situation had earned her admiration once more, and she felt an overwhelming sense of relief that she hadn't tried to locate Stacey without his help. When he climbed into the car and handed Stacey her case, Rachel reached for his hand in gratitude.

But it was Stacey who spoke first. "Thank you, Cole."

"Did anyone harm you?" he asked, jamming the key into the ignition.

"No, but I'm not sure they wouldn't have if you hadn't come when you did." She shuddered at the thought.

"What exactly was going on?" Rachel demanded, as Cole backed the car out of the driveway.

"Steve told me he was having some friends over for the weekend. You know, to fish and swim and have a good time. He told me I wouldn't have to do anything I didn't want to, but once I got out here..." Sobs muffled her final words.

"Couldn't you have talked to me about it?" Rachel asked. "Why didn't you tell me about Steve? Bring him home so I could meet him?"

"Do we have to discuss this now...in front of him?" Stacey sobbed.

"Cole is the reason you aren't still back there with them," Rachel countered. "And what were you doing in that van? Was that fellow who was driving drunk? You could have all been in a serious accident."

"Let it go for now, Rachel." Cole reached across the short distance separating them and placed his hand on hers. "She looks done in and we're almost home."

Two pair of eyes met in the rear-view mirror, one dark and understanding, the other blue and troubled, not quite sure whether to trust the message hidden in the depths of the brown eyes.

After seeing that the two of them were safely home, Cole took a cab back to the airport and caught the last commuter flight of the night. He had hated leaving, especially when Rachel had pleaded with him to stay with her, but now he was the one who felt she needed the time alone with her daughter.

He had been distant with her because it had suddenly occurred to him that before they could be happy together, she would have to let go of Stacey. Stacey was the stumbling block in their relationship, not Floyd. As long as she could manipulate her mother's feelings, Cole didn't stand a chance. He tried to tell himself that Stacey would have objected to any man's serious interest in her mother, but he had to believe that she'd found his rejection a bitter pill to swallow. And although he was not normally one for self-recrimination, he couldn't help but look back and question why fate had put him in that bar.

Yet he could understand Rachel's wavering emotions. Children could pull at heartstrings you didn't even realize you possessed. Melinda Sue had taught him that. He knew what lengths parents often went to for their children, the sacrifices they made for them. God, he could only pray that he wouldn't be one of those sacrifices.

Rachel was disappointed that Cole had returned to Minneapolis on what was to have been their weekend together. She was beginning to see the stress involved in a long-distance relationship. And as much as she loved her daughter, it was hard not to blame her for Cole's absence. Before he had gone, he had had a private talk with Stacey, which, as far as Rachel could tell, had only succeeded in lengthening her daughter's long face. Although it was late, Rachel decided that she couldn't wait until morning to talk with her daughter.

"I'm trying to understand why you would run off like that." She stood with her hands on her hips in front of Stacey. "You must have known what that cryptic message would do to me. I felt terrible, as if it were all my fault and you were punishing me." Rachel's voice held no anger, only fatigue.

"I'm sorry, Mom. I really am. But I've been feeling so confused lately. I guess it's because I thought you'd finally found a man to make you forget about Dad."

Rachel sat down on the edge of the bed and took Stacey's hands in hers. "Oh, darling, I could *never* forget him. You're my constant reminder of the love we shared. You're like him in so many ways. I've seen you with your friends, the way you always champion the underdog. Even as a little girl you could never bear to see anyone left out at school. That gentleness deep within you reminds me of him. If I could have one wish it would be for your father to see what a beautiful person you've grown up to be."

Stacey started to cry and turned her face away from her mother. "How can you say those nice things when you know I did what I did to get even with you?"

Rachel's hopes brightened. "People do strange things when they're hurting, Stacey."

"Aren't you even mad?"

"Would it make you feel better if I were? What do you want me to do, Stacey? Stop seeing Cole?"

"No." The word was barely a whisper. "It's just that . . . sometimes changes are so hard to accept."

"Oh, darling, don't I know," Rachel said on a long sigh. "But there's one thing that will never change. You're always going to be my daughter and I love you."

"Oh, Mom. I love you, too," Stacey said, flinging her arms around Rachel.

After the Steve Granger episode, Rachel became aware of a change in Stacey's attitude toward Cole. Her hostility was replaced by indifference, but Rachel also detected a hint of her daughter's acceptance of Cole as a father figure. Her own relationship with Stacey had progressed to the point where she finally felt that she was speaking to an adult and not an impetuous teenager. When Rachel was to fly to Minneapolis for the Braxton's golden-anniversary celebration, Stacey agreed to go along.

"They're absolutely wonderful, Rachel." Cole beamed as the models lined up in a semicircle on the stage. The Mr. B. collection was ready in time for the launch of the fall fashions and Rachel was amazed at the speed with which the Braxtons had expedited the entire plan.

"You don't think they're too trendy?" Rachel asked.

"I think they're exactly what Braxton's was looking for. You ought to be in your own studio."

"We've been through this before. I haven't had enough experience, and besides, it's a competitive field," Rachel argued.

"Every field is competitive. And you've just designed an entire collection alone... I stand corrected, nearly alone," he added when he saw her eyes flash. Her loyalty never ceased to amaze him.

"I don't think Julian would appreciate my taking all the credit," she affirmed.

"You deserve the recognition. Braxton's is going to want to keep you as the designer for the Mr. B's label. Why have Annalise get all the credit? I wish you would think about my offer to finance you."

"I'll think about it," she said with a smile.

"You are a tough woman at times, Rachel." He squeezed her affectionately. "But soft at the right times," he added, close to her ear.

"Has Stacey made any decisions about college yet?" he inquired as they walked back to his office.

"She's applied, but she hasn't decided if she's going to register. She seems to be drifting and I don't know how to help her." Worry clouded her blue eyes. "I'd like her to study music—you've heard how well she plays the piano."

"Do you think a change in scenery would help? I have to go on a business trip and I'd like you and Stacey to come with me."

"Are you sure you want to drag us along?"

"Actually, I have ulterior motives. You see, I promised my younger sister, Alicia, I'd take her along because the shopping is so fantastic, and I thought Stacey would be a good companion for her. That would leave you for me." He grinned wickedly. "Besides, it couldn't hurt you to meet some of the textile people I'll be seeing, in case you decide to open your own shop."

"You haven't said where it is you're going," Rachel reminded him.

"Hong Kong."

"Hong Kong!" she echoed. "I was expecting you to say New York or Los Angeles! But Hong Kong...it sounds so mysterious."

"It is a unique place to visit. Will you come?"

Except for a couple of Rachel's business trips to New York, she and Stacey hadn't even traveled outside of the Midwest. The money she had set aside in a vacation fund sat untouched and now they were being given the opportunity to fly halfway around the world to the Orient. Rachel felt a strange sensation prickle the hairs on her arms at the thought of such an adventure.

"Does that dreamy-eyed look mean yes or no?" Cole asked when she didn't immediately reply.

"Yes," she told him, ignoring the tiny niggling doubt that warned her that such a trip would change her life forever.

RACHEL FOUND IT INCREDIBLE that in Hong Kong there were even more chaotic throngs of people than in frantic Chicago. From the moment the plane touched down on the runway in the middle of Victoria Harbor, Rachel was captivated by Hong Kong's breathtaking beauty, and once again, she felt the unfamiliar sensation that somehow this trip would change her life.

Rachel could have used a day to adjust to the jet lag she had experienced after the sixteen-hour flight and to adapt to the time difference. But Alicia and Stacey were ready to sightsee the minute they arrived at the hotel and caught a glimpse of the luxurious shopping arcade connected to it. Alicia Braxton was a soft-spoken, younger version of Patsy, whom Stacey took to immediately, much to Rachel's delight. The two girls discovered they shared many of the same interests, and Rachel was pleased to learn that Alicia was a college sophomore and an advocate of campus life.

In the days that followed, Rachel came to depend more and more on Cole. The more she saw of him, the more she wanted to be with him. Although Cole had said the trip was in the interest of business, they didn't do much that was business-related for the first few days of their visit. She felt like a fairy princess being escorted around fantasy island.

To Rachel, Hong Kong was the most romantic city in the world. Cole, being familiar with the British crown colony, knew all the right things to see. One evening, they rode the tram up the side of Victoria Peak to catch the breathtaking view of the city's nighttime brilliance. A carpet of neon lights flickered like glowworms and silhouetted the anchored ships. On another day, they took the Star ferry across to Kowloon, instead of using the quicker, more modern Mass Transit Railway, which ran under the harbor. Stacey complained about the crowds and the noise and the greasy smell of bunker oil, but Rachel found beauty in the midst of the harbor, where freighters, ferries and barges tumbled over and around the wakes of the pleasure cruisers that competed for space with the junks.

On the third day of their visit, they were invited to dine at the home of a Chinese business associate of Cole's, who owned several textile factories in Hong Kong. Cheung Kai and his wife, Ling, had attended a university in London and spoke fluent English, as did their two teenage daughters, Mei and Ping, and Ling's parents, who also lived with them. Rachel found the visit fascinating and appreciated the opportunity to sample the Chinese hospitality and observe the cultural differences. By the end of the evening, both Stacey and Alicia had become advocates of wok cooking and adept at the use of chopsticks.

Cole and Cheung were occupied with business meetings over the next few days, and Rachel had enthusiastically accepted Ling's offer to accompany Rachel, Stacey and Alicia to the shopping district. Ling and her daughters proved to be excellent tour guides. Rachel was amazed at the number of exquisite fashion stores Hong Kong boasted, although she personally preferred shopping in the small lanes where flower stalls added bright colors to the open displays of herbs, paper lanterns and hand-carved jade. While the girls went swimming, Ling and Rachel squeezed their way down the narrow aisles of the street market, where food stalls spilled out on both sides of the pavement. Watching Ling select her fresh fruits and vegetables for dinner, Rachel marveled at the abundance of fresh food. After two days in Ling's company, Rachel felt she had been exposed to a Hong Kong few tourists see.

"This is traditional urban Chinese life," Ling assured her as they walked past a picturesque mixed residential and commercial area.

"Is all of this dried fish?" Rachel asked, as they paused in front of a retailer selling shark's fins behind glass.

"This shop, yes. See the shrimps and oysters? They are easy to recognize. But those yellowish papery squares in the jars are jellyfish with the tentacles removed." She pointed to Rachel's left. "Next door you will find the dried fruits you are more familiar with."

As they left the markets behind, the streets narrowed and became steeper. The fruit stands were replaced with stalls selling joss sticks and paper offerings to be burnt in the surrounding temples.

"This is the temple of Man Mo," Ling told her as they stopped in front of a fire-screening door. "It is dedicated to two Taoist deities—Man, who is the god of intellectual skills, and Mo, who is the god of military. Come, we can go in."

The atmosphere was thick with smoke as Rachel followed Ling into the temple. Hanging from the ceiling were giant incense coils. Two stone incinerators stood in the center of the hallway and the pungent odor of joss sticks stung Rachel's senses.

"The coils will burn for two weeks," Ling explained. "The red tag that hangs from the coil is the worshipper's prayer." She led Rachel up a small row of steps to a long marble-topped table in front of the main altar. "These brass deer symbolize long life."

They wandered around the ornately decorated temple and admired the elaborately carved sedan chairs and the statues of gods on display while worshipers carried on despite the tourists.

"You wish to have your fortune read?" Ling asked, pointing to a stall as they left the temple. "You choose a bamboo stick and he will tell you what the gods have in store for you."

Rachel glanced skeptically at the elderly man dressed in black. "All right," she agreed, not wanting to offend her hostess. Rachel selected a piece of bamboo and handed it to the soothsayer who studied the stick for several minutes before speaking in Cantonese. Ling's eyes widened, then her brow became furrowed.

"What is it, Ling?" Rachel asked.

"He says the gods have destined that you will meet up with someone from your past who will make you both sad and happy. He says that for many years you were unlucky in love, but now your luck is changing. You will have to make a decision that will require strength of the heart and many prayers, but do not be alarmed, because after this cloud passes, your future will be filled with prosperity and happiness."

Rachel experienced a feeling of déjà vu, the same eerie sensation she had felt when she landed at the airport. The words of the soothsayer reminded her of the premonition she'd had about her visit to Hong Kong changing her life. Over the course of the day she tried to put her uneasy feelings about the fortune teller's prophecy aside, but was unsuccessful. He had been unfailingly accurate in assessing her past love life. And he had had no way of knowing she had been separated from Floyd for so long. By dinnertime she was still feeling a little restless, and was grateful she would be seeing Cole.

Alicia and Stacey had been invited to attend a rock concert with Ping and Mei, which meant Rachel and Cole would be dining alone. Rachel chose a red cheongsam that she'd purchased from a small shop in the Repulse Bay district. The high-necked, close-fitting dress flattered her tiny figure. She knew the slit up the side was daring, and although she was as petite as the Chinese women, she was definitely more fully figured and the silk fabric clung seductively to her breasts. It fit her mood, Rachel thought, as she stared at her reflection in the mirror. This was the first evening she and Cole would have any privacy and she could picture his hands sliding sensuously down the length of silk. His fingers would discover the provocative slit and then they would...

"Mom, we're leaving now."

Rachel was jerked back to the present as Stacey's voice called out from the sitting room of the hotel suite.

"I'll be right there," Rachel returned.

"Wow! That dress looks great on you!" Stacey complimented from the doorway to the bedroom.

"Thank you. Have a good time, won't you?"

"You, too, Mom." And with one last look over her shoulder, she left.

The dress had the same effect on Cole as it had on Stacey.

"I think you're bringing new meaning to the cheongsam," Cole told her as he drew her into his arms and ran his fingers caressingly over the smooth silk. Rachel melted under his touch, just as she had imagined she would. He cupped a breast with his palm while his thumb caressed the side of her neck. "I want this night to be special for us, Rachel." He reluctantly removed his hands. "But first, we must have dinner."

"We could order room service," she suggested in a low whisper.

"Don't think the thought hasn't crossed my mind," he said lazily, kissing her lightly on the lips. "But tonight we have Hong Kong waiting for just the two of us. I want to make this a night you won't ever forget."

If Rachel had thought the harbor beautiful by day, it was even more splendid at night. After hiring a taxi to take them to Aberdeen, Cole led her across a pedestrian bridge to the waterfront where a sampan waited to take them over to a floating restaurant. Painted red and gold and outlined by numerous golden lights, the three-story restaurant cast a blazing sheen over the quiet waters of the harbor. The sampans and junks that carried diners to the pagoda-shaped restaurant suddenly seemed minuscule in size.

"I'm glad you wore that dress, because tonight we're dining Cantonese style," Cole told her as they landed at the pier to the restaurant.

A Chinese waiter escorted them to a room that exuded an atmosphere of grandeur. Chinese gold carvings decorated the onyx-faced walls and Venetian chandeliers hung from the ceiling. The soft sounds of a Gershwin melody could be heard as they passed the piano bar, and for just a moment, Rachel felt a wave of cool air dance lightly across her bare arms. Gershwin had been Floyd's specialty, and the words of the soothsayer came to mind. She shivered.

"Are you cold?" Cole asked as the waiter showed them to a table overlooking the glittering harbor.

She shook her head. She was too captivated by the atmosphere and Cole's presence to let anything distract her from the feelings of bliss. The floating restaurant was noted for its seafood, but Rachel thought it wouldn't have mattered what she was eating. They were alone in the most romantic of settings and everything was right in her world. Each time she looked at Cole she found herself more in love with him. When they were ready to leave the restaurant, a jetfoil was waiting at the dock.

"Where are we going?" Rachel inquired.

"You've just eaten on a floating restaurant. Now we're going gambling on a floating casino. I feel lucky tonight," he said close to her ear.

Unlike the floating restaurant, the casino was not in Hong Kong but off the waterfront of Macau. After the quiet intimacy of the restaurant, the crowded casino was a dazzling contrast. Rachel was surprised at the number of Chinese people gambling, the lines often three deep around the tables. Upstairs, where the stakes were higher, the crowd was thinner and Rachel found herself seated next to Cole at the roulette table, gambling for the first time in her life.

After only a short time, a tall stack of chips rested in front of her and her eyes sparkled with excitement. "I can't believe I'm winning."

"Do you want to cash in while you're ahead? We could try blackjack," he suggested.

"Have I won a lot of money?" she asked.

"Enough to cover what Stacey's been spending," he told her with a smile. But Rachel didn't hear his comment. All the color had drained from her face and she sat staring, unseeing, across the room.

Cole turned to see what had caused her face to turn ashen, but saw nothing out of the ordinary. "Rachel, what is it?" he asked, placing his arm around her trembling shoulders.

"He's alive. The soothsayer was right." Her voice was distraught, her eyes clouded.

"Rachel, you're not making any sense," Cole told her, pulling her away from the table. "What did you see?"

"I saw Floyd."

## *CHAPTER THIRTEEN*

COLE'S EYES DID A QUICK SCAN of the crowded casino, but he saw no one who even slightly resembled the soldier whose pictures he had seen. Nearly all the patrons of the casino were Chinese; a Caucasian would have easily stood out.

"Where did you see him, Rachel?" Cole asked.

"He walked through the doorway, looked around and then left again without stopping. I know it was him. Don't you see? It all makes sense. When I was with Ling today a fortune teller read my bamboo stick and he told me that I would meet someone from my past. Now I know what he was talking about. Floyd is alive." Her fingers clutched at his coat sleeves. "I've got to find him."

"Rachel, wait a minute." He grabbed her shoulder as she turned to leave. "I don't doubt that you saw someone who reminded you of Floyd, but I think you're overreacting because of what some fortune teller happened to tell you."

"I can't waste time arguing with you, Cole. I've got to find him before he leaves the casino. Are you going to help me?" It only took one look from her soft, pleading eyes and Cole was following her out the door.

They searched the entire casino, from the top deck, down through the various gaming rooms, to the main floor where a cabaret was performing in the nightclub, but there was no sign of anyone resembling Floyd. When they had searched every place Cole could think of, including the rest rooms, he stopped alongside the railing overlooking the water and pulled her close to his side.

"Rachel, we've looked everywhere." He put a protective arm around her shoulders. "The chances that it really was Floyd are very slim."

"You don't believe me, do you?" she accused, biting her lower lip.

"I don't doubt that you saw a man who reminded you of Floyd. But I think you've been affected by the mysterious aura that seems to float in the air in this part of the world. I myself can feel it. Floyd has always been such an intense part of your subconscious, it's only natural that you would associate some of those feelings with this part of the world. Your visit to the fortune teller heightened your awareness of how close you actually are to where he disappeared." He placed his hands lightly on her shoulders and Rachel could feel the warmth of his palms through the red silk.

"But the soothsayer was so accurate. He told me I had been unlucky in love and that I would meet someone from my past." She paused. "He said this meeting would necessitate my making a decision. And don't forget about my book of poetry that had a Hong Kong postmark on it. I've told you I've always felt Floyd was alive and right now that feeling is the strongest it's ever been." The night air was cool off the water and Rachel shivered.

"You're tired and it's too cool to be standing out here. Let me take you back to the hotel," he said softly.

She didn't want to leave. He could see it in her eyes as she looked over his shoulder toward the casino entrance, as though expecting to see Floyd standing there.

"Look at me, Rachel." He lifted her chin so that she was gazing into his eyes. "I'm real and I want you to come home with me." His mouth descended upon hers, warm and moist. Rachel's nostrils were filled with the clean fragrance of his after-shave. She laid her head on his shoulder and her arms encircled his solid torso.

All the way back to Hong Kong, Cole held her in his arms. She looked so fragile, her usually bright eyes troubled and opaque. The confusion she was experiencing was evident in the preoccupied expression that kept her brow furrowed. Cole drew her closer to him and inhaled her musky fragrance, as though he could physically bridge the mental distance he sensed was widening between them. He felt as though he couldn't reach her, and the thought frightened him.

The special night that had started off so right was ending up so wrong. He had planned everything so carefully. The girls were to be out with the Cheung sisters, he was to have taken Rachel to dinner, then on to the casino for a little excitement, and when he brought her back to the hotel they would have had champagne in his suite and he would have asked her to be his wife.

He was tempted to take her to his room when they arrived back at the hotel, but he knew she wouldn't be completely with him. Tonight it wouldn't be Stacey's presence that kept her from his bed, but the ghost of Floyd Andrews. So instead of making passionate love with her and giving her the emerald-and-diamond ring he had in his pocket, he found himself saying good-night and kissing her cheek.

Rachel stood for a long time under the shower with her eyes closed, willing her mind to go blank. She turned her face up to the pelting spray of warm water, as though it could wash away the images of the soothsayer and the man she knew she had seen. It was Floyd. There had been a look of recognition in his eyes, only for a moment, but his eyes had met hers. She couldn't have imagined it. Her thoughts were not easily disposed of, and long after Stacey was asleep in the bed beside her, she lay awake.

The next day was to be Cole and Cheung's final day of business negotiations. As well, Cole had arranged for Rachel to meet with representatives of Aiku Textiles. Cole was concerned about how pale she looked at breakfast; he knew she had slept poorly, and before leaving he suggested she cancel her plans to meet with Ling. He also cautioned her about looking for Floyd.

Rachel paid no heed to Cole's warning. After eighteen years of struggling with the government for information concerning Floyd's whereabouts, she was not about to be deterred. She decided not to tell Stacey what had happened at the casino and suggested that she and Alicia accept an invitation to spend the day with Ping and Mei. Ling arrived shortly after the two girls left, expecting to take Rachel sight-seeing. But Rachel had other plans on her mind.

"Ling, will you take me over to Macau?" she asked as they stepped out into the crowded city street.

"But why, Rachel? Shopping is not nearly as good there as it is here. I thought you wanted to see the botanical gardens?" Ling looked confused.

"I don't want to go for the shopping. We can do the gardens another time," Rachel explained.

"You are bored with Hong Kong?" She looked disappointed.

"No, I love Hong Kong," Rachel reassured her with a smile. "But I want to see Macau. Do you mind?"

"I can take you, but you will need to go to the Portuguese embassy first... to get a visa." Ling advised her.

"I have a visa," Rachel admitted. "Cole and I were gambling there last night."

"You wish to go gambling this afternoon?" Ling asked, her eyes wide.

"No, I simply want to look around."

"I will call Cheung to let him know where we will be." She started walking back into the hotel, but Rachel's arm detained her.

"No, please. I'd rather that Cole didn't know. Will that cause a problem between you and Cheung?"

"No, it will be fine," she hesitantly agreed, but Rachel could see that the Chinese woman did not understand her reluctance to tell Cole of her plans. "If you are in a hurry we can take the jetfoil. Otherwise the ferry can take us," Ling explained as they reached the Macau wharf.

"Oh, the jetfoil, please."

"I hope you will not be disappointed in the sights. Macau is mainly for gamblers," Ling cautioned.

Once they were seated in the glass-enclosed craft, Rachel confided to Ling her reason for wanting to visit Macau, relating her experience in the casino and Cole's reaction, and explained how the whole episode tied in with the soothsayer's prophecy.

"Cole thinks that I saw a man who only reminded me of Floyd. He doesn't understand that there are some things a woman can feel in her heart. What do you think, Ling? Could a missing serviceman possibly be living in Hong Kong?"

"Hong Kong has always been a community of refugees, Rachel. That is why the Chinese in Hong Kong are such hard workers. They are the survivors, the ones who have left intolerable conditions and have risked difficult circumstances to search for what they believe is a better way of life. If there was one place you would find a refugee, it would be Hong Kong. But what I don't understand is, if your Floyd is one of those who has escaped from the POW camps, then why hasn't he gone back to the United States, or at least tried to contact you?"

"Don't you see? He could have amnesia...or maybe he's been brainwashed." Rachel had asked herself that same question, and lain awake half the night trying to find plausible explanations.

Ling's face was sympathetic. "I know how your heart hopes, but Rachel, I have not heard of any such cases in all the fifteen years Cheung has been involved with the diplomatic services."

"Oh, Ling," Rachel sighed. "It all feels so very strange. I know I saw him. And now I must find him."

When they arrived at Macau, Ling suggested they hire a taxi to take them from the hydrofoil wharf to the casino. Rachel was grateful for Ling's presence, as she was able to communicate in Cantonese and was familiar with the street names. Starting at the top of the floating casino, they searched from one gaming room to the next, until they had covered all floors of the gambling palace. The casino was relatively quiet in comparison to the previous night, with the exception of a Cantonese opera being performed in the nightclub.

Rachel didn't know what she had expected to find. In fact, she wasn't even sure why she had come. Now that she thought of it, Floyd could just as easily be in Hong Kong or Taiwan. Maybe he, too, had only been visiting Macau as she and Cole had, or maybe it hadn't been him at all.

"Ling, if you were to visit Macau as a tourist, where would you stay?" she inquired.

"Probably at the Lisboa Hotel. It is very big and it also has a casino."

"Is it far?"

"No, we can walk from here, or take a pedicab."

"Let's walk."

Rachel absently listened to Ling's singsong voice explain the history of Macau as they walked past beautiful old European villas in various stages of decay. With each step she took, she wondered if Floyd had walked down the same cobbled street. In her mind she was formulating what she could do if Floyd was not listed as a guest at the Hotel Lisboa. Luckily, Ling would be able to check with the other local hotel registers using her Cantonese.

But the hotel registers proved useless. Not one of Macau's hotels listed a Floyd Andrews, nor had anyone seen a Caucasian resembling him.

"Rachel, I think we should have some lunch, then head back to Hong Kong," Ling suggested.

"You're probably right," Rachel conceded. "Thank you for coming with me, Ling. I'm only sorry that I dragged you around on this wild-goose chase."

"What is this wild-goose chase?" Ling looked puzzled.

"That means a futile expedition."

"It did not ease your heart?" Ling inquired softly.

"No, but after eighteen years of trying to find answers, one day does not discourage me," Rachel assured her. "I only hope I haven't put you in an uncomfortable position with Cheung."

"Cheung is like Cole—overprotective. But women in Hong Kong are learning to be more independent, like the women in the Western world. But some men, both Western and Chinese, prefer to be a bit masterful. Do not worry. Cheung and Cole will not be upset."

Rachel didn't know about Cheung, but Cole was definitely upset. Forced to wait for a vacant hydrofoil, it was nearly dark by the time the two women arrived back at Hong Kong Island. Stacey, Alicia and Cole were waiting for Rachel in the lobby when she walked in.

"Where have you been?" Cole demanded. "Do you realize that you nearly missed your appointment with the Aiku representative?"

"You'll have to give my apologies to the Aiku people. I've just got back from Macau and I'm exhausted." Rachel's feet were aching, as was almost every part of her body.

"Macau? You went back to Macau after last night?" Cole raised his voice slightly.

Rachel glanced at Stacey, then back to Cole. "I had to. But I don't think we should discuss it just now, do you?" Her tone was a bit haughty.

"Look, Cole, why don't Stacey and I meet you in the arcade?" Alicia suggested, casting a perceptive glance at the two others.

"Fine," he agreed, waiting until they were out of sight before he turned to Rachel. "Why didn't you tell me you were going? Didn't you realize how worried I would be?"

"I'm sorry." She ran her fingers across her forehead. "Listen, I'm really not feeling well enough for dinner."

Cole took her arm in his and led her across the lobby to the elevator where they rode in silence to her room.

"I know I saw him last night." Rachel was the first one to speak once they were in the suite.

"So you went wandering about the Orient alone." He tried to keep the anger out of his voice, but was unsuccessful.

"I had Ling with me," she corrected.

"Ling has led such a sheltered life she doesn't even realize there are street gangs in Hong Kong. Don't you realize what a lone Caucasian woman can run into?" He ran his hands through his hair.

"For your information, Cole Braxton, I've been taking care of myself for the past eighteen years without you holding my hand." She looked defiantly at him, her cheeks flaming.

"God, how I hate it when you start that. I want to take care of you, Rachel."

"I've gotten along pretty well without your help," she retaliated.

The arrow went straight to his heart and found its mark. "I had hoped you'd begun to want it," he said quietly, his anger dissolving.

"I have," she moaned, not daring to look at him. "But finding Floyd or whoever this man is who looks like him is something I have to do."

He wanted to grab her, shake some sense into her, make her trust him. But instead he found himself saying, "At least let me help you." Even if it meant losing her, he knew he had no choice.

"You will?" She seemed surprised by his offer.

He felt like some kind of martyr, and only hoped he wouldn't be the instrument that delivered the woman he loved into another man's hands. He leaned over and smoothed a strand of hair away from her cheek. "Why don't you tell me what happened today."

She went over the details of the trip to Macau, telling him about their casino search and the checking of the local hotels.

"Do you have any pictures of Floyd with you?" he asked.

"Just this one," she said, pulling the locket out of the pocket of her silk blouse. Cole felt as though a knife had pierced his heart. She hadn't worn that locket since their first date, yet now it rested near to her heart. He watched her slender fingernails pry the tiny image out of the gold setting, and he was unable to prevent the jealousy that consumed him as she tenderly handed him the photo.

"You won't..." She had started to say, *You won't lose it,* but had caught herself.

"No." Cole knew what she was thinking. "I'll have it enlarged, then we'll ask around and see if we can't find someone who recognizes the face. Macau is a tourist hangout for gamblers; this man could have been visiting from any of the surrounding countries."

There was something in her eyes that Cole did not want to recognize. He only knew that he felt as though he had already lost her. Or worse yet, that he had never really had her.

"I'll phone the Aiku people and arrange another meeting. Stacey and Alicia are going to want dinner. What about you?"

"I think I'll go straight to bed. I'm exhausted," Rachel said wearily.

Cole was disappointed. He had hoped that they would at least share dinner together. And for the second night in a row, he found himself leaving her when he needed to be with her the most.

"Good night." He paused, then lifted her fingers to his lips, kissing each one individually.

"Good night."

Once in her room, Rachel kicked off her espadrilles, then made her way into the bathroom, where she swallowed two aspirin before collapsing on the bed.

COLE AWOKE during the night in a cold sweat. He had been dreaming. Rachel had been alone on a sampan in the middle of a terrible storm, drifting farther and farther away from him. He got up and poured himself a glass of water, unaware that in the room next door the woman slept just as restlessly, plagued by dreams of a soldier locked in a bamboo cage.

THE CHINESE ARE great believers in fate. Cole had to agree that only fate could have accounted for his visiting the small village of Stanley. Had it not been for Stacey's wish to purchase jeans at a ridiculously low price, he wouldn't have been there the next morning. It was in Stanley that he found the man he was certain Rachel had mistaken for Floyd Andrews.

He was leaning up against a market stall where embroidered linens and hand-stitched blouses were displayed. Sitting behind a table was a Vietnamese woman, her hands busily stitching a colorful floral piece of fabric.

"You look American." Cole smiled, not missing the flicker of surprise in the man's eyes.

"At one time I was, but I've been absorbed by the Orient," the man returned.

"It's a fascinating part of the world," Cole replied, peering through the locked glass case at the gold jewelry inside, his attention caught by a sapphire ring.

"You like the sapphire? It would make your lady happy, no?" He extracted a key from his pocket and opened the case, pulling the ring out for Cole's appraisal.

"It's lovely, but I really should bring her to see it first. Will you be here later this afternoon?"

"Only until three o'clock on Thursdays." He shrugged apologetically.

"Perhaps you have a card with your name and address where I could reach you?" Cole asked.

"Are you staying on the island?"

Cole nodded. "At the Mandarin Hotel."

"If you think your lady would be interested in the ring, you could stop by the Excelsior Hotel. I play piano in the lounge every evening." He offered his hand and said, "Frank Sullivan."

"I'll probably do that." Cole replied, returning the handshake. Before he turned to go, he pulled out his wallet and removed a picture. "This is my lady. You can see how blue her eyes are...perfect for sapphires," he said with a false smile, carefully noting the man's reaction to the photo of Rachel. Cole wasn't surprised to see a startled expression cross his face that was almost instantly masked with a smile.

"It would indeed be perfect for her." Cole heard him say as he walked out of the shop.

By the time he located the two girls, he had already decided that he would take Rachel to the Excelsior Hotel for dinner.

Rachel received the news less enthusiastically than Cole had expected. "If he says his name is Frank Sullivan then it can't be Floyd," she rationalized.

"But it might be the man you saw at the casino." He was praying that he was wrong, but the only way he would find out if the man was Floyd Andrews was by Rachel's positive identification. Maybe he had imagined the flash of recognition in those eyes. "Would you come with me and see? We can go for dinner."

With as much courage as she could summon, she agreed.

But Rachel didn't need to wait for dinner to hear from Frank Sullivan. Shortly after lunch a knock on her door announced a delivery boy. When she opened the door, she was greeted with a bouquet of daisies. Her heart began to palpitate. Daisies were Floyd's favorite flowers. Trembling fingers removed the tiny card from its envelope and wide eyes read the message:

Please come to the Harlequin Bar, Kitten.

Only Floyd had ever called her Kitten.

Rachel couldn't remember slipping into the blue-and-yellow-flowered sundress or her two unsuccessful attempts to apply her lipstick evenly. She had tissued all traces of the creamy gloss from her lips, and now, as the elevator whisked her up to the twenty-fifth floor of the hotel, she began to worry about her appearance. Had she combed her hair or even put on matching shoes? A quick glance at her feet alleviated that fear. As the gilt elevator doors slid open, she had to force her feet to move out onto the thick-piled carpet. She felt like a robot as she stepped into the lounge and paused to grab onto the back of a bar stool while her eyes surveyed the occupants. They came to rest on a man sitting next to the plate-glass windows, the man she knew in her heart was Floyd.

His eyes met hers from across the room and Rachel stopped breathing. Here she was, face-to-face with the man she had been dreaming about for eighteen years. She had imagined this meeting with him thousands, no, probably millions of times, yet now she felt paralyzed.

Disregarding the onlooking patrons, he stood hesitantly, then pushed back his chair and walked over to her. His skin was darker, more lined, and the planes of his face were sharper, thinner, more defined. Then he smiled, and the crooked tooth was visible and Rachel knew that this was no illusion.

"Floyd!" Her voice was breathless with emotion.

"Yes, it really is me, Kitten." Floyd's voice was as choked with emotion as hers. "God, Rachel, you don't know how many times I've prayed for this moment."

Suddenly he was holding her in his arms in a tight squeeze. "You're alive! You're alive!" she repeated with a rush of tears as they swayed in an emotional embrace.

They stood in the middle of the bar, oblivious to everything around them. Rachel rained kisses all over his forehead, his cheeks and his eyes, so happy to know that he was alive. Nothing mattered; no one else existed. All the agony and uncertainty of the past eighteen years was being purged from their memories. Neither of them saw the tall, dark American who stood in the entryway to the bar. Cole watched the pair, laughing, kissing, hugging, weeping for joy, and a coldness settled in the pit of his stomach. It was like watching a scene from a bad movie, only this was his life and he was the odd man out. He unconsciously slid his hand to his jacket pocket and felt the outline of the jeweler's box, then did an abrupt turn and walked out of the bar.

"Come, we'd better sit down." Floyd led Rachel over to his table next to the window.

"I must look a mess. I bet my eye makeup is running down my face," she said, still half laughing, half crying.

"You look beautiful," Floyd said as he pulled out her chair, then sat down across from her, holding her eyes. "I can't believe how pretty you are.... All these years I fantasized that you would still look the same as you did at seventeen... but you're even prettier."

Rachel glowed under his words, pleased that he hadn't changed either. Oh, he was older, the gray hairs just starting to pepper his temples, but he was still her sweet, gentle Floyd.

"Your hair still shines like corn silk." He reached across to finger a few strands and Rachel was lost in nostalgia. "I've never stopped loving you, Rachel."

Rachel reached across the table to place her hand over his, but as her fingers met his she felt the cool metal of the gold wedding band. Her elation began to wane. This was not a man suffering from amnesia, nor was he brainwashed. He was alive and healthy and he hadn't contacted her.

"Floyd, where have you been? And why didn't you let me know that you were alive?" She pulled her hand back away from his.

"I can explain." He signaled for a waiter, then ordered something in Cantonese, and Rachel was brought back to reality. Floyd was obviously fluent in Cantonese and no stranger to Hong Kong. Where had he been for the past eighteen years?

"You speak Cantonese quite well," she observed after the Chinese waiter had disappeared.

"Although English is used in most of the tourist sites, the majority of people here do speak Cantonese." He struck a match and lit the cigarette he had placed between his lips.

"Floyd, I don't understand what you are doing here."

"I go by Frank now," he corrected. "Frank Sullivan."

"But why? Where have you been for eighteen years? Why haven't you tried to contact me? Were you a POW?"

He stared at her through a gray cloud of smoke. "I wish it were that simple."

"Floyd, you're not making any sense," Rachel persisted.

"I'll try to explain the best that I can. I need your word that I can trust you, Rachel."

"Trust me? Floyd, I've been keeping a vigil for you for eighteen years."

"It isn't easy for me to tell you this." His fingers were turning the matchbook around in a circle on the table.

"What is it, Floyd?"

At that moment the waiter arrived with their drinks. Floyd stared out the window until he had departed, then turned back to look Rachel straight in the eye and say, "I'm a coward."

## *CHAPTER FOURTEEN*

"FLOYD, WHAT ARE YOU TRYING to tell me?" Rachel knew she wasn't going to like what she was about to hear.

"I've been out of Vietnam for twelve years."

"Twelve years!" she said, gasping. "Why didn't you contact me? Don't you realize what I've been doing for the past eighteen years? I thought you were an MIA!"

"Oh, God," he said with a sickening groan. "I had no idea. . . ."

"No idea?" she broke in bitterly. "What were we supposed to think? There hasn't been a day that's gone by when I haven't worried that you were being tortured in some prison camp or suffering from disease." She made a desperate effort to control the break in her voice. "And now you sit there and tell me you haven't been in Vietnam for twelve years? I don't understand. Why didn't you come home?"

"War changes people, Rachel. It makes them do ugly, atrocious things, and I was so damn stupid." He took a long sip of the exotic-looking cocktail, then lit another cigarette from the glowing tip of the one he had just about finished.

"Floyd, what happened?"

"Rachel, please, I need you to just listen without interrupting me." He crushed the empty cigarette package in his fist. "Eighteen years ago I was only a boy. We were both so young. Remember how worried you were before I left for Nam that something would happen to me?" He made a derisive guttural sound. "I was so green, I didn't realize just what kind of a hell I was being sent to. If you remember, I actually told you that it would be good for us; that as long as I was in Nam I would get combat pay, which would mean more money for us when we married. I thought that it would mean an early out. The talk about boot camp was that all the guys who did a tour in Nam got an early drop. The sooner I was discharged, the sooner we could be married, the sooner we could start a life together." His hand swept across his forehead and back over the side of his head, and Rachel noticed that his hair was thinning on top.

"When we first landed in Saigon, it was hard to believe that there was a war there. That's where I met Tex, the closest friend I made. He was a lot like me, thinking he was doing some patriotic duty that his country would be forever grateful for. And looking around Saigon, we thought, hey—this isn't going to be so bad. It was hot and humid, but at least it didn't look like the pictures we had seen.

"But that was before we were shipped out to Quangtri, which was right up next to the demilitarized zone. There, I discovered the war that the television cameras back in the United States had failed to reveal. It was ugly and it was scary, and I knew that my chances of ever seeing you again were growing slimmer each day. You don't know how many sleepless nights I lay awake in the dank, humid air wondering what I was doing in a country where life seemed meaningless, where Americans were suspicious of children, women . . . any human being with slanted eyes. You know me, Rachel. I'm not the kind of person to even hit another human being, let alone kill someone." Floyd turned his face to the window and continued.

"Do you know what it's like to see piles of dead human beings? Their eyes were glazed over like the eyes of the dead fish in the market; they were like mannequins. Their flesh had turned a waxen gray and it was as though they had never even been alive. I looked at a pile of dead human beings and I saw myself lying there. I thought, I could be the one looking like a dead fish. And then, suddenly, the reality of the war and the part I was playing in it could no longer be denied." Floyd's eyes turned to stare straight into hers, but Rachel knew he wasn't even seeing her.

"Why are you telling me this, Floyd?" she asked, his pain seeping into her senses with an indelible force.

"I have to explain to you why things happened the way they did." His face revealed an urgent need to make her understand. He summoned the waiter and signaled for one more cocktail. Rachel's drink sat untouched.

"Shortly after I arrived at Quangtri, I wrote to you to tell you that we would get married in Hawaii when I was on my R and R. I wanted you to have a diamond ring, so when one of the fellows from the platoon went for his R and R, I gave him the money to pick one out for you. I know that doesn't sound very romantic, but I needed to know that you were back home for me, wearing my ring.'' His eyes automatically flew to her left hand. ''Did you like the ring?'' He couldn't help but ask.

Rachel swallowed back the sob that had risen in her throat. ''It was beautiful. I still have it.''

''I figured we would be married in Hawaii and I would pick out the wedding band myself, although I knew in my heart that my R and R would never come. I was an infantryman—a grunt—the most susceptible to attack.''

''After several months of living in the bush, I was assigned to be the point man on a search-and-destroy mission. All that day I could feel that something wasn't right. It was my turn to be the lead man on the patrol. Everything was quiet, hot and still, until a machine gun rat-tat-tatted, and then all I could hear were screams. I could hear guys yelling that the squad leader had been cut down and I turned to look back at Tex to see his once strong, healthy body lying in a heap in the tall grass. He was crying, 'Help me, Floyd,' but I knew he was a goner. Everywhere I looked there was death. It seemed as though I was the only one left alive. All I could hear was screaming, crying and the sound of death.''

He reached across the table and took her hands in his. ''You can't imagine what I was feeling. I didn't want to die. I didn't want to be captured. So I crawled on all fours, desperate, determined, not thinking about the United States Army or the reason why I was in Vietnam, only thinking about one thing...not ending up in a stinking, decaying pile.''

Rachel could feel his hands tighten on hers as he spoke. An overwhelming flood of empathy poured through her. Floyd was silent, his eyes lowered, his head drooping.

"It's okay, Floyd," she said gently, and he lifted his head.

"I never went back to see what had become of the rest of the squad. I couldn't. It had all happened so fast I hadn't even realized that a bullet had grazed my leg. I kept running and running, until I collapsed. When I awoke, I was in a hut, being nursed back to health by a Vietnamese woman. It took several weeks before I was even able to get out of bed. When I regained my strength, I tried to repay her by helping her plow her fields, even though I knew that the longer I stayed, the harder it would be to go back. Finally, the day came when I knew I couldn't go back. I was a deserter. I had faced the enemy and run. I could never face my dad again, and more important, I could never face you."

"So you chose to let us believe you were missing in action. Don't you realize the agony you've put your family through? We never gave up looking for you."

"I presumed that I would have been reported dead...like the rest of my squad. But believe me, Rachel, death might have been easier. I lived with the constant fear of either the United States Armed Forces or the Viet Cong finding me. When the North Vietnamese overran the country, the family I was living with was forced to flee also. I helped them travel to Hong Kong, which is when I thought about contacting you. But I couldn't bring myself to subject you to that kind of embarrassment or shame."

"And so you sent me the Elizabeth Barrett Browning poems," Rachel said solemnly.

"I knew I could never come home. If I hadn't been so paranoid about being caught, I would have sent you more of a message."

"What about your parents?" She thought of all the nights they had sat together, the prayers they'd said, the candles they'd lit. She thought of the letters they'd written to Washington, the phone calls they'd made to senators, the agony, the frustration.

"I really believed they would have reported me as dead. Besides, I wouldn't have been able to disappoint my father with the news that his only son was a deserter."

"Floyd, there's something I have to tell you about your father." Her voice softened.

"Is he dead?" He said it coldly, like a man who had little respect for life.

She nodded solemnly. "He had a heart attack four years ago, but your mother is still well. Floyd, she deserves to know you're alive."

"You really believe she would be happier knowing that her son is a coward and not a war hero?" he sneered.

"Don't you know that a mother's love can forgive anything?"

"What about a fiancée's? Can you forgive me, Rachel?"

The emotions were raw, too confusing, too fragile at this point. "Will you come back to the United States?" she asked.

"I can't." He finally released her hands.

"Why not?"

"Rachel, desertion is a crime. Why do you suppose I go by Frank Sullivan? I have a new identity here in

Hong Kong. I've built a new life for myself. I'm no longer an American."

Rachel looked at the man across from her and couldn't believe that her Floyd, the man who used to march in the Fourth of July parade in Colby and proudly sing "The Star-Spangled Banner" at baseball games, was now an expatriate. This wasn't the boy she had kissed goodbye at the airport and sent off to war. Of course it wasn't. This was a man who had been through an experience no man deserved. He needed her compassion, not her condemnation. But then he raised his glass to his lips once more, and the gold metal on his finger caught her attention.

"You're married." She was surprised at how normal the words sounded when her brain was focusing on the fact that while she had been crying at night over his absence, he had been in the arms of another woman.

"Rachel, I didn't think I'd ever see you again, and..."

"No, you never stopped to think that I would be waiting for you." Her face was strained. "What is she like?" Some demon curiosity dragged the words from her.

"She's Vietnamese... she's the woman who nursed me back to health in Nam. We have a modest life, but after the intolerable conditions we've lived through, it seems like paradise. We have a small shop in Stanley where she sells her needlework and some jewelry. I also play the piano in the lounge of a hotel here in Hong Kong."

"Do you have any children?"

"Two stepchildren... both girls."

"That's nice." Rachel suddenly felt detached, until his next question.

"Rachel, what happened to the baby?"

"She's not a baby anymore."

"It was a girl?" His face softened a bit.

"Yes. I named her Stacey." Rachel opened her purse, withdrew her wallet and flipped through the plastic-covered envelopes until she pulled out a photo. "Here's her graduation picture."

"It's almost like looking at you when we first met, except she isn't even a girl anymore."

"Heavens, no. She's going to be eighteen tomorrow." She took the picture from his hands.

"Tomorrow's her birthday?" At Rachel's nod, he continued, "I've thought about the two of you so often, Rachel. You must believe me. And I never doubted that you would raise our child to be a fine person. I know I've no right to ask this, but I'd like to see her."

"No!" The refusal was instant. "You haven't thought about her for eighteen years. I've had to be both mother and father to her because you chose not to."

"Rachel, do you realize what would have happened to the two of you if I had come home? There would have been a trial resulting in lots of media attention, focusing on the fact that I chose to stay with a Vietnamese family, which would have raised questions about my allegiance. I couldn't disgrace you that way. No child deserves to be teased all her life because her father's labeled a coward or possibly even a traitor."

"Oh, Floyd, it's all so complicated," she said with a sigh.

"You wouldn't have to tell her who I was, Rachel. I simply want to talk to her, to see for myself what she's like."

"But I'm sure she'd recognize you. We do have photo albums at home, and you haven't changed all that much." She looked at his gaunt features and realized that he really had. "I'll have to think about it," she told him, but silently she wondered if she really did have a choice.

"You never married, Rachel?" He stole a look at her left hand.

"No." The word was short and curt.

"Rachel, I'm sorry. I know that words mean nothing to you now. But I figured you would have learned of my death, met a good, decent man and married... especially with the baby."

"I thought I had met that good and decent man. I thought that Uncle Sam would find him and send him home to me." There were tears in her voice.

"God knows I didn't deserve you, Rachel," he admitted soberly. "Would you have preferred it if I hadn't seen you in the floating casino?"

"That was you," she accused.

"I couldn't believe my eyes when I saw you sitting at the roulette table. I thought I'd been dreaming, but then this morning, when your friend came into the shop, I knew I had to see you just one more time."

"I always knew in my heart that you were alive," she confessed.

"We had it all at one time, Rachel. Now, we only have our memories." They sat in silence for a few minutes before he said, "This Cole Braxton, are you in love with him?"

"Yes."

"Was I the reason for your never marrying?"

"I'm not really sure anymore," she said frankly.

"I should be going. Here's the number of the hotel where I work. Leave a message for me as to your decision concerning Stacey."

Rachel rose to leave, but his hand on her arm stopped her.

"You won't turn me in to the authorities, will you?"

It was like the final stab wound. Rachel shook her head sadly. How could he even have asked such a question, she didn't know. She watched him walk away, only a shadow of the man she had known.

She didn't return to the hotel room, but went for a long walk. Her thoughts were fragmented, full of the past, full of anguish. Eyes downcast, tears sliding down her cheeks, she walked with an ache in her heart and wondered if it would ever go away. She wasn't even aware that she had ended up outside Cole's suite. Her breath caught in her throat when he opened the door. His face was filled with kindness and concern as his eyes gazed at her splotchy face. She wanted to fall into his arms.

"Frank Sullivan is Floyd." Her voice was little more than a whisper. "He's not an MIA, he just never wanted..." Overcome with emotion, she began to sob heavily.

Cole scooped her up into his arms, inhaling her scent, feeling her warmth. "Shhh, it's all right." He kissed her forehead. "Everything's going to work out." God, how he hated to see her cry. He wanted to take away her pain, protect her. After her sobbing subsided, she lay against his shoulder.

"How are you feeling?" He gently wiped the tears from the corners of her eyes.

"I hurt."

Seeing her like this was tearing Cole's soul out. He needed to know what had happened between her and Floyd. But a knock on the adjoining door prevented him from finding out.

"That must be the girls," Cole said before calling out for Alicia to come in.

"Mother! What's wrong?" Stacey demanded as she entered the room and saw her mother's obvious emotional distress.

"Stacey, I'm fine, honestly," Rachel assured her, shrugging out of Cole's grasp.

"You certainly don't look fine." She faced her mother with her hands on her hips. "What's going on? How come you've been acting so weird? Yesterday you run off across the ocean, then today you disappear right after lunch."

"Stacey, I think your mother could use some rest." Cole placed his hands on Rachel's shoulders.

"Cole, it's all right. I need to talk with Stacey. Maybe you and Alicia could have dinner without us this evening?"

Cole did not look pleased, but acquiesced. Back in their hotel room, Rachel indicated that Stacey should sit beside her on the divan.

"I have something to tell you."

"What?" Stacey's face was cautious, and Rachel was sure she was expecting news that she and Cole would be getting married.

"Well? What is it, Mom?" Stacey asked after several moments of silence.

Rachel knew that she had to tell her daughter about Floyd, but the right words simply wouldn't come. Finally, she said, "Your father is alive. He's here in Hong Kong and I've seen him."

"Dad's alive?" Stacey's eyes were jubilant as she flung her arms around her mother. She jumped up off the divan and twirled around the room. "I can't believe it! Dad's alive! So where is he? When can I see him?"

"Sit down, Stacey, please. I have to tell you a few things first." Rachel's tone was not to be overlooked.

"What's wrong? He's not crazy, is he? Has he been in a POW camp?" Stacey looked frightful.

Rachel suddenly found herself unprepared for the questions. Should she be the one to tell Stacey about her father's past? Or should she simply let Stacey meet Floyd without knowing the truth?

"Well, Mom, what is it?" Stacey insisted.

"What happened to your father in Vietnam is very difficult to understand. Promise me when you meet him you'll remember that he has been a victim of war."

"Mom, you're scaring me."

"He's perfectly healthy, darling." She placed her arm about Stacey's waist. "It's just such an emotional story I don't think I can go through it again. I'll let him explain it to you."

"When do I get to see him?"

"I'll call him tonight and we'll go first thing tomorrow."

They ordered room service, then Rachel went to bed. When Alicia and Cole returned from dinner, Cole stopped at the Kincaid suite.

"Can I see your mother for a few minutes?" he asked Stacey when she answered the door.

"She's already asleep. She was so exhausted from all the excitement." Stacey's cheeks were flushed. "Have you heard the good news, Cole? My father is alive, here in Hong Kong."

"Yes. I'm happy for you, Stacey. I know how difficult it has been all those years he was missing."

"It's just like in the movies . . . a dream come true. We are actually going to be a real family." The words were spoken without malice, just with the anticipation and enthusiasm of a child. The muscles around Cole's heart contracted, and he couldn't help but feel he had truly lost Rachel.

"If your mother should wake, tell her I stopped by."

"Sure." Impulsively, she gave him a close hug. "Thanks for bringing us to Hong Kong. If it hadn't been for you we might not ever have found him."

Cole needed to get out of the hotel. When he reached the street, he jerked the door open on the rental car and climbed inside. He drove too quickly down the crowded streets, but his insides were churning. There was no air conditioning in the tiny car and the humidity was stifling. He pulled off the road and jumped out of the car, his shirt clinging to him as sweat trickled down his arms and neck. Damn! He slammed his palm on the roof of the car. He couldn't lose Rachel, not now.

He was feeling so insecure. Cole Braxton, insecure over a woman. But then, never before had he met a woman who gave him such a feeling of completeness. All those years he had only been a half; now he was whole. Would the wholeness be snatched away from him?

God, he wished she were with him right this minute, confiding her deepest feelings about what had happened with Floyd. But he hadn't had fifteen minutes alone with her since she had met with Floyd Andrews, and for all he knew Stacey was absolutely right about her parents. But while Rachel was confused and going through a difficult period, he knew she loved him. Even if she didn't know that, he did. What the two of them had was special, and Cole Braxton wasn't going to give up so easily on something he wanted so badly. He would stand by her through the confusion until everything worked itself out.

Only Cole wasn't able to stand by Rachel. During the night he received word that his grandfather had suffered a severe stroke, and he was forced to make immediate flight arrangements back to the United States. All the doubts he was experiencing resurfaced the next morning when Rachel told him she couldn't leave with him. Having arranged to take Stacey to see Floyd that morning, she was only able to meet briefly with him before he left.

"Rachel, I hate leaving you like this," Cole told her, the frustration apparent in his face.

Rachel wanted to close her eyes and plead with him not to leave. When she had awakened this morning her first thought had been that she needed to be with Cole, and now she was wondering how would she cope after he left. But she knew she needed to be strong...for Stacey's sake.

"I'm sorry about your grandfather, Cole, but Stacey and I just can't leave yet."

"Stacey is ebullient, isn't she?" He really wanted to ask her how she was feeling.

Rachel nodded her head. "We're meeting Floyd at the hotel shortly."

"Would you see that she gets this? I know it's her birthday today." He handed her a shiny red package with a white bow.

Rachel's heart ached. "Thank you, Cole. It was sweet of you to remember."

"Do you have any idea when you'll be flying home?"

"We haven't thought that far ahead."

"No...I suppose not. Oh...I've made another appointment for you with the Aiku people this afternoon." He waited for her response but she only nodded absently. "Well, I'm going to have to get moving." He looked at Rachel, a thousand words on his tongue, but all he could do was kiss her tenderly and say, "I love you, Rachel." Then he left.

RACHEL QUESTIONED the wisdom of her decision to tell Stacey about Floyd right up to the moment they left the hotel. Her doubts increased as they traveled across the island to Causeway Bay in a taxi, for Stacey was enthusiastically making plans for her father's return to the United States. Rachel had successfully evaded her questions as to how he happened to be in Hong Kong. Stacey had assumed that he must have been a prisoner of war who was just now being released. All her life Stacey had waited to meet her father. Rachel could only hope that she wouldn't be too terribly disappointed. Learning the truth about Floyd had come as a shock to her, yet subconsciously she had been mentally preparing herself to admit that her future did not revolve around him. And then she had Cole to turn to. Whom would Stacey turn to?

Rachel looked at her daughter as they entered the Excelsior Hotel. She was no longer a child, but an adult, and she needed to know the truth about her father. After eighteen years of frustrating hope, she had that right. Looking at her in her white sundress, and knowing how much time she had spent getting ready for this visit, Rachel wished she could shelter her from what she knew was coming. And Stacey's next words made her want to turn around and go back to Chicago without even seeing Floyd again.

''Mom, this is the best birthday present I could have ever asked for.''

Rachel could only smile weakly. She had finally come to accept the fact that she simply could not protect her daughter from some things.

The piano bar in the hotel was deserted and chairs were piled on tabletops. One lone custodial worker was pushing a vacuum cleaner across the thick red carpet when Rachel and Stacey walked in. Floyd was seated at the grand piano, and when he saw Stacey and her mother, he began to play ''Happy Birthday.''

Rachel felt she should break the silence after the music had ended. ''Floyd, this is Stacey. Stacey, this is your father.''

''I knew you'd come back,'' Stacey said through a stream of joyous tears. Rachel met Floyd's eyes.

''Hey! Dry those tears. Let me get a good look at you.'' He pushed her back in an appraising way.

"You're beautiful... just as I always dreamed you'd be. But you get red blotches on your cheeks when you cry... just like your mother." He lightly ran a fingertip across her cheek, then handed her a tiny silver package with a pink ribbon. "I'm only sorry I missed the other seventeen birthdays."

Stacey's fingers quickly opened the package—a lot more eagerly than she'd tackled the lovely earrings Cole had given her. She let out a little cry of delight at the sight of the carved jade butterfly. "It's beautiful. Thank you."

"The Chinese believe jade has the power to ward off danger and disease," Floyd told her. "Here, sit down beside me. I want to hear all about you." He made room for her on the piano bench.

Rachel excused herself, giving Floyd and Stacey the privacy they needed. She walked over to the window overlooking Victoria Harbor and reflected on the significance of all that had happened since she had come to Hong Kong. The words of a Chinese proverb Ling had used came back to her. "Every blade of grass has its own share of dew." She glanced across the room and saw the two familiar faces that would have been all she needed to make her happy at one time. Stacey was engrossed in what her father was saying, and Rachel could feel a tightness in her chest, knowing what was coming. How did one make sense of all that had happened? How did one rationalize a war, a missing soldier, a girl growing up without her father? How had such a kind, dear boy gone off to war and ended up a refugee?

She turned and stared at the fish in the aquarium, bemused that the Chinese should regard the carp as a prized fish when back in the Midwest cartoonists mocked the "garbage" fish. One man's junk is another man's art, was what her mother would have said.

"I'd like to leave, Mother," Stacey said solemnly over her shoulder.

Floyd was standing with his hands in supplication. "Let me get you a taxi."

"Thank you. That would be nice."

He walked with them down to the lobby, hailed a taxi and looked imploringly into his daughter's eyes. Stacey uttered a cold "Goodbye" before climbing into the taxi.

All the way back to the hotel she was silent. Rachel tried to question her, but she refused to be anything other than morose. If there was one thing Rachel had difficulty dealing with, it was the way Stacey could go inside herself when she was troubled.

As soon as they were back at the hotel, Stacey said, "When are we going home?"

"Whenever you like."

"I want to leave as soon as possible."

"Stacey, will you please talk to me about it? I know you're upset, but we have to discuss this," Rachel pleaded.

But when Stacey's mind was set on something, a rocket wouldn't budge her. Just a few hours later, Rachel was seated on a 747 at Kai Tak airport. The soothsayer had been right, she thought. Her heart had broken a little in Hong Kong. Would it be mended once she was back in the United States?

## *CHAPTER FIFTEEN*

SEPTEMBER IN CHICAGO was crisp and refreshing after Hong Kong's oppressive humidity. Rachel inhaled the bright morning air outside her apartment, happy to be back home. Only now was the shock of meeting Floyd beginning to wear off. Her abrupt departure from Hong Kong had left her little time for examining her feelings. While Stacey packed, she had gone back to the Excelsior Hotel to say goodbye to Floyd. Compared to their emotional reunion, their parting had been detached, cool.

"I hope that somewhere in your heart you'll find a place to forgive me," were Floyd's last words.

"Take care of yourself, Floyd," was all she could find to say to him in reply. In just a few short hours, eighteen years of illusions had been shattered, and she could only feel an emptiness toward him. War had left only a shell of the man she had known, and looking at his desolate face, all her anger had fallen away. He was not a coward, but a human being, Stacey's father, a man she had once loved. When the plane took off, her one thought had been that she needed to see Cole....

Both she and Stacey were feeling the effects of the long flight and the time change. Once in the apartment, Rachel groaned in relief, then fell down onto the sofa and thought how good it felt to be home. She leaned back and closed her eyes, but Stacey's voice had them open almost immediately.

"Why didn't you tell me he was a coward?" Stacey's vigil of silence was over. She had been uncommunicative on the flight back, and Rachel had been too engrossed with feelings of her own to worry about her daughter's ego, although she hadn't missed the way Stacey had fingered the jade butterfly.

"What was I supposed to say? 'By the way, I bumped into your father and it turns out he's not an MIA but a deserter. How about coming along and say hi to him?'" Rachel rose from the sofa.

Stacey took Floyd's picture from the desk top, shoved it into a drawer, then jerked the framed purple heart and bronze star off the wall.

"Stacey, he's your father, no matter what kind of a life he has led. He wanted to see you."

"You could have prepared me for the experience," she retorted. "I thought he was a hero. He doesn't deserve these. He's nothing but a coward." She waved the medals in front of her, then tossed them into the wastebasket.

"Don't you ever talk about him in that tone of voice again. Do you hear me?" Rachel retrieved the medals from the trash and set them on the desk. "Now, I know you're hurting, but I'm hurting, too. And in my eyes he is no coward, but a victim. They took him away from me, a good, kind decent human being who was only a boy, and sent him off to fight a war he shouldn't have been in. He didn't want to kill people, but he was thrust into an insanity no man should have had to endure. And because he couldn't live that kind of life, he was forced to become a refugee. He may not have been tortured in a prison camp, but he has suffered a mental torture that will haunt him the rest of his life. Can't you try to understand that?"

"No, I can't!" she cried out bitterly. "You can think whatever you like, but as far as I'm concerned, I have no father." Then she burst into tears. Rachel took her in her arms and let her cry, gently rocking her back and forth and smoothing down her hair, just as she had done when Stacey was a child.

"Oh, Stacey, I know what you're feeling," she comforted her. "It's just going to take some time to get over all the anger and the pain." Rachel only hoped that it wouldn't take too long. They needed to get things back to normal.

If she had expected to return to Chicago and find everything the same, she was mistaken. When she went into Annalise Fashions the next day, she learned that Julian had taken on a new apprentice. Suddenly Rachel found herself wondering if her job with Annalise was as secure as she had originally thought. She had phoned Cole twice in the past two days, but he hadn't returned her calls, which only added to her feelings of uncertainty. She had spoken to Owen Braxton, Sr.'s housekeeper and had learned that he was still hospitalized, but his condition was improving. When Katie joined her for lunch, Rachel was feeling tired and melancholy.

"Welcome back, stranger!" Katie set a cheeseburger down in front of her. "Here...my treat. I'm so happy to have you back."

Katie always managed to elicit a smile from her. "Thank you. You know, I actually missed these greasy hamburgers." Rachel removed the bun and splashed on some catsup.

"Are you kidding? With all that exotic food?"

"It was wonderful, too," Rachel agreed. "But unusual. You should have seen Stacey's face when she found out that this delicious soup we were eating owed its savory taste to fish lips."

"It sounds as though you had a great time."

"We did...." She paused to look up as Julian's new assistant walked past. "Am I being replaced?"

"I'd say Julian is taking precautions. Good news travels fast. We've all heard about Braxton's interest in you. Everyone's been speculating that you went to Hong Kong to check out textiles for branching out on your own. Any truth to those rumors?"

"I haven't made up my mind yet, but you'll be the first to know," Rachel assured her.

"So tell me. How was Hong Kong?"

"Full of surprises."

"What kind of a cryptic comment is that?"

Shrugging, Rachel said, "Don't pay any attention to me. I'm in a terrible mood."

"It's probably jet lag. How about coming over tonight? I'm having a few people over to commemorate the first day of autumn."

Rachel smiled. Leave it to Katie to think of a reason to party. "Maybe I will."

"Great. You can tell me all about your Hong Kong surprises then."

When Rachel arrived at home she found a large manila envelope in the mail from Patsy. Enclosed were several advertisements and newspaper clippings from the Minneapolis papers concerning the Braxton's golden-anniversary celebration and the new Mr. B's collection. Rachel could hardly believe that she was the chic designer they were describing so eloquently. She played back her answering machine, but there were no messages from Cole. Was he angry with her? Not that she would have blamed him. She had been so wrapped up in her own emotions that she had completely ignored his feelings. She hadn't even explained the outcome of her meeting with Floyd to him, and she couldn't help but wonder how Cole felt about her after her inconsiderate behavior in Hong Kong.

After a revitalizing shower, she dressed with care for Katie's impromptu party, choosing a sleek-fitting pair of black slacks that clung to her tiny legs and a Chinese silk blouse that flattered her figure.

Katie's party turned out to be just the prescription Rachel needed to forget about Stacey's melancholy and her own uncertainties concerning Cole. She laughed, played games, drank just enough wine to feel light-headed... and Bud doted on her. When he offered to see her home, she accepted. Bringing the car to a stop in front of her apartment building, he pulled her into his arms.

She knew she should resist, but the wine had her feeling mellow. "Bud, you're such a dear," she said, putting her head on his shoulder, the fatigue catching up with her.

"Rachel, you're the one who's special." He kissed her hard on the lips.

Rachel was startled. When he drew back, she said, "I think I'd better go in."

"Can I see you on Friday night?"

*You're not being fair to him,* a little voice called out to her. She straightened and said, "I'm sorry, Bud. I can't."

"I understand. Katie told me you were serious about someone, but you can't blame a guy for trying." He gave her his lopsided grin.

Rachel kissed him lightly on the lips before getting out. She fumbled for her key at her apartment door and nearly screamed when a voice said, "I thought you disliked parties?"

"What are you doing here?" she said angrily. "You nearly frightened me to death."

"I heard you blew the appointment with Aiku again." He wanted to grab her and kiss her, but damn, it irritated him to think that while he was wondering if they had a future together, she had been off socializing with Katie and her friends.

"I've told you a hundred times I don't want to be out on my own." She didn't care that she was sounding ungrateful.

"I also heard that Julian's hired a new apprentice."

"Are you implying that she's my replacement?" Why were they standing there arguing when she only wanted to be in his arms?

"She is your replacement. I told Julian you would be quitting."

"You did what?" she shouted, unmindful that they were still out in the corridor.

"You're a fantastic designer who should have her own label. Instead, you're giving all your wonderful creativity over to someone else."

Stacey's sleepy form opened the door and stood before them. "I can hear you two all the way in my bedroom."

Cole took Rachel by the arm and propelled her down the stairs and out into the street where he hailed a passing taxi. Despite her protests, he shoved her in when it stopped.

"Where to?" the driver asked.

"Anywhere!" Cole shouted.

"Stop this taxi," Rachel demanded to the taxi driver who hadn't left the curb yet. She scrambled out. "You think you can just storm into my life and make decisions for me. Well, I don't need you, Cole Braxton," she screamed at him and slammed the door.

RACHEL CRIED HERSELF to sleep that night. For three days she had waited for Cole to call her and when he finally showed up on her doorstep, they had shouted at each other. More than anything in the world she had wanted for him to take her in his arms so she could tell him that he was the one she loved, not Floyd.

Stacey was already having breakfast when Rachel got up the next morning. She took one look at her mother's red-rimmed eyes and said, "Mom, I think we should talk."

"What about?"

"About us."

She had Rachel's complete attention now.

"I'm sorry, Mom. About what happened in Hong Kong and about the way I've been behaving since we've been back. I realize now that finding out about Dad came as just as much of a shock to you as it did to me."

Rachel hugged her daughter. "What brought about all of this?"

"Cole."

"Cole?"

"He came by earlier last night after you had already left for Katie's party. We sat and talked for a long time. He really made a lot of sense, Mom. He straightened me out on a lot of things."

"He did?"

"Yes. He made me realize that Dad wasn't a coward. You see, when Cole was in Vietnam..."

"Cole was in Vietnam?" Rachel interrupted.

"Yes. But he said he was more fortunate than Dad because he wound up a supply clerk in Saigon and was never really forced into combat the way Dad was. But he said he saw the effect that the war had on people. And he told me I should think of Dad as a hero. Back then, there were a lot of protesters and draft dodgers who refused to serve in the military, but he told me that at least Dad went to fight for his country. That alone took a bravery some men didn't have."

"Cole said that?" Rachel said in a near whisper.

"Mmm. Did you two have a big fight? I heard you crying last night."

"That's because I can't believe I said the stupid things I did."

"He really loves you, Mom."

"Do you really think so?"

"Why else would he tell me about Melinda Sue's death? Do you know what he told me, Mom? He said that even though he knew he couldn't take the place of my real father, he would be proud to call me his daughter. He thinks the three of us could be a real family."

"And how do you feel about that?" Rachel needed to know.

"I think that if he makes you happy, then I'm happy, too. He's really nice, Mom."

"Yes, he is," Rachel said, smiling.

"So what are you going to do about it?"

"Do?"

"Yeah...you know, like call him and tell him you're sorry."

"Call him?"

"Mom, you sound like you're having trouble with words that are longer than one syllable." Stacey chuckled. "I thought you were with it! You're a woman of the eighties...call the man and tell him how you feel."

"You know, as a daughter, you're okay," Rachel said, hugging her closely. "But I'm not going to call him. I'm going to call Auntie Kay to come stay with you so I can fly to Minneapolis."

Stacey's hand stopped hers. "Mom, I'm eighteen. Don't you think I can get by for a few days without Auntie Kay?"

"Yes. I do." Rachel looked at her daughter and felt a surge of pride.

"Good. Because I'm going to be on my own beginning next week. I've enrolled at Marquette University."

And once more, Rachel hugged her daughter close.

IT WAS A COOL CRISP Autumn night on Cole's landing. Fallen leaves crunched underfoot as he trudged up the bank to the deck overlooking the lake. At the sound of the car door slamming he leaped the railroad-tie steps leading from the receding shoreline two at a time, thinking it was news of his grandfather. He rounded the front of his home and saw that it wasn't any family member standing on the step, but Rachel, a helium-filled, heart-shaped balloon tied to her wrist.

Cole was suddenly conscious of his worn flannel shirt and his hip waders. And the fact that he hadn't shaved yet today. And that his rubber boots squeaked when he walked. He had been fishing, and here she was looking as if she'd just stepped off the pages of

*Vogue* and he could smell her musky scent. He thrust his hands behind his back, hoping the fishy odor wouldn't find its way around his thick frame.

"Hello, Rachel." It was the same, lazy drawl she had come to anticipate.

"Hello, Cole," she returned, almost shyly. She was grateful that he hadn't asked her what she was doing here.

As Cole got closer, he was able to read the Heaven or Bust that was printed on her silver balloon. "I think it might bust first," Cole told her, a wide grin sweeping across his face as his finger flicked at the string on her wrist. On the other side of the heart-shaped balloon were the words, "Rachel + Cole."

"Do you think we can make it to heaven?" Cole asked.

"You need to ask?" she said coyly. She smiled at the tenderness that was in his eyes. She wanted to reach over, put her finger to his mouth and trace the fine, strong curve of his lips. She longed to be in his arms, to feel his strength, his warmth, the beat of his heart. "You're the only man I know who can take me there." She looked at the smooth brow, the assertive chin and the dark brown eyes.

"Oh, Rachel," he groaned before his arms went around her, crushing her to him. The big green waders stood in the way of his feeling her body pressed against his, but he didn't care. For days he had been dreaming about holding her in his arms and now he couldn't resist. His mouth found hers and he kissed her with a passion that demanded reassurance as well as excitement.

"Cole, I'm sorry about last night," she managed in between kisses.

He pressed his forehead up against hers and released a long sigh. "Let's go inside; we need to talk."

He turned to open the door, then let her precede him into the entryway. He kicked off the hip waders, then followed her inside. "Let me take a quick shower and get rid of this," he said, rubbing his palm across his jaw. "Help yourself to something to drink." Rachel nodded as he walked past her down the hallway. She untied the balloon and let it float to the vaulted ceiling.

She was too nervous to remain seated. As if drawn by a magnetic current, she found her way to Cole's room. When she stepped inside, she could see him standing in the adjoining bathroom, shirtless and shoeless, a hand towel draped around his neck while his razor cut paths across his lathered face. A steady stream of water flowed from the faucet as he alternately rinsed the blade and scraped the razor across his skin in a tempo that had Rachel fascinated. When Cole became aware of her presence, the razor stopped in midair. He stared at her with clear eyes, as if waiting for her to say something.

"I lied last night, Cole. I do need you." She looked at him with such a longing he dropped the razor into the sink.

With one swift movement, he brushed the towel across his face and drew her into his arms. His firm, warm lips covered her mouth in a kiss that filled Rachel's nostrils with the scent of lime shaving cream. Then he let his tongue trace the outline of her lips.

"You should have let me finish," he breathed against her cheek.

"Why?" Her fingers were exploring his naked torso, causing Cole to emit little gasps. His lips brushed her throat while his hands undid the front of her dress. Rachel held her breath while she waited for the feel of his hands against her breasts. She thought it exquisite torture, feeling his thumb gently stroke her nipple through the nylon cup. He held her gaze as his fingers undid the hooks of her bra, and the look on his face made Rachel tremble.

Her small hands traveled across warm, hard flesh as she reveled in the feel of his solid strength. And then his arms were around her, and the mat of dark hair on his muscled chest was against her breasts. Cole's mouth urgently sought hers, his lips warm, his tongue searching and thrusting, and Rachel felt herself sinking into a whirlpool of sensations.

Cole picked her up into his arms and carried her over to the king-size bed. He laid her down gently, then removed his jeans, his eyes never leaving hers. Undressed, he lay down beside her and helped her eager fingers finish undoing the buttons on her dress. When she was completely naked, he expelled a soft moan, and his eyes traveled over the curves and angles he had come to know intimately. Then he was kissing her tenderly, on her lips, her throat, her breasts. His hands caressed the curve of her hips as he gently rolled her on top of him. Rachel, straddling him with one palm on each side of him, pushed herself up until the tips of her nipples were tantalizing him. Cole pulled her back down against him, his hands on her buttocks, pressing her to feel his urgent need. Then he was rolling her over again and he was on top, looking down into her face as though he was searching to find her very soul. He was kissing her, exploring every sensitive part of her body with lips that burned a fiery trail from her head down to her thighs, until Rachel wanted to shout with excitement. She let her fingers slide smoothly over his shoulders, down his back, feeling the muscles tense, his skin warm and moist.

As she parted her legs, he moved between them and thrust deeply inside her. Rachel arched hungrily toward him, meeting his desire with a passion equal to his. Clinging to him, she felt the beginnings of ecstasy flow through her veins like liquid fire. Together, they moved as one as wave after wave of shuddering sensation engulfed them, until neither one had any thoughts, any awareness, only an exquisite feeling of intoxicating passion.

Cole collapsed beside her, breathing heavily, one leg resting across her thigh. "I think we made it...at least I know I did," he said, burying his face in her hair. "That had to be as close to heaven as we'll ever get."

Her only response was her kittenlike purring as she cuddled up to him, replete with his love, wanting to wallow in the afterglow of passion.

"Maybe it's because this past week has been hell for me." He lifted her chin so that her eyes met his. "I've wanted to be with you so badly, yet every time I tried to get close to you..." He broke off, at a loss for words.

"I know. I'm sorry." She touched his cheek with her fingertips. "It almost feels as though Hong Kong was a bad dream." She shivered as the cool autumn air drifted in through the open window, prompting Cole to pull up the covers and wrap the two of them inside.

"I need to know what happened, Rachel."

"I thought Stacey told you."

"I'm not talking about Floyd. I need to know what's happened inside you."

She pulled her knees up and wrapped her arms about them. "I think it must be true what they say about first loves. They're the most painful and probably the hardest to let go of. And when that first love is a memory you are clinging to, it's even more difficult. For eighteen years I nourished such a love because I'd thought it would last a lifetime, that there would never be another man I could love the way I loved Floyd. And of course, there was Stacey. I hadn't wanted to give her false hopes that she had a father alive somewhere in the world, but I truly believed he would come home to us."

"Rachel, you were as much victims of the war as Floyd."

"I suppose so...but as I think back now, how much easier it would have been to accept that he had died. Maybe Stacey wouldn't have had to suffer quite so much."

"Do you realize you're always thinking about someone else's happiness? What about you, Rachel? You still haven't told me how you feel about Floyd."

"At first I was hurt, angry that I had spent eighteen years waiting for a man who didn't even want to come home to me. I wanted to hate him, but I couldn't. It was so sad, Cole, to hear about his awful experiences in Vietnam. All I could do was pity him, and try to remember the good and gentle man he had been."

"I saw you kissing him in the bar," Cole confessed.

"You didn't think I was still in love with him?"

"I didn't know what to think." Rachel was surprised to see a hint of uncertainty in his usually sanguine features.

"But I thought you knew how much I loved you," she said gently.

"Do you realize that you've never told me?"

"I guess I thought I had. I do love you, Cole," she said sincerely. "I love you, not Floyd. When you had to fly home to be with your grandfather, I had to force myself not to beg you to stay with me. I needed you so badly, but you seemed so cool."

"Just uncertain. That night before I left, I came to your room but you were sleeping. Stacey told me the three of you were going to be a family. I didn't want to believe it, but Rachel, you're the most loyal person I've ever encountered in my life. I thought you loved me, but I worried that maybe you'd go back to Floyd out of some misplaced loyalty to him."

"Floyd is married. If only we had had some time to talk I could have told you. There was no question of the two of us resuming a relationship."

Cole pulled her back against him and rested his chin in her hair. "Do you know how frustrated I was? When I flew to Chicago, needing to be with you, I found you off at some party. Then when I tried to talk to you about the Aiku business you snapped my head off."

"I snapped *your* head off?" she protested in mock indignation. "You show up out of the blue on my doorstep, then without so much as a welcome kiss or hug you get on my case about missing the Aiku appointment—which I truly am sorry about—and then you tell me that you've told my boss I'm quitting, when all I really wanted was to be in your arms. For days I'd worried that you had finally grown tired of me."

"I'll never grow tired of you." He nuzzled her ear, gently biting its lobe. "I'll love you forever, Rachel." Holding her against the length of his body, he felt the familiar heat running through his veins. He would never get used to the way his hands and mouth brought her alive, the way her body responded to his caresses. They moved together rhythmically, intuitively, accelerating to an erotic tempo until they both were complete. And finally, Rachel was deeply satisfied and at peace. Bodies entwined, they fell asleep.

THE FIRST THING Rachel did when she awoke the next morning was to turn to look at Cole. But instead of his dark head lying on the pillow she found the heart-shaped balloon. It had lost its buoyancy, and now rested beside her so that the "Rachel + Cole" stared back at her. She smiled to herself, then raised herself up on one elbow. Attached to the balloon's string was a small velvet box.

She reached for the box as Cole stepped out of the bathroom, a towel wrapped around his waist.

"What is this?" she asked shyly.

"It's supposed to be a balloon floating from the ceiling with a package dangling from the string. But I guess my package was a little too heavy for the balloon." He dropped down beside her on the bed, a smile on his sensuous mouth. "We seem to be better at communicating with balloons."

As Rachel's fingers opened the jeweler's box, he said softly, "Will you marry me, Rachel?" While she stared at the diamond, he reached across to pick it off the velvet cloth and slip it onto her finger. "Well?" he asked, when she seemed to be at a loss for words.

"You want to marry me?" she repeated.

"I have wanted to for a long, long time. After Melinda Sue died I wasn't able to really get close to anyone. Then I met you, and I found myself wanting to share everything with you—my thoughts, my laughter, my disappointments. I wanted to be everything for you: a lover, a friend, a protector. But there was always Stacey or Floyd. I figured that in time Stacey would accept me as a father figure, but I wasn't sure about Floyd's ghost. The night we went to the casino I had planned on proposing to you, but..." His words trailed off. "When Floyd turned up in Hong Kong I felt impotent. I couldn't protect you from the hurting, I couldn't make any decisions for you. I could only hope that the love I thought we shared would be strong enough to guide you back home to me."

"It was." She sat up on her knees and looped her arms around his neck. "I probably just didn't want to admit how much I did love you because I knew that if I did, I would be closing the door on Floyd. My feelings for you were so strong, so frightening. But thank God you were there for me. Because for the first time in eighteen years I feel alive."

"Can I take that as a yes to my proposal?" His hands explored her silken flesh.

"Absolutely," she agreed, bestowing a lingering kiss on his lips.

Cole dragged his mouth away from hers reluctantly. "We have to get dressed. The weather is perfect for the balloon and I want to take you up in the clouds. Today I will take you halfway to heaven."

"We definitely don't need to get dressed for that," Rachel said, and pulled him back to her.

# Harlequin Superromance

## COMING NEXT MONTH

**#238 TEMPTING FATE • Risa Kirk**
Reya Merrill thought that handling public relations for the controversial Geneticon account would cinch her promotion. But when Colin Hughes, owner of the genetic research laboratories, defies her every move, she loses her job... and her heart.

**#239 A DISTANT PROMISE • Debbie Bedford**
Advertising copywriter Emily Lattrell seemed to have it all until she met handsome real-estate magnate Philip Manning. Almost overnight she quit her job, moved to a northern Texan farm and became adopted mom to Philip's nephew and two nieces. Now she'd truly have it all... if she could learn to accept Philip's love.

**#240 SEASON OF MIRACLES • Emilie Richards**
Schoolteacher Elise Ramsey had chosen duty over love once. Then, in the middle of her life, she was offered another opportunity to find joy in the strong arms of Sloane Tyson. Her first lover. The boy was gone forever, replaced by a man impossible to deny.

**#241 GYPSY FIRE • Sara Orwig**
After star witnesses Jake and Molly escape the watchful eye of the Detriot police, they find themselves holed up together in the Ozarks. Molly can't bear Jake's workaholic lists and thirst for success. But Jake discovers he can't bear to take his eyes off Molly....

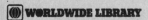

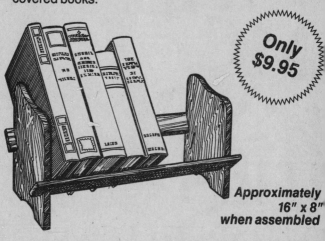